# ALSO BY SAM LEE JACKSON

All formats, ebook, paperback and hard back
available now at Amazon.com

# DEEP WOODS WARRIOR

## SAM LEE JACKSON

Deep Woods Warrior

Piping Rock Publications
3608 E Taro Lane. Phoenix AZ 85050
www.samleejackson.com

ISBN 979-1-88534737-8-2 (paperback)
ISBN 978-1-7351654-9-3 (€)
Library of Congress Control Number 2023912661

# ACKNOWLEDGEMENTS

I gratefully thank my long-time editor Ann Hedrick
May God rest the soul of my very talented illustrator Spomenka
"Ladybyrd" Bojanic who passed away last year
Sarah Plante, who excels in sales, marketing,
and all things social media
Marina@Polgarusstudios for her consistent formatting skills

**And especially many thanks to my readers
who comment on and review my work.**

Most of all, to Carol. An accomplished proofreader and counselor. She is my lighthouse. When I am lost at sea, she is always there to guide me.

# 1

Captain Rand couldn't have ordered up a better day. Mild temperatures, mild breeze, open bar. Hollywood pretty people with gleaming teeth and tanned skin. My friend and neighbor Pete Dunn had finally gotten a screenplay greenlighted and casting had started. Some really big names had been floated and the press was sucking it up. Phoenix hadn't hosted a big movie in a long time, so every political wannabe was on Captain Rand's triple decker party boat.

Pete had invited me and Marianne, Blackhawk, Elena, Nacho and Esperanza to join him. He had also invited Old Eddie and young Jimmy. Every male of us had politely declined and then after Elena had threatened mass castration, we all ended up standing on the upper deck with a drink in our hands. We stood in a small cluster toward the stern with every man, from movie stars to waiters sending clandestine glances toward our women.

Pete was once again surrounded by a gaggle of pretty people trying to describe his movie. He had told me about it, and it made me uncomfortable. It was about an ex-Navy Seal who gets involved with trying to rescue the young granddaughter of a

1

foreign dignitary from a street gang. A gang that is run by a murderous cartel. At first the protagonist was missing a foot, but I protested so strongly that Pete had changed it and made the guy one-eyed. There is always something rakish about a one-eyed hero. It still didn't mean I was happy.

Everyone was decked out in summer boat finery. Some of the girls were in bikini's, the men in flashy Hawaiian styled shirts. Very few men were in long pants. I was one of those. I wanted to cover my prosthetic. What made me the most nervous was a crew from the local TV station roaming around taking random shots and interviewing people. Wherever they were I'd try to be on the opposite side of the deck. Of course, Elena was dying for an interview. Why not? She was an entertainer and could use some free publicity. I looked at Blackhawk. "I'm going to the bar. Want anything?" He shook his head. Marianne threaded her arm through mine.

"I'll take one, big spender," she said.

We started through the crowd when she tugged at me. "That's downright stupid," she said. I looked to where she was looking. A man had a small child, hardly more than a baby, standing up on the safety rail while he held its tiny hands, making like it was dancing. He was laughing and even from here I could tell he was drunk.

Captain Rand blasted his horn as a loaded cabin cruiser cut across our bow. Captain Rand swung across the wake to minimize the bounce, but the wake threw us sideways. Several women screamed, but not at the sudden dip. They screamed because the baby was gone over the side. The father was looking stupidly down to where the baby had fallen.

I was at the guard rail in two bounds. I leapt to the top and pushed off the top rail in one motion, without thinking. It was a pretty good vertical dive, but it was two stories down. I sliced the water and went deep. As soon as I could, I brought my knee to my chest and pulled the prosthetic off. Then the other shoe. The water wasn't clear but thank God it wasn't murky like it is sometimes. On my way down I had automatically calculated where I thought the baby had entered the water and tried to hit it as close as possible.

The baby was nowhere in sight. From then on, it was all luck. I swung around but she was nowhere in sight. I flipped onto my back so I could look back up toward the surface. I guessed I was twenty feet under. I started swimming in circles. It wasn't long before my lungs began to burn. Then the baby was there, floating face down. Its eyes were wide open and were looking at me. There were no bubbles coming from its nose or mouth.

Three strokes and I was there. I grabbed it, covered the baby's nose and mouth with my mouth and blew what was left of my air into its lungs. I kicked for the surface. It seemed forever but was only seconds. I burst into the air. I was too busy shaking the baby, trying to get a response, to hear the cheering.

I took a deep breath and blew it all into the baby's face. Furiously treading water, I began chest compressions. Babies are tricky. It is very easy to crush their little bodies. I held it by the back of its baby shirt and with two fingers applied compressions very rapidly. After what seemed like forever, the baby vomited water and began to cry. I finally glanced around, and Captain Rand and Eddie were in the emergency skiff and were putt-putting my way.

When they pulled alongside, I reached high and handed the baby to Captain Rand and then clambered up the outboard motor and into the stern. As soon as I fell into the boat, Eddie kicked it and we raced to the party boat, if you could say we were racing with a 9.5 HP motor. Captain Rand wrapped the crying baby in a thick white towel. There were several in the boat. I grabbed one and pulled it over my head and shoulders. It wasn't cold but I was shaking.

# 2

The news said the baby's name was LaDonna May Wilson. The film crew on the boat had footage of the father dancing the baby on the rail. You could hear a woman calling for the man to get the baby down. Then the cameraman stumbled and when the picture was clear again the baby was gone. Suddenly, a man streaked from off camera, leapt to the top rail, and went over. The cameraman was late to the rail and there was nothing but roiled water on the screen. They had done an edit and suddenly I was there, surfaced with the baby. You could hear the people on the boat shouting and cheering. There was another edit and Captain Rand came up the gangway with the baby in his arms and I was behind him climbing on board, but I had a towel over my head and my chin was ducked into my chest. If you didn't notice I only had one foot, you would never know it was me.

Marianne and I were at the El Patron watching the news with Blackhawk and Elena and Nacho and Jimmy. Marianne squeezed my arm, kissed my cheek and told me I was a hero. This stuff made me very uncomfortable. I had waited in the cockpit with Marianne while Captain Rand got the big boat turned around and headed back to the marina. The last thing in the world I wanted was TV footage of me coming off the boat. As he was docking, I slipped over the starboard stern side, where I couldn't be seen by anyone on shore and swam the length of the marina to Tiger Lily. The news talkers had a field day with speculation as to who the mystery man was. Jimmy told me that when Blackhawk and Elena came off the boat Blackhawk had to bark at Elena to shut her up. She got over it when Blackhawk gently and forcefully explained how notoriety could ruin all of us and especially put me in a dangerous situation. I had made some friends in the underworld of Phoenix, but I had made some dangerous enemies at the same time.

There are three nightclubs under the same huge roof of El Patron. Marianne was, what in the day, had been called the torch singer. Her club was in the first space. Blackhawk had named it Rick's American, named after the nightclub in the old Bogart movie Casablanca. Marianne excelled at the old jazz standards of Sinatra, Ella Fitzgerald, and Nat King Cole. It didn't hurt that she was one sexy lady.

The last room was the one the whole building was named after. It was the largest room. The El Patron was where Elena and her large mariachi band packed them in four nights a week. The middle room was a Texas style honkytonk steakhouse. Elena had recently renovated the room to add the steakhouse kitchen feature. There was still country music on weekends, but the dance floor was much smaller. She had ingeniously set up a hybrid kitchen that could serve all three clubs at the same time. Above the El Patron space was another space. The ceilings in El Patron were so tall that the other space made the outside of the building look three stories tall. This space Blackhawk had made into a small office and waiting room and all the rest was living area. He had filled it with three baths, four bedrooms and fine furniture and fine art. You could access this part of the building though a staircase from the inside of the saloon. Steps went up to a landing that had a narrow walkway around three sides. At the top of the stairs was a door that opened into a hallway. That led to the office and living quarters. Connected to the back of the El Patron was a large storage room with a loading dock. The building itself was built to be a large commercial looking building that squatted in the middle of a large parking lot. The lot was well lit and monitored. Each street entrance was fitted with a Vegas styled sign with flashing lights.

Elena had hired a James Beard award winning chef and had encouraged him to come up with a menu that was a cross between New York and Mexico City. Marianne and I were sampling one of his latest inventions. He was a fabulous guy and a talented chef if he could stay away from the booze while he cooked. Like all creative people he could get excited. He had concocted his own special mole poblano, the famous Mexican sauce made any number of ways, depending on who makes it. This one he had drizzled over shredded pulled pork and fried bananas. The Midwesterner in me wrinkled my nose at it, but boy, was I wrong.

Jimmy brought me another beer. "Have you tasted this, Jimmy?"

"Yeah, it's fabulous."

Elena came down the stairs and joined us. She sat beside Marianne.

"I know of another dish you should add to your menu," Jimmy said to her.

"Hot dogs," Elena said, smiling.

"No, no. Elk tenderloins. Elk steak."

"Where would I get elk steaks?"

"Place on Sixteenth street," I said. "Another one at Cave Creek and Utopia."

"Easier than that," Jimmy said. "I'll hunt them. I just got drawn for elk this year. In fact, I can get my hands on three elk tags. One is for bow."

Nacho came strolling in, his customary newspaper under his arm.

"Hey Nacho," Jimmy said. "You want to go elk hunting?"

Elena snorted. "Nacho, elk hunting?"

"What's wrong with that?" Nacho said, offended. He sat on his usual stool.

Elena laughed, "Ignacio is a city boy. The only meat you could count on him to bag would be a triple stacker cheeseburger."

"Bugs," he said, unfolding the paper.

"Bugs?"

"The outdoors is filled with them. Drive me crazy. What about Blackhawk?"

"Does Blackhawk look like Daniel Boone?" Elena snorted.

"Now hold on little lady. You'd be surprised," I said. "One of the problems they gave us in training was a one-month course in forest survival. Then to test us with winter coming on, they dropped us stark naked deep into the forest with only a K-Bar knife and we had to make it out over thirty miles and survive at the same time. Blackhawk came out in the top ten percent."

"I suppose you were number one?"

I shrugged modestly.

Blackhawk came down the stairs and Jimmy turned to fix him a drink. He sat on the other side of Elena from me.

"Jackson says you were in the top of your deep woods survival test," Jimmy said. He set the drink in front of Blackhawk. Blackhawk took a sip.

"Jackson don't lie," Blackhawk said.

"That true Marianne?" Elena said.

I turned my head to look at her.

"So far, so good," she said. I raised my glass, and we touched rims.

"So, you're good in the woods?" Jimmy said. Blackhawk gave him a one shoulder shrug.

"Set the team record coming out," I said.

"What was your secret?" Nacho said.

Blackhawk took another drink. "I just thought of something no one else thought of. I climbed the highest hill, then climbed the highest tree."

"You could see a long way?"

"I could see forever. In all directions."

"So how did you decide which way to go?"

"Well, that was the easy part. I waited until it got dusk, and I could see the head lights on the highway, so I slept the night then hiked to the road and hitchhiked to the next motel."

"I thought you were naked?" Elena said.

"I got lucky and flagged down a van full of nuns coming back from Vegas."

Elena just shook her head. Nacho said, "Boy that was lucky."

# 3

It was late. After Marianne's show at the El Patron we were at Marianne's place getting ready for bed. "Did I tell you I got an email from my sister?" she said.

"I don't think so," I said.

"Got it this morning. Tiffany's coming out to hook up with ASU. She's decided to go to school here. She wants to stay with me until she gets settled."

"Tiffany? Mariellen's daughter?" Marianne nodded. "The whole time?"

"No. I'll just show her around until she gets settled in a dorm room."

"I assume she's been accepted."

"She came out while you were in Albuquerque, remember?"

"Oh, yeah." I didn't remember.

Marianne was leaning into her dresser mirror, detaching her earrings. We had been together for a while, and I still found things to notice about her. Her ears were delicate. Perfectly formed like God had taken special care. She applied cold cream to her face and began to remove the stage makeup. Because of the harshness of the spotlights that played on her while she sang, she always took extra care with her skin.

"How come an email?" I said. "You guys talk on the phone every day."

"She does that when she has something she doesn't want to talk about."

"What don't you think she wants to talk about?"

She turned from the mirror to look at me. "Don't be obtuse."

"What?"

"She'd have to talk to me about it before I knew what it was."

I shook my head. "If you had to guess, what do you think it is."

"Could be Tiffany. They've been having trouble."

"What kind of trouble?"

"Only child growing up trouble. Empty nest syndrome trouble."

"You always led me to believe that Tiffany was the good child."

"She's wonderful, she's my favorite niece."

"She's your only niece."

"That simplifies things. Maybe it's Dad's health. He has problems. He's been getting dizzy lately."

"How old is he?

She looked at herself in the mirror. "Turned eighty-three last birthday."

"You were a late baby."

She smiled. "He was forty before he married Mom, and it was ten years before I came along."

"He still have VA benefits?"

"They are going to run a battery of tests but he has to go to the VA in Orlando." She looked at me. "What are you doing?"

"Scratching," I said. "You know why God gave men a pair of balls?"

"Do tell me."

"So, he'd have something to scratch in the mornings."

She just looked at me. "You aren't in the Army anymore, surrounded by juveniles. Go to bed."

# 4

The next night was Marianne's night off. Her favorite restaurant was called Chaz's, named after the chef that owned it. He was nationally known. When Elena decided to put a full high-end restaurant in part of the space that had been the hard rock club, she had tried to hire him, but he had all the awards he wanted, and his own place so she settled on Texas BBQ and steaks. Worked for me. She had the best country bands of the area play there and while it was the smallest of the three clubs in size, it did very well. Whole lot of shit kickers in Phoenix.

Chaz's was not a large place, but it had its charm. The kitchen was in full view of the dining area. The walls were decorated with large fine art. Several were nudes and there were enough of them to make the uptight prigs nervous. The restaurant was only three blocks from one of the largest evangelical Christian churches in the Valley.

Chaz had a habit of wandering through the dining area talking to his customers. Once Marianne mentioned to him that he had lost a couple at the table next to us. They had said a blessing when they sat down. A loud and long blessing, meant to be heard, that spoke directly to the decline of American values.

He had laughed. At least they didn't want to burn them. There was no worry about him not having enough customers. You had better call a week ahead to get your reservations. One of his practices that made him popular was only making two entrees a day. One was usually a standard American dish. Prime steak or sea bass or shrimp and grits. The other would be a little more exotic. Usually something from another country that Americans usually don't get to taste. Letting his creative juices flow. That was your choice. The choices were listed on a board by the front door. Tonight's was Wagyu beef medallions cooked to order, with mashed potatoes and roasted asparagus with Chaz's original hollandaise, or white Crystal crab direct from Australia. And he meant fresh caught. Shipped within ten hours from the waters off Australia. Served with his own pepper sauce. Marianne was a midwestern girl. I completely understood why this was her favorite restaurant. It was so exotic compared to what was at home. All the waiters and waitresses wore starched, long sleeved white shirts and black aprons wrapped around their waists.

Another reason it was her favorite place was because Chaz had brought his wife into Rick's American two or three times to catch her show and was very complimentary. He always made her a special dessert.

Our waitress took our drink order and was back inside two minutes. I had an old fashioned and Marianne ordered a glass of Chardonnay.

"When do you go elk hunting?" Marianne asked, taking a tiny sip of wine.

"Day after tomorrow, oh-dawn thirty. Jimmy is anxious. When does your niece arrive?"

"She flies in tonight, or should I say tomorrow. She arrives at 2:30."

"AM? You mean this morning? Holy crap. Why so late?"

"Because my sister is a cheap skate. I offered to pay but she wouldn't have it."

"Here's a dumb question. "Who is picking her up? A taxi, I hope."

She smiled. "Oh, no. Auntie Marianne will pick her up. Mommy insists."

"Has Mommy thought about the inconvenience she's putting you to?"

"Hasn't crossed her mind."

"That doesn't make sense."

"Sometimes family doesn't make sense. You don't have a sister, do you?"

I shook my head.

They brought the food and got us all arranged. I sliced a piece of beef and popped it in my mouth. Delicious. I chewed it thoughtfully.

"So," I finally said. "How do we handle the situation?"

"What situation?"

I looked at her across the rim of my drink. "Now you don't be obtuse. Our situation. Our relationship. I've been spending a lot of nights at your place."

She cracked and chewed on her crab. She took her time. She swallowed and took another sip of wine. "Oh, that situation."

"I've never had the impression that you were fully forthcoming to your family about the complete nature of our relationship. *Complete* being the operative word."

I watched her and this was one of those rare times that I couldn't read her. Her eyes were on her plate. She was silent for a long while. She chewed some more. Finally, she looked up at me and said, "I told you, the girl is screwed up and a little wild."

"You told me," I agreed.

"She is only nineteen."

"Just a baby."

She took another drink of wine. This one larger. "I don't think it's a good idea to promote a relationship like ours to someone that young and impressionable."

"Like ours?" I said.

"Now don't do that. You know what I mean. It's bad enough that these kids go off to college and immediately start screwing around. No more boundaries."

"I don't think that describes our relationship."

"No it doesn't but…" She stopped. She took a deep breath. "I have been the only one in the entire family, aunts, uncles, cousins, anybody that tried to maintain some resemblance of a moral code. My sister didn't. I haven't told you this, but my sister had three abortions. Two of them were selective. When we look at Tiffany, it just scares the hell out of us."

I drained my old fashioned and caught the eye of the waitress. "So, what do you want us to do, not see each other?"

"No, not that. You are going hunting. You'll be gone, how long?"

"Not sure, probably ten days to two weeks."

"By the time you get back she will be entrenched in her new life. We can handle it then."

16

"Never put off till tomorrow what you can put off till the day after tomorrow."

The waitress brought my drink.

"I am hoping you will work with me on this."

I looked at her. "Do you want to get married?"

"Huh, what? What are you talking about?" She looked at me like I was crazy.

I nodded. "Yeah, me neither."

# 5

Marianne had never been to Sky Harbor this late before. She couldn't remember being at any airport this late before. The good news was that the expressway wasn't busy. She had no trouble pulling onto the cylindrical parking ramp that wound up and up and up, round and round and round, until an electronic sign told her she could pull off into the garage and find parking. She made a note of which floor she was on and what the identifying directions and numbers she would need to find the car again. She turned the wrong way and so had a longer walk to the elevators. She glanced at her watch. She was a little late, but she knew her niece was always late, so she wasn't bothered.

She took the elevator down to the luggage claim area. It was a huge area with at least twenty carousels. When she stepped off into the wide-open area the first thing she heard was her name on the loudspeakers. She stopped, shocked. It was fifteen seconds before the message was repeated. She was requested to proceed to the lost luggage room, located midway down and outside the barriers that enclosed the carousels. It had a sign. She could see it from where she was. She was confused. She didn't have any lost luggage. Maybe Tiffany had used her name. She headed for it.

Usually, this area was always crowded but now there weren't many people there. She made her way to the room and stepped through the door. The first thing she saw was a security guard lounging against the wall. Next to him was a maintenance guy with a bucket on wheels and a mop handle sticking up from the bucket. Sitting on the floor next to him was Tiffany, spraddle legged, her head on her chest, her hair a mess. She was out. There was a large Starbucks next to her. The security guard looked at Marianne with a relieved look on his face.

"Are you Aunt Marianne?"

"I'm not sure I want to be."

The security guy said, "Could I see your I.D.?"

Marianne got on her knees and took Tiffany's face. She pinched it. The girl just grumbled. She shook her. She still didn't want to open her eyes.

"Jesus Christ, what the hell happened to her?"

"May I see your I.D., please," the guard said again.

Marianne dug it out and gave it to him. He looked at it then handed it back.

"Ma'am," he said. "I'll just be a happy camper if I can turn her over to you and get her the hell out of here. It's too late to arrest anyone. It would be noon before the paperwork is done, and I get off shift in an hour."

Marianne shook the girl again. Tiffany started mumbling. "How'd she get like this. Jesus, she reeks."

"Evidently it was a going away party that got out of control. When she boarded, she seemed normal. What we didn't know was she had a bottle of tequila in her carryon and some pills we haven't been able to identify."

"Didn't that go through security?"

He shrugged. "Evidently, she ended up with it on the other side. I think it was in a Green Tea bottle, but I can't prove it. Let me help you get her up."

"Her luggage?"

He took Tiffany by the shoulders and lifted her. "It's that matched set by the wall. The purple ones."

Tiffany grumbled and came awake. "What the hell?"

"Tiffany? Are you okay? Can you walk?"

The girl looked distressed. "I think I'm going to be sick."

The maintenance man picked up her oversized coffee cup and poured its contents into the mop bucket. He handed it to her.

"Use this," he said.

She took it. "Fuck you," she said.

"You think you can get her home?" the security guard said unfazed.

"Can you help me get her luggage to my car? It's in the parking garage."

"Small price to pay," the guard said.

"And fuck you too," Tiffany said and belched.

# 6

I intended to sleep late but I awoke with a mixture of elk hunting images and thoughts of marriage to Marianne in my head. I thought about that for a while. I did love Marianne but was I *in love* with her? Could I live with any woman for the rest of my life? Could I be domesticated? Was it fair to her? What do women expect in a man? Would I have to get a job?

I stopped that crap right there and went back to thinking about elk hunting.

I put on my trunks and my swim foot and dove in and did ten furious laps to the buoy and back. I showered and fixed sausage patties and eggs for breakfast. I started packing. I stopped by the storage unit and got what I thought I'd need, then went to the club.

When I got to the El Patron, I piled my stuff by Jimmy's truck and went inside. Nacho and Jimmy were watching the news. There was a seven-alarm fire at an automobile tire storage facility and the plume of black oily smoke could be seen from just about anywhere in the city. Even the space station could see it.

"See! What did I tell you," Jimmy said, setting a glass of beer and half a tumbler of tomato juice in front of me. "As soon as you have another piece of news, the baby saving hero of Lake Pleasant will be forgotten. What's it been, a couple of days?"

"They are charging the daddy with reckless child abuse," Nacho said.

"As they should," I said.

Jimmy brought some topo maps over and we moved to where we could spread them on a table. He had previously marked up the one we would be interested in. While he spread the map out and was studying it, I called Blackhawk.

"Yeah?"

"Jimmy and I are looking at maps. You want to join us?"

"Be right down."

Jimmy went back to the bar and dug out a magnifying glass. He began to search the map. "Here," he said, putting his forefinger on a spot on the map. "See where it says Mogollon Plateau? Just east of there is the section, at least one of them. The elk are probably moving to lower elevations where it's warmer and the grass is beginning to pop up." Blackhawk walked up to hear that last part.

"How many days do we have?" he said.

"Most hunts last 10 days. If you get one on the first day, the remaining days go back into the barrel for someone else to draw. The bad news is that there has already been a batch of permits put out for that section. I think we need to move deeper up the rim and hike back in." He tapped the map with his forefinger. "Very few elk hunters, especially from the valley, are in the shape to hike through the unimproved forest. I'm figuring we can out-hustle them. Get up there a couple of days early and use that time to find the herds that haven't started down yet."

"Is that part of the forest legal for us?"

Jimmy shrugged. "That is about as remote as you can get. You think a ranger will be wandering around up there in zero-degree weather hoping to find a needle in that haystack?"

"So, you don't mind if we bend the law a little bit?"

"Look at the map. Tell me where the section ends. There are no markings, and it goes all the way north to the highway."

"And we hike back in and each kill one and have to lug it back through that rugged forest, and get back before the meat begins to spoil."

"Got that figured out," Jimmy said. "We drop my truck on an old, unused logging road I know of. It's pretty far north and isolated from the well-known areas. We pull the twenty-three-foot flatbed trailer with minimal gear and two quads on it. We ride the quads in another ten miles then snug them and backpack in until we find the pastures where I think the elk will be." He looked satisfied with himself. "That way we can get our two critters and one guy dresses out the meat, so the guts don't spoil and the other two get the quads. There's a place outside of Payson that will process the meat."

"Unless we want to do it ourselves," I said.

He smiled at me. "The processors up there probably do ten elk a day. Guys like you and I are amateurs. Let the pros do what they do."

"Good idea," I said.

The double doors that were between the El Patron and the hallway to the other two nightclubs opened. Marianne came in leading a very beautiful girl that could have been her younger twin. Jimmy almost swallowed his tongue.

They stood a moment, letting their eyes adjust to the lower light. I moved over to them.

"Hi," I said. "You must be Tiffany." I saw her glance at my feet. "I'm Jackson," I said, offering my hand. She took it gently with barely a squeeze. I kissed Marianne on the cheek. "Come on in." I led them to the table with Jimmy and Blackhawk.

"This is Jimmy," I said. He said hi. "And this is Blackhawk, he is the owner of this fine establishment.

"Hi," Tiffany said demurely.

I looked at Jimmy. "Why don't you get Elena on the intercom and tell her we're bringing a guest up to meet her." Jimmy moved to the intercom.

Elena was waiting for us in the living room of the apartment. When we came in the front door, she came across the room and in Elena fashion, took Tiffany in a big hug.

"I've heard so much about you." She held her at arm's length. "My goodness, you are as beautiful as your auntie."

"Thank you."

Elena said, "Can I get you guys anything?"

Marianne shook her head, as did her niece. "Too early for me and I have to work tonight."

"Have you seen your auntie perform?" Elena said.

"No, not for a while."

"You are in for a treat," I said.

"That's what I've heard."

"Are you staying with Marianne?" Elena asked.

"For a few days," Tiffany said. "Until ASU has a dorm room available."

"Which I don't understand," Marianne said. "They have known for a while how many students to expect. I'm planning on going down tomorrow to shake their tree."

"Who's going tomorrow?" Elena said.

"Just the two of us," Marianne said.

"I'll go with you," Elena said.

"Uh, oh," Blackhawk said.

Elena gave him a look. "When do you boys leave to go kill those poor defenseless animals?"

"Tomorrow or the day after tomorrow," Jimmy said, his eyes still on Tiffany.

"What are you killing?" Tiffany said. She sounded a little shocked.

"They are going elk hunting," Elena said.

"You kill elk?" she shook her head. "Just for sport?"

"No, not just for sport," Jimmy said. "We harvest what we kill and process it and eat every animal we kill."

"That's disturbing," Tiffany said.

"What did you have for supper last night?" I said.

Marianne looked at me. "I took her to Alfredo's."

"What did you order?" I asked Tiffany.

"I had their special."

"Which was?"

"Chicken parmesan," she said.

"Was it good?"

"Delicious," she said.

"What animal died so you could enjoy it?"

She looked at me and anger flashed across her eyes. "It's not the same."

No one said anything. Tiffany stood and looked at her aunt. Her aunt was looking at me and it wasn't very friendly.

"I want to go home now," the girl said.

"I'm sorry…," I started, but Marianne cut me off with the wave of a hand. She followed her niece out the door.

"Señor subtle strikes again," Elena said.

# 5

My living arrangements had been pretty easy lately. I had choices. Spending a lot of time at El Patron, I could spend the night there as a guest of Blackhawk. I usually slept on the couch in his office. The office had a half-bath, so I didn't have to disturb anyone. I had a key, so sometimes they didn't even know I was there. I could stay at Marianne's, which I was in the habit of doing on her days off. Her workdays she needed her rest. But now with Tiffany staying there, the message was clear. Stay away for now. That left one option. I took it. I trekked back to the boat. I had my stuff in the warehouse already. Jimmy had said tomorrow or the next day. Mox nix to me.

I sat on the Sun Deck and nursed a drink and began a list of things I would likely leave behind if I didn't have a list. After I filled a page, it was obvious that most of that stuff Jimmy would bring. I crossed off half of it. I stood up and looked at the lake. It was late enough that most people out on the lake had their running lights on. I turned and looked at the marina. The dock lights were on, that soft glow that haunted everything, bulbs designed to keep the bugs away. The bar lights were on but not many people were there. Eddie's old River Runner was there, I couldn't tell if his skiff was. I reached under the captain's cockpit console and pulled out the binoculars. The skiff was missing. He was out night fishing. Pete Dunn's Thirteen Episodes was dark.

I came out here to be alone. To live alone. It was just complete happenstance that Blackhawk had come to the same city. He had stopped at a dive called El Patron for a drink. He met Elena and decided he wanted both, the club and the girl. He made the owner an offer the guy couldn't refuse. He had been here ever since.

I had sought solitude, but I had never been lonely. Tonight, for some reason, I felt lonely. Maybe it was because I knew I had peeved Marianne. Maybe it was because I had not been invited to join her and her niece. Marianne was very private when it came to family. I don't know what I expected. I didn't have family to share and don't know if I would if I could. Probably wouldn't know how.

I decided to fix a bigger drink and count the stars. I made it through about half the drink before I nodded off. I was awakened by footsteps on the dock. I roused myself and looked over the side. Sherrie, the marina bartender, was coming my way with a bottle in her hand. She stopped at the bow and called out in a low voice, "Jackson."

"Hi there," I said standing. "What's up?"

"The place was dead, so I closed the bar early and I knew you were here. I thought we could have a drink."

I stood for a moment. Sherrie had always, in subtle ways, let me know she was interested. I didn't encourage her, and she didn't push it. Every time it might have been a good idea, one or the other of us was tied up. I had many thoughts about her, but I never followed them anywhere. I tried to tell myself to be the good man my mom would want me to be. But, hell, I didn't know what that was. I had lost her too early and couldn't remember what she would have wanted.

Here I had been musing about being alone and the gods had sent a gift. With her own bottle. A damned good-looking gift. We could always just talk, I thought. Be a fool not to.

"Come on up," I said. She stepped aboard and, luckily, I hadn't activated the alarms. I pulled two lounge chairs to face out at the moonlit lake and close enough for quiet conversation. She came up the steps and came over to me. She was wearing her bikini with a wraparound scarf at her waist. This wasn't unusual. She usually wore a bikini top and cut-off shorts when she was behind the bar. On crowded weekend nights when the tips were flowing, she would replace the cut-offs for her bikini bottoms to help the tips along.

"What've we got," I said. She handed me the bottle. Captain Morgan spiced rum.

"I thought we'd have this with Sprite. Very popular."

"I have Coke," I said.

"Any port in a storm," she said.

"Where did you hear that?"

"Either you or Eddie."

"I'll be back." I went down and filled two tall glasses with ice, grabbed two Cokes and climbed back up. She was standing at the rail watching the moon on the water. I fixed the drinks and handed her one. I picked up my old one and tossed the remains over the starboard side. I came back to where she stood. She turned and offered her glass for a toast. I touched it with mine and we both had a drink.

"I've been trying to make this happen for a while," she said, watching me.

"I know. God knows why."

She took another drink, her eyes looking at me over her glass. They were dark and beautiful, like her hair. "I'm not an easy girl," she said. "I want you to know that."

"I know that. I've known you for a while. And conversely, I'm not an easy guy. I can't balance more than one girl at a time. You know I have a girlfriend."

"Yes, I know that. I'm not here to change that."

"Why are you here?"

"Lonely. Broke up with the last jackass I was with, and I saw an opportunity for you and me to have a drink together. So I took it."

"I'm not sorry you did."

We looked at each other some more. Finally, I said, "Let's sit down before I kiss you."

"Good idea," she said. We walked over and sat on the chaise lounges. There was a breeze moving her hair. She brushed it back. "Doesn't mean it's not going to happen."

I shook my head, not sure what I was thinking.

We sat silently, taking a drink once in a while. "That was really something you did for that baby," she said, looking at the moon that was just rising.

"How do you know it was me?"

"I was there," she smiled.

I gave her a sharp look. "Oh, yeah. I forgot. Look, I'd

appreciate it if you don't say anything."

"Like that teenager you helped find and getting Eddie's nephew out of jail and cleared of murder."

I shook my head, "You know what they say."

"What's that?"

"Shit happens. I didn't go looking for any of that."

# 6

"You seem to get your share of it."

"You noticed that, did you."

"Where's your girlfriend, or is it fiancée? Where is she tonight?"

"Not fiancée. Her niece is in town. The niece is going to ASU and Marianne is helping her get settled."

"She sure can sing."

I nodded. "She sure can." I took another drink and noticed my glass was almost empty. "Would you like another drink?"

She looked at her drink. "No, not yet. I didn't come down here to get tanked."

"Do you have a boyfriend?"

She shook her head. "I just told you I broke up with my last jackass. I really don't want anything steady."

"You expect me to believe that?" I said with a laugh. "I thought all girls wanted a steady guy."

"I really don't. I'm perfectly happy doing what I'm doing. I did have boyfriends, I mean exclusive boyfriends, but it seemed always to end up the same sad way."

"Sad? Why sad?"

"Things would be great. I like to have fun and we'd be having a lot of fun. Then, it's like they began to get too serious. They started to get possessive. I'd go do something and they'd be like, where have you been? They'd start coming to the bar, and at first that was okay. But when I would do what I'm hired to do, which is be happy and friendly with everyone, not just the guys, but everyone, they would get jealous. Then if they got drunk, they would start trouble. After the third guy did that, I just decided it wasn't worth it."

I drank the end of my drink. "Would you like to have one more, a night-cap?"

She looked a hole into the bottom of her glass. "Sure," she said finally and drained her glass. She handed it to me, and I went down for two more. I brought them up and handed hers to her. We clinked our glasses and drank.

She was still watching the moon. "You thinking about getting married?"

That caught me by surprise. I looked at her, but she wasn't looking at me. I looked across the water and for the second time that day I thought honestly about it.

I finally answered, "No." I took another drink and said, "No, I don't think so. I'm stuck in my ways. I like living on my boat. I like reading all day if I want to. I like fishing with Eddie on the spur of the moment. I don't like obligations like taxes and retirement funds and health insurance. How could I bring a girl, no matter how much I loved her, into that?" I hitched around to look at her. "You mentioned some of the situations I got into. If I had to worry about a wife or someday maybe a child and I got into some bad situation, maybe I'd hesitate, or make the wrong call or take too long to make a decision and get killed. Or get someone else killed." I was silent. "No, I would be a bad choice for any girl to marry."

She set her glass down and stood up. She stepped across me, straddling me. She sat on me and taking my face into her hands she kissed me. Long and hard and relentless. I dropped my glass as my arms went around her. She kissed me with everything she had. And I kissed her back and did it again. While her mouth was locked on mine, she reached around her back and unfastened her bikini top. She dropped it to the side and my hands found her breasts. No store bought these. I felt my body reacting to her. I am male and sometimes at times like these, some things are unavoidable. Time stood still. All there was, were her breasts, her tongue and my body reacting.

Finally, she stood and slipped out of her bikini. She pulled my trunks off. She sat on me again in a way that interlocked our bodies. I pulled her face down to mine and my pelvis tried to get as far up into her as I could. Maybe it was because it was so unexpected, maybe it was because I have always liked her and just like Eddie, she represented the carefree independence of my lifestyle. It didn't hurt she was very good looking. I can't tell you how long it was, but both of us raged through the first encounter. Without a pause we moved into a quieter dance. Softer, gentler, more aware of pleasing the other. When we finished, she lay on top of me until we caught our breath. I scooted to the outside of the chaise lounge, and she snuggled me, her head on my chest. We lay there for a long time, then fell asleep. Two hours later I awoke, and we hadn't moved. I roused her. The air was chilling. She gathered her bikini and scarf and followed me down the staircase. I found a clean sleep shirt for her and one for me. She protested, saying she should leave. I said, not unless she had a really compelling reason. It would be foolish not to get some sleep. She kissed me and climbed into the bed, and I climbed in beside her and we spooned up. Within a very short amount of time, we were both asleep.

I usually was an early riser unless I set my body clock to sleep later. The sun was up when I awoke. I hadn't pulled the hurricane curtains and the morning light was creeping through the salon and the galley and was working its way down the hallway to the master stateroom. I had been smart enough to take the outside of the bed and slipped out as quiet as a mouse. I went to the front head so I wouldn't wake her. I relieved myself, splashed water on my face and ran my fingers through my hair.

I started a pot of coffee and went through the oversized locker to see what I had for breakfast. I started a half-pound of bacon sizzling and scrambled some eggs and shredded cheese with a splash of half and half in a small mixing bowl. I had chopped mushrooms and white onion and was sautéing them in butter when Sherrie came yawning down the hallway.

"I smell bacon," she said.

"Yes ma'am," I said. "Coffee and orange juice if you like. Hope you like bacon."

She leaned her hip against the counter as she fixed her coffee in the cup I had set out. "I grew up outside Livingston, Montana," she said. "Hell yes, I like bacon. My granddad always said, if you have eggs and anything else, you have a meal."

"I think I'd like your granddad."

"Yeah, you would." She blew on her coffee and took a

tentative sip. She set it down and came to me and put her arms around my neck. She kissed me, then kissed me again. "Thank you," she said as she released me.

"For bacon?"

"No. Any of my past boyfriends would be pulling at me to go back to bed for more sex."

"Am I your boyfriend now?"

She smiled. "Nope. But, maybe one of my best friends."

"Perfect," I said.

"But not friends with benefits. I won't be behind another woman's back. As long as you are with Marianne, don't count on this again."

"Yeah," I said. "Exactly. Breakfast is ready, can I dish yours up?"

"I'm famished," she said.

After we ate, I walked her down to the gate that was supposed to guard the dock. She turned and kissed me, looked me in the eyes and then was gone. As I turned away, I saw Eddie standing two docks over rinsing seagull crap off his dock. He smiled at me and then extended a hand and shot me with his thumb and forefinger.

# 7

Late afternoon I headed for the El Patron. I don't like to talk on the phone and drive, but I thumbed Marianne's number. It immediately went to voicemail. I swung into her neighborhood and drove to her house. I kept telling myself it wasn't guilt. Her car was gone, and no one answered the door. I drove over to El Patron, trying her number a couple more times. It always went to voicemail. I sat out front for a few minutes and thought what a pathetic stalker I would be. I locked up the Mustang and went inside.

There were few customers. Blackhawk was at the bar with a raft of papers spread in front of him. It looked like invoices. He was never in a good mood when he paid invoices. I sat a few stools from him. He looked at me and nodded then went back to his paperwork. Jimmy was stocking the lockers, preparing for the night. Nacho came from the back with a keg on a dolly and wheeled behind the bar.

Jimmy came down, "Getcha something?"

"Gimme a coke," I said.

He looked at me. "You feeling okay?"

Nacho said, "What'd he say?"

Jimmy said, "He said he wanted a coke."

Blackhawk was laughing. "Give the man a coke," he said.

Nacho got the keg in place and came down with my coke and a beer for him.

"I guess I'm getting in a rut," I said. Nacho slid in next to me. I looked at him. "Is Marianne working tonight?"

Nacho looked over to Blackhawk. Blackhawk didn't look up. "She and Elena took the night off."

"They out on the town?"

"They took off this morning with Marianne's niece to make sure she's properly enrolled and to see about finding her housing at ASU."

Right on cue the doors burst open and the three girls came giggling in. "Three tequilas," Elena called out. "Por favor."

Jimmy jumped to the tequila bottle. Elena led the girls to Blackhawk, and she sat next to him and leaned over and kissed the side of his face. The other girls sat next to her. It was noticeable that Marianne didn't look at me. At least it was noticeable to me.

Jesus, I only said that eating meat was normal. As soon as that went through my mind, I knew it was more than that. I looked at my coke. It couldn't be Sherrie. No way. I looked at Tiffany. Her blond hair was windblown, and she was flushed. As soon as Jimmy set the tequila in front of her, she didn't wait for Elena's toast. She downed it and waved at Jimmy for another.

Elena toasted. "Here's to a successful day. Miss Tiffany has a very nice townhome, and a very nice roommate, all furnished. Ready to move into. Walking distance to the campus."

"Thanks to Aunty Elena, who seems to know everyone in this whole fucking town."

Marianne looked strained at Tiffany's language. "Just lucky," Elena said modestly. "My cousin, well I have a hundred cousins, but anyway, one of them has a daughter out there. The girl has a townhome apartment and her roommate bailed on her, so she was ecstatic to meet Tiffany." She twisted around and said to Tiffany, "What classes are you two taking together?"

"PolySci and Near Middle East Studies."

"Can you believe that?" Elena said. "I don't even know what that is, and these two kids are studying the same stuff."

I was watching Marianne. She was toying with her shot of tequila. I jumped in.

"You think this place will work?" I said to her.

She glanced up at me. "Elena says it's perfect."

"Which cousin is this?" Blackhawk said.

"You remember Frank and Gabriella. Frank's the carpenter. Helped you set the bar up. Their daughter Rosie. A real sweetheart. I love Rosie."

"That's because she brings forty of her closest friends down here to cheer everything you do," Blackhawk said.

"You wish you had forty friends," Elena said. Blackhawk opened his mouth, but she had already turned. "It's going to be great, Tiffany."

"Let's get this party started," Tiffany said. She waved at Jimmy. "Come on, good looking. Leave the bottle this time."

A group of customers had come in and came to the other side of the bar. Their chatter filled the room. Just under the new voices I heard Blackhawk lean into Elena and ask, "This is the Rosie that was in rehab?"

I didn't hear Elena respond. An hour later Marianne literally had to drag her niece out of the place. She glanced at me. "Need help?" I said.

She shook her head.

"Let me know when we can talk," I said.

She nodded, then helped her niece across the floor and out the double doors. Jimmy came over. "You want something else?"

"When do we leave for the elk hunt?"

"I figure early morning, day after tomorrow. That work with you guys?"

I nodded. "Give me a scotch," I said.

# 8

The day Jimmy had chosen to leave for the elk hunt was the same day Tiffany decided to move into her new condo. Luckily, she didn't have anything to move. So, I felt I wouldn't be needed. Clothes, a few pictures, a laptop and Marianne got her a small desk she could set up in her room to study. Elena enlisted Nacho and two of her cousins to help. I didn't have much to pack either.

I had a pretty good rifle, a Proof Tundra. Expensive as hell, but I got it from a discreet dealer in New Orleans. I bought it because in an accuracy test against other popular rifles it had proven to be the most accurate. I also had a Kabar Marine fighting knife. I kept it razor sharp and strapped to my leg when I was out in the wild. I had a 4-inch razor sharp folding knife I kept in my pocket. I could use it for skinning. I made a trek to the sporting goods store and bought meat bags and a 30 degree below zero sleeping bag. Jimmy said not to worry about kitchen things. We were hiking back in, so we would be minimalists. Blackhawk had checked the online weather and warned me that at that elevation it would be cold, especially at night. I packed some extra warm socks and dug out my long johns. I found a snug old watch cap in one of the storage lockers and dug out my insulated service boots. They were high-topped and waterproof. It had been a while since I had treated them. I rubbed them down with Otter Wax. One of them was set up to accommodate my prosthetic. I found an old pair of walkie talkies. Unfortunately, the contacts were corroded so I called Jimmy while I was at the store and he had enough for all of us.

I called Marianne a couple of times. One went to voicemail and I left a message. The second time she did pick up but told me she was busy with her niece and couldn't talk. I told her I was leaving for the elk hunt, and I was hoping we could get together when I got back. She said that would be fine. She sounded preoccupied but other than that, nothing unusual. I gave a mental shrug and got ready for the hunt. Most of my stuff was already at the club so all I had to mess with was clothes, toiletries, things I had just purchased and munchable stuff I would carry with me.

After I piled it all together on the bow, I stood looking at everything. Then I started putting things back. I narrowed it down to eating, sleeping and hunting. If it wasn't a critical necessity for one of those, I put it away.

I walked over to Eddie's River Runner. His skiff was tied up to it, so he wasn't fishing. He wasn't there. I figured he was working at the bar. It was early yet, and the place only had a few customers. Sure enough, Eddie was behind the bar. I wondered if Sherrie would be there, but she wasn't. I had been wondering what we would say to each other once we did see each other. Probably nothing out of the ordinary. We had made it pretty clear we were just friends and didn't want anything else.

The first thing Eddie said to me as I seated myself at the bar was, "Sherrie'll be in a little later."

I laughed. "Good to know."

"Thought it would be. Beer?"

"That'll be a start," I said. "Dos Equis."

He set the bottle in front of me. "When's the big elk hunt?

"Tomorrow morning. O'dawn thirty."

We talked fishing and elk hunting and how Eddie's legs were too old to take the strain of mountain hiking. I finished the beer and declined another one. I walked back to the Tiger Lily, and swam ten laps to the buoy and back. I toweled off, broiled a steak and scrambled some eggs. I took a quick shower and went to bed. I lay there a long time before I went to sleep.

One thing I never get used to is how eerie a big city looks when you travel through downtown really early in the morning. Even the streetlights had a different glow. Jimmy was already there. I parked next to the garbage bins, on the side that shielded the car from the distant street. I popped the trunk and unloaded my stuff, laying it on the asphalt next to the truck. I pulled the custom-made canvas cover and draped the Mustang, tying the cover down.

"You want to pack this stuff in any particular design?" I said.

"I try to keep it at or below the height of the walls of the bed."

He directed where he wanted my stuff. This wasn't his first rodeo. The warehouse door started up. Blackhawk came out carrying a duffel and two bottles of Wild Turkey. He handed them to Jimmy.

"Night warmer," he said.

"Stuff them somewhere they'll be protected. Precious cargo," I said.

Once packed there was nothing left to do. No one to say goodbye to. So, we started away. The El Patron looked gray and lonely in the eerie light of the parking lot. I had decided to park down at the El Patron instead of leaving the Mustang in its parking spot at the marina. If they had to pick me up, it would be miles out of the way. We were headed to the rustic little town of Payson. There was no easy way to get there from the houseboat. We'd have to take I17 to the 101 East, then all the way around the north end of the city to Shea Blvd, then east to the Beeline Highway. This way we only had to get over onto the SR51, then up to Shea.

Blackhawk took the passenger seat. I settled into the back seat of the dual cab truck. I got comfortable. We'd be driving a while. The sky was just becoming light when we reached Fountain Hills. Jimmy topped the gas tank off. Once out of Fountain Hills we were in the desert and headed up. Payson was a mountain town. When I first came here, I spent some time exploring the state. I was familiar with Payson and the surrounding area. I'd driven all the passible logging roads. I got into the habit of driving up to the Mogollon Rim to hike and camp. I tested myself to see if I could live off the land. Fish and squirrels were my main diet. On the way back to the boat I would stop at Christopher Creek at the little bar there and celebrate with a big old fat cheeseburger and fries.

As we left Fountain Hills, I suggested we stop at a café in the middle of Payson named Café 260 after the highway it was on. Best biscuits and sausage gravy from that part of the state. Jimmy agreed.

"Thought we were going to push to get to the elk," Blackhawk said.

"We'll need food for energy," I said. "After today, hot food will be scarce."

He didn't argue. I snuggled back and dozed, but the curving road kept tossing me around and kept me awake. We pulled into Payson and came to a halt at the first stoplight. I remembered a large saloon down the road to the left. Big place. Had a large bandstand and dance floor. I hadn't been there in a long time. We drove on through town and turned right, out of our way, to make for the restaurant. Despite the early hour, the café was nearly full. We were lucky to get a table. I was right about the biscuits and gravy. We finished, paid, and piled back into the truck. Since we had turned out of our way for the biscuits and gravy, we turned back toward the highway we had come in on. Jimmy pulled into a gas station to top off again.

"Keep an eye out for Houston Mesa Road," Jimmy said. We pulled out of the gas station. We saw no road sign. We went a while, "I think this is it," Jimmy said. Eagle-eyed Blackhawk saw the sign laying in the ditch. Someone had sheared it straight off. I guess I was expecting to turn onto a dirt road, but it was asphalt. At least for the first several miles. It wound through the pines and homes that lined the road. After six or seven miles we turned onto an unimproved road. After several miles of boiling up dust behind us we saw a sign proclaiming the area to be Brody Hills and after a while we came to very small developed community called Whispering Pines.

"You gotta be a recluse to live way out here," Blackhawk said. "Almost as bad as living on a boat."

"Worse," I said. "Got no place to fish."

"We were driving alongside a creek back there," Jimmy said.

"Starve to death, living on trout that small."

"Crawdads and turtles. Yum, yum," Blackhawk said.

"You a spoiled city boy now."

"Pull over," I said. "I need to take a leak." Jimmy obliged and we all got out and stretched and relieved ourselves. We climbed back in.

Jimmy said, "Up ahead is a dot on the map called Washington Park. There is a really rough road heading directly north from it. Goes straight up the rim. I almost didn't make it the last time but now I've done it I'm confident I can get us up north."

"He's confident," Blackhawk said.

"I'm all for getting me up," I said.

"All you have to do is look at Marianne for that," Blackhawk said. "That girl is hot."

"Marianne is a lady," Jimmy said.

Blackhawk glanced over the seat at me. His mouth wasn't smiling but his eyes were.

# 9

What a lot of people don't get about Arizona is that it's not just desert. A whole bunch of it is mountainous. Thick with tall ponderosa pines and aspen and spruce. Forest fires were a monumental problem every year. By the time we pulled into Washington Park the forest was too thick to see twenty yards into it. No wonder the elk thrived up here. The place was marked with parking to accommodate the hikers. Trails led off into the dense forest.

"I hear banjo music," Jimmy said.

"I don't," Blackhawk said.

"He's talking about the Burt Reynolds movie *Deliverance*," I laughed. "These four wasp office-type guys are taking a canoe trip to see the last of a wild river before it's flooded. That and the hillbilly people along the way. It was the banjo music of these inbred people that gave you the creeps."

"Three wasp type guys not four. Burt Reynolds was a bad ass guy with a bow and arrow," Jimmy said.

"John Voight turned out to be a badass, too."

"At first you didn't know he was badass. By the end you did."

Jimmy turned into the parking area at the trailhead and put the truck in park. He was looking around.

"Thought you had been here?" I said.

"Two years and a forest fire ago," he said. Blackhawk and I sat silently, waiting. Finally, he put the truck in gear and pulled ahead. He circled and slowly pulled to the north end. A faint pair of tracks led off into the trees. He followed the tracks. The trees and brush had grown and the branches scraped the sides of the truck.

"Arizona pin striping," Jimmy said. He forged ahead. It was very slow going and after a while I could tell we were headed up. Of course, my optimism was telling me that I just might spot some elk out the side window, but I couldn't see twenty yards into the forest.

After a very long drive we came up into a meadow. It was about twenty acres across. The leaves were turning, and it was quite beautiful. The trailer we were pulling was banging and clattering. Enough to scare animals away. Jimmy stopped.

"The road stops on the other side," he said. "That's where we'll switch to the quads."

He pulled straight across, and in the middle the truck sank into muck. Jimmy expertly didn't stop, and goosed it enough to pull us out of it and on across the meadow. On the other side he pulled up on flat solid ground. He got out and we followed.

Jimmy expertly unstrapped the quads. I helped him pull the right and left ramps out. He backed a quad down. I followed with the other one. Blackhawk was unpacking the totes that held our gear.

It took time, and we were all sweating in the cold air, when

48

we had the quads loaded. I felt like we had enough to feed a small army. We strapped our rifles on the special racks that held them to the handlebars. Blackhawk kept his across his lap, wedged between him and Jimmy. We fired them up, looked at each other and started through the thick forest. Jimmy took the lead. He knew where he was going. The deep silence of the forest was now broken by the growl of the gasoline engines. I lagged back from Jimmy far enough to allow the mountain breeze to carry his exhaust and dust away from my nostrils.

Despite the quad noise, there is something soothing and mesmerizing about the deep forest. The dew had evaporated, and the sunlight splashed through the trees in mottled patches of light that made the surroundings magical. This is one of the things that drew me to love Arizona. Places like this don't exist in the breadbasket states.

After a short time, we popped out of the forest and came to a maintained road. Jimmy stopped in the middle. I pulled up beside him. He cut his motor and so did I.

"General Crook Recreational Trail," he said.

"We taking it?" Blackhawk said.

Jimmy shook his head. "Up ahead a few miles, is the Blue Ridge Reservoir, which is a narrow canyon lake. Man made. In the meantime, just ahead are Clearwater Creek, Big Creek and General Springs. Plenty of water for elk. If we were in a hurry, we could swing left here and grab the Crackerbox Trail. It heads north and is improved like the Crook Trail here."

Blackhawk looked over at me. "What think you?'

"I'm in no hurry."

"Let's go up ahead and stay off the trails. Get some miles

behind us," Jimmy twisted to look at me. "Stop every once in a while, and scout around for sign."

"Neon lights," I said. "Elk R Here."

"More like elk scat," Jimmy said.

"The plan was," Blackhawk said, "to set up a base camp, leave the quads and hike in until we find the critters."

"Let's find a base camp, then," I said.

Jimmy started his quad and kicked it into gear. Blackhawk grabbed his shoulder, one handed, to hold on.

I followed. I thought briefly about Marianne. Wondering if she had her niece moved yet. The thought didn't last as every dark shadow began looking like an elk.

# 10

By the time they had Tiffany moved into Rosie's condo, Marianne was exhausted. Elena had come along to help, and Marianne was very grateful for that. It wasn't that Tiffany had a lot of stuff, she didn't, but Tiffany was practically worthless. She jabbered on and on about stuff Marianne not only didn't know about, but stuff she didn't care about. Elena was a saint. She not only helped with Tiffany, but she cleaned her niece's apartment also. Like every young girl living alone, the place was a mess.

After a while Tiffany said she wanted to take a walk around the neighborhood, just to familiarize herself with it. When Marianne offered to walk with her, she very quickly declined. She said she wanted to clear her head. Elena and Marianne just looked at each other. Sure enough, when she returned she reeked of marijuana. The good news was that while she was gone, Elena and Marianne got everything done.

"She's like her mom," Marianne said. "If my sister had been an only child my dad would have killed her. I spent my childhood covering up for her."

"She smoke dope a lot?"

"Pills, booze, then cocaine. When she got pregnant and was told she couldn't abort again, dad got her to agree to rehab. She straightened out enough to be a mom. At least got Tiffany raised. But, even now, she's still a slob. The acorn didn't fall far from the tree."

Both Marianne and Elena were scheduled to perform. As soon as they had the girl's room as good as it could be, they headed back to the nightclub. Elena and Blackhawk's apartment, on the second floor of the nightclub, had two full bathrooms. Both girls could take showers and a nap. Marianne always kept performance clothes and make-up in the spare closet. After her shower and before she lay down on the queen-sized bed in the guest bedroom, she tried to call Jackson.

The phone rang until it went to voicemail. His voicemail announcement was the generic one that just repeats the number dialed. She tried again with the same result. This time she left a message that it was her and to call. She put a sleep mask on and took a nap. Later, just before going on stage, she called Tiffany, no answer. She called Jackson again. No luck again. When she got home she felt like she had given a lackluster performance. After her shower, she tried again and got the same result.

She took two sleeping pills, so it was the next afternoon when she finally awoke. She tried again. Same thing. She was getting irritated. She dug out the number Elena had given her for Rosie, Tiffany's roommate. Rosie answered with a groggy voice heavy with sleep.

"Hey Rosie," Marianne said more cheerfully than she felt. "This is Tiffany's Aunt Marianne. I'm trying to reach Tiffany."

"Did you call her?"

Marianne wanted to bite her lip. "Yes hon. I called her; she doesn't answer."

"Probably sleeping," she said. "We were out late at a party last night. I wanted to introduce her around."

"I'm sorry to be a pain, but could you sneak a peek and if she is just sleeping, let her sleep."

There was silence. When you are this young these things can be very hard requests. Finally, she said, "Okay, let me check." She laid the phone down and Marianne could hear her muttering to herself. It wasn't very long before she was back.

"She's not here. It doesn't look like she's been here. The bed's still made and there's still stuff on it you guys had put there yesterday."

Marianne's heart went to her throat. She swallowed. "When was the last time you saw her?"

There was silence as she thought. "She was hooked up with a group that was partying pretty hard. She told me she would Uber home."

"When you got home, she wasn't there yet."

"Yeah."

"When did you get home?"

"Around one. I had a class this morning. Which I barely made. After class I came back and went back to bed. I didn't think to look in on her. She's a big girl."

Marianne thought, yeah but she's Momma's little girl and if something happens to her Momma is going to kill me.

"Thanks for checking, Rosie. If you see her, have her call me, would you please?"

"Sure thing."

Marianne hung up and looked at the wall.

# 11

Jimmy was leading us through the dense forest as quickly as he could. He knew what we were thinking; the noise of the quads would push any elk within hearing distance away. Just trying not to crash the quad took all my attention. As intentionally as he was driving, I assumed he had a destination in mind.

An hour later he pulled off into a small meadow surrounded by thick bushes of chokeberries and some crabapples. He cut the engine and Blackhawk stepped off and stretched and rubbed his butt. I did the same. Jimmy walked out into the opening and looked around.

"This must be the place," Blackhawk said.

"Ain't no place around the place but this place," I returned.

"Which one is Amos and which one is Andy?" Jimmy said, walking back to us.

The countryside had gradually opened and the brush that had been choking it had lessened. Jimmy walked around studying the ground. Finally, he joined us.

"Elk sign?" Blackhawk said.

Jimmy shook his head. "Don't see any. I'm looking for bear scat.

This looks like a good place for base camp but with all the berries that ripen in the fall the bears will be filling out their fat for the winter. I just don't want to set up a camp on their dinner table."

"Good idea," I said.

"I studied the maps pretty hard," he said. "This area is good because it has a lot of bunchgrass and the summer grasses haven't all gone yet. There are also groves of cottonwoods, and the elk love the bark of cottonwood and there's plenty of that around."

He pointed off to the east. "In that direction there are meadows and ravines as you get closer to the edge of the Rim."

"So, we set up camp here and hike out to hunt?" Blackhawk said.

"That's what I figure, unless you guys want to do something else."

"By the time we get the camp up, there won't be much light left for hunting."

"Really didn't figure on hunting today anyway," Jimmy said. "Hoping we might get lucky and run across one. He bent down and picked up a piece of basalt the size of a softball. "Hard to believe this was underwater a million years ago or so."

I spread a large blue tarp and began to unpack the quads, laying our gear on the tarp. Jimmy and Blackhawk assembled the lightweight nylon tent that supposedly slept six. In reality, it was just big enough for the three of us. Maybe the manufacturer was used to short Cub Scouts. Depending on the wind or rain or both, it wasn't any warmer than sleeping outside by the fire. If it rained and with this area getting five times the rainfall of the valley this time of year, that was the only reason we had brought it.

While they set up the tent, I set up the throne. The throne was our bathroom accommodation while here. It was a frame of two by fours with a wooden toilet seat tacked to the top. It's open at the bottom. You dig a hole for stuff to go into, balance the throne over the hole, and at the end of your business a shovel load of dirt made you one with the earth. It was a lot better than squatting on a log.

There was always a hearty amount of crude male humor when we were on an operation. Blackhawk took an amount of ribbing as to whether he really had Native American blood or not. After doing his business out in the brush he would suggest that if there were non-believers, he had left a good sample of his DNA for them to test.

Once I had the hole dug deep enough, I went back to camp and set up a small fire ring. We had been taught the old adage; Indian make small fire, sit close, white man make large fire, sit far away.

The light was falling quickly. The night promised to be clear. Once the fire was set up and arranged, I set up my sleeping gear. The cuisine for the night was corned beef hash from a can and biscuits. Blackhawk had the El Patron chef make the biscuits. Did I say they were exceptional? I tried to talk him into bringing the cook with him. Jimmy agreed, but we were outvoted, one to two.

Later Jimmy said, "You guys are probably used to overnighting in places like this. Out under the stars. Fresh air. Listening to the night birds sing."

"It's quiet out there," I said in my movie tone voice.

"Yeah, too quiet," Blackhawk said.

"One big difference. We never had a fire. Makes you a sitting target."

"Another difference was instead of birds chirping we had barrages of mortar fire to lull us to sleep."

It was a pleasant night. We didn't have a big fire, so it didn't take long to burn down to coals. I filled the coffee pot for the morning. It was old fashioned pot metal. You filled it with water and then added the coffee grounds and let it boil. You sifted the grounds out as you poured. It was a mistake to put the grounds in the night before. For some reason that made the coffee bitter.

We all decided we'd rather sleep outside the tent, under the billion stars that would fill the sky. In the last of the light, we each scraped a cot sized area beside the fire, removing any stone big enough to dig into us. From under the trees, we gathered leaves and nettles, and branches we made smaller by chopping them up. We hung our rifles about seven feet up on limbs of a close by pine tree. Keep them out of the dew line. The pistols went to bed with us.

After we settled in, Jimmy said, "Good night, John Boy."

I said, "Good night, Mary Ellen."

"Shut the fuck up," Blackhawk said. "I hate the Waltons." I chuckled at that. How could anyone hate the Waltons.

The moon had traveled half-way across the night sky when a loud crashing in the underbrush brought me wide awake. My fingers curled around the grip of my pistol, and I lay frozen, listening as hard as I could. I heard some more rustling through the underbrush, this time farther away. And then, there was silence.

"Blackhawk?" Jimmy whispered.

"Yeah, I heard it," Blackhawk said. After a full minute of listening, Blackhawk said, "It's gone now. Could have been anything. We'll check at light."

I rolled over and went back to sleep. Holding my pistol. As the sun was just beginning to lighten, I climbed out of my sleeping bag. I had prepped the fire the night before. I started it with a kitchen match and fed larger and larger sticks to the flame until I had a decent fire going. I added coffee grounds to the coffee pot and set it on the folding wire rack Jimmy had brought.

By the time the coffee was boiling there was enough light in the east to see by. Blackhawk rolled out of his sack.

"Coffee's on," I said.

"That's why I'm up," he said.

Jimmy came over and added a couple of sticks to the fire. He had an old Army issue backpack aluminum frying pan in his hand.

"What's for breakfast, cookie?" I said.

"Breakfast of champions," he said. "Spam and bagels."

"Yum, yum," Blackhawk said.

"Hey. You better enjoy it. I figure we'll be at least two days out before we're back here. So those mornings will be slim-pickin's. Bagels only. I wonder what was out there wandering around, last night?"

"Let's eat, pack up and head out. We can look for tracks then."

So, that's what we did. We backpacked, taking just enough to survive on. Water, sleeping bag, ammunition, some food, binoculars and rangefinder and a rain poncho. Our clothing was too heavy to begin with, but we toughed it out. It was going to get colder. I had us all check our phone GPS's. Easiest way to find each other in the forest. GPS was fine but none of us had a phone signal.

We spread out looking for sign of whatever had made the racket the night before. I was the one that found it. Under low hanging fronds of the mallow plant was the largest bear track I've ever seen. I laid my hand in it and it still extended two inches farther.

# 12

Marianne didn't know what to do. Tiffany was a touchy one and Marianne knew if it appeared that she was hovering it would just piss the girl off and she would complain to her mom. What swirled back around in Marianne's mind was that Tiffany was a small-town girl in the big city. Worse yet, a small-town girl at one of the nation's largest party universities and she had been out partying with kids she didn't even know. *Kids*, she thought. She remembered that age and if you want to see how stupid college kids, especially girls, can be, Google *college coeds gone wild*. Those sites never meant coeds being boys. Everyone expected boys to be ruled by their genitals. Hell, boys will be boys. And stupid activity was usually expected. Marianne shook her head. Boys don't get pregnant. If the one-night stand did get the girl pregnant, the boy would be, *see ya wouldn't want to be ya.*

Marianne needed someone to talk to and it couldn't be her sister. And her mom and dad were just too old now to be able to understand what kids now days were like. They both had been to college, but their colleges had been conservative midwestern Christian colleges. She decided to wait until after her show tonight. Elena's show ended after hers, so she'd wait till then and if Tiffany hadn't shown she would talk to Elena. Elena had a lot of relatives in Phoenix. They could usually track down almost anyone.

She told herself that it was dumb to work herself up over this girl. She hadn't even been here that long. She could do nothing but wait. She picked up a novel she was reading and forced herself into it. She finally went to the club and went up to Elena's apartment and let herself in with the key Blackhawk had given her. She lay on the couch and dozed until she couldn't anymore. She washed her face and brushed her hair, applied lipstick, then studied herself in the mirror. People had always told her she was beautiful, but she didn't see it.

She went down. At the bottom of the steps, she realized that someone sitting alone at one of the tables that bordered the dance floor was waving at her. It was a woman with long dark hair, wearing a tailored suit. With a start, she realized it was Boyce, the police detective. They had spent time together with Elena shopping and been to lunch together. She found that she liked Boyce very much.

She moved across the room, dodging dancers that overflowed the dance floor. She pulled a chair out and sat with Boyce. She scooted her chair around to watch Elena better.

She smiled at Boyce, then spoke above the band, "You alone?"

"Almost always. I was out late on a case in this neck of the woods, didn't want to go home right away. Thought I'd stop by and watch Elena. Where are the boys?"

"They decided to go elk hunting."

Just then Nacho came up to their table, "Hey, Marianne. Get you a drink?"

"White wine spritzer," Marianne said.

"You got it." He looked at Boyce, "Another scotch?"

Boyce gave him a big smile, "One more then I have to go," she said.

"Yeah, right," Nacho said then moved away. They both watched him walk away.

"Be like dating my brother," Boyce said.

Nacho was a shadow less than six feet four inches tall. He didn't have an ounce of fat on his body and his hair, black and as shiny as a raven's wing, hung down his back, past his shoulders. His real name was Ignacio Pombo. If you used it, you would suffer his wrath. "Kinda like me," Boyce said out loud.

"Beg your pardon?"

Boyce laughed. She shook her head, "Sorry, I was thinking about how he hates his real name. Kinda like me."

Marianne thought about that. "You know, you're right. I've never heard you called anything but Boyce."

"Let's keep it that way."

"Would you call him handsome?" Marianne said, still watching Nacho.

Boyce thought about that. "Kinda weird," she said. "It's like you took a handsome face and waved a wand and changed each feature just slightly. Like it's sort of out of focus."

"Yeah, you are right. Still good enough looking but just out of focus."

"But he is sexy," Boyce said.

Nacho brought their drinks back. "Get you anything else?"

"No thanks, how much longer is Elena on?" Marianne said.

"Probably two more songs unless she feels the need."

The last song turned out to be American Pie which she sang in Spanish. Marianne thought it was a great idea. She regretted she didn't know Spanish. After the ovation Elena spoke with several fans then finally broke away. She waved at Nacho and came and sat down. Nacho brought a tall glass of ice water, a rock glass half filled with tequila and a cold, damp, hand towel. She drank half the water, drank half the tequila, and mopped her face with the towel.

"What brings you here this late?" she said to Boyce.

"Had interviews down the street. Thought I deserved a drink."

"You certainly do darlin'." She looked at Marianne.

"I'm glad Boyce is here. I need some advice," Marianne said.

"What kind of advice?"

Marianne laughed. "Motherly advice."

"You're laughing because you know none of us are mothers."

"Yeah. Just thought of that."

"So, what's going on?" Elena said.

Marianne explained the problem she was having with Tiffany. The other two listened.

"When was the last time you tried her?"

"Just about a minute before I came downstairs and joined you. Went straight to voicemail."

"It's the time that's gone by that is worrisome to me," Boyce said. "What's the girl's name again, the one she's staying with?"

"Rosie."

"When is the last time you talked to her?"

"Yesterday. I don't want to come off as a helicopter aunt. Like Rosie said, Tiffany is a big girl."

Boyce looked at Elena. "Maybe you could call Rosie tomorrow morning, you know just seeing how the girl is working out since you recommended her."

"I can do that," Elena said. "But I won't be able to reach her until noon. Rosie doesn't get up before that."

# 13

I spread my hand over the top of the bear print to show the guys the print was bigger than my hand.

"Do you have your running foot on?" Blackhawk said.

"Of course not," I said.

"Good," he said. "I'll stick with you."

Jimmy laughed.

"Nice," I said. "Real nice."

Jimmy moved out a few yards and was studying the ground.

"What do you think, Deer Slayer?" I asked.

"I think it would behoove us to determine which way the old boy is heading."

"Behoove?" Blackhawk said.

"I concur," I said.

"Don't make me sorry I invited you guys," Jimmy said.

With Jimmy's direction, we spread out to search for more tracks. We found them heading away from our camp. Maybe he already had a belly full, or maybe he didn't like the smell of humans.

"How are we going to do this?" Blackhawk said.

"Do you have your walkie talkie's?" Jimmy asked.

We dug them out of our backpacks. "Turn them to channel eight," he continued. "We should be the only ones on that frequency. If you want to communicate, click the on switch twice. If we hear the double click and we can talk out loud, we click three times. If you are stalking and can't make noise, click once, wait five seconds, and click again." He demonstrated. "You get it?"

We both nodded and clicked the speak button to test it. "Let's spread out, stay a hundred yards apart," Jimmy continued. "If we haven't, we need to touch base with each other at least every fifteen minutes."

"Agreed," Blackhawk said.

"Let's put Jimmy in the middle," I said.

"There's a really rough trail from here that goes straight north about twenty miles to the Blue Ridge Reservoir. We should hit elk anywhere along there. I'll stay close to the trail. Unless something silly happens, if you are on my left you can turn to your right, and you'll hit the trail."

I looked at Blackhawk. He shrugged. "I'll take the left," I said.

"What if we run into a herd and we don't want to talk?" Blackhawk said.

"Click once. Wait, then click once, then wait, then click once and wait, then click again. If you don't get a response, do it again."

Jimmy nodded in the direction where he thought the trail was. "Okay. That's where I'm going, you guys ready?"

"Let's do it," I said.

Blackhawk and I split off and I began making my way

through the forest. It didn't take long to lose sight of the other two. I admit I felt exhilarated. A pine wood forest has a smell all its own. Home décor stores are filled with aerosols that proclaim to be pine this or pine that, but they never smell like this. There is also a dampness to a forest. The rainfall hits the canopy of leaves and limbs then drips its way to the ground where it soaks into a foot of thatch. The sunrays don't find the moisture very well and the ground cover is almost always damp.

As I walked along, I kept my head on a swivel. Constantly alert. Just like patrolling the Cambodian border. Old Eddie had told me a tale of elk hunting with some guys and how they had insisted on getting out before daybreak. Pulling a homemade single axel cart behind, they drove way back into the designated area. Even on the gravel road it clattered and banged and set up such a noise Eddie was sure every elk in ten miles could hear it. Then the driver pulled off the road into the raw forest and it became even worse. Finally he stopped and they set up a camouflaged stand. They found three trees close together and they wrapped a camouflage cloth around it and they hunkered down in the middle. The deaf leader of the pack, that couldn't hear the cart banging, had brought coffee. He had a propane rig that you could set the coffee pot on. To Eddie's disgust, soon the odor of coffee wafted through the trees. Eddie said, by now he had given up. So he leaned against a tree and waited while the others laced their coffee with generous pours of Jim Beam. Eddie laughed about it now. He said, "Two of us had done everything we could to neutralize the human scent of everything we brought along, and these bozo's boil up coffee and lace it with bourbon. It's a wonder they didn't smoke cigarettes."

He went on, "We only had one tag, so the kid that had gotten drawn was the only one that could shoot. We had agreed to share the meat and had gone along just to go. The kid was a rookie. It wasn't even an hour when the coffee drinkers decided they had to pee. Eddie told them to make sure they were a long way from the stand. One guy said, "How far?" Eddie said "Far enough that we can't shoot you."

They laughed like they thought that was funny. Eddie didn't laugh. They clumsily climbed out of the blind and stumbled back into the forest. They had barely gotten gone when Eddie could hear the elk slowly walking toward him. A small family, maybe twenty at the most. The tag was for bull elk so the cows and youngsters were off limits. They were looking for antlers.

The kid said to Eddie, "I should probably get my binoculars." Eddie said, "You probably should get your rifle."

The kid got his rifle and was so nervous he almost dropped it. "I'm shaking," the kid said.

Eddie said, "I was patient with him. I told him to slowly raise up and lean against the tree. Hold the rifle on the trunk to steady it. The elk came plodding out of the forest into an open area with a sparse stand of trees. Just across the open and slightly below, there was a thicker stand of trees. If they got in there, the kid would have no shot. They were beautiful. Mostly calves and cows. I whispered to him, "That's a young bull next to last. Zero in on him. Right behind the shoulder. Take a deep breath and hold it. Squeeze the trigger. Don't jerk it."

The kid came up beside the tree, pressed into it so hard Eddie was sure the elk would hear him. The kid stared through the scope for a very long time. Just before the young bull stepped out of sight behind the trees, just when Eddie was sure the kid would wait too long, the rifle exploded. It scared the kid. He dropped the rifle to the ground. The elk scattered into the trees.

"Get your rifle, boy," Eddie yelled and jumped out of the blind. He raced to the clump of trees, with the kid right behind. When he got there the elk was down. It was a small male, but it was legal. It was still alive. "Well son, it looks like you shot junior. He's still alive, put him out of his misery."

He said the kid stood for the longest time then finally said, "I can't do it."

Eddie took the rifle and touched the elk behind the ear and pulled the trigger.

"What happened to the other guys?" I had asked.

"They came running up pissed because they had missed it," Eddie said. "We hadn't been there an hour and now their hunting trip was over. Wait all year, only get one tag pulled and it only lasts an hour. And you are off behind a tree pissing."

A breeze had come up and rustled the tops of the trees. The air was crisp and cold. I rewrapped my wool scarf so my nose was covered. I stopped and unlimbered my canteen and took a drink. I wasn't thirsty. I just wanted a moment to get focused. I looked over toward Jimmy but couldn't see anything but pine and brush. The same with Blackhawk. I pushed on.

# 14

You ever have the experience where you suddenly become aware of a sound, then you realize you've been hearing it for a while? I was making my way down a small ravine then back up the other side, when I realized I had been listening to a low register humming. Or, more like a deep throbbing buzzing sound. I remembered where I had heard this before. I stopped, alarmed.

As a SEAL recruit I had been assigned to a patrol, led by a shirt-tail lieutenant who had made the decision to prove himself by being the lead man. He walked right into a large swarm of hornets and instead of freezing and slowly backing out, he began yipping and yelping and swatting and within seconds the entire tribe was in a murderous rage. They swarmed him and would have killed him if a big farm kid, from Iowa, hadn't rushed him with a ground cloth, got him covered, and then outrun the murderous bastards himself.

I was halfway up the other side of the ravine when I turned and looked toward the sound. It wasn't hornets or even bees, it was flies. A million of them. And they were focused on something I couldn't make out, lying at the bottom of the ravine.

I stood for a long time trying to decide whether I really wanted to see what it was or not. It wasn't that far away but I took out my binoculars and studied it. It was large and had been worked over pretty good. I thought one part I was looking at were ribs, but I couldn't be certain. Then I focused on something that made the hair on my arms and the back of my neck stand up. You have always heard the expression. Believe me when I tell you it can happen. It appeared to be an arm, with what appeared to be a watch on the wrist.

I don't believe I've vomited five times in my life. I almost made it six.

I dug my walkie talkie out and clicked it twice. A few seconds went by then my walkie talkie clicked three times, then another three times.

"Hey guys," I said. "I need you to come find me. I'll make sure my phone is putting out my GPS location. I've got something to show you."

"What is it?" Jimmy said.

"I'm not sure I know enough to tell you. Come find me."

I tightened the scarf around my nose and mouth and slid my hood up and put on gloves. I worked my way over to the mass of death and bones. The flies were awful. Big green bottle fly suckers. Before I got to it, I selected a sturdy palo verde branch and trimmed the thorns off and cut it long enough to make a good poking stick.

Before I got to the corpse, I saw bear tracks in the sandy bottom of the ravine. They were fresh enough that I figured a week at the most. It's hard to tell with sand. It blows easily in the wind and the edges on the prints don't take much to erode. It was obvious it was a bear that was feeding on the corpse. What the bear had left, the coyotes had taken care of. Parts of the carcass were scattered. The birds had taken all the entrails, but the skull was missing.

It was almost a half hour before the guys came to the top of the ravine. In the meantime, I had found the skull. I picked it up on the end of my stick and found a hiding place for it. I climbed out to where they could see me. I waved.

I got on my walkie-talkie and said, "You need to cover up before you get to me. There're a billion flies." They took my advice and put their hoods up, gloves on and bandannas across their mouths and nose. When they got closer, they knew why.

"Bear?" Jimmy said.

"Mostly," I said.

"What do you mean *mostly*?" Blackhawk said.

With my stick I pointed at the coyote tracks. "Coyotes," I said.

"Look at the feet."

"Not much left, gnawed down to the ankle bone."

"See anything strange?"

"What?" Blackhawk said.

"Where's his boots?"

They stood silently for a minute. "Maybe a coyote took it away to chew on."

"His whole shoulder is still available. Why would they take a chunk of processed leather and rubber?

"Where's his head?" Jimmy said.

"Good question," I said. "Follow me." I turned and climbed the ravine. They followed. A few yards out there was a bunch of sage that was pressed down. "This is where the bear bedded down after he ate his fill."

"Came out here and took his time with it. Where's the skull?"

"Over here." I had examined the skull then placed it into the center of an ocotillo. I had taken a strip of bright orange ribbon from my pack and cut off a three-foot piece. I tied it to a bush that was a dozen feet from where I placed the skull. I figured we'd need it to find the skull again.

"I don't figure we'd want to cart it around with us. Figured the critters wouldn't bother it in here."

"Probably not with all that down there," Blackhawk said. "What'll we do? Walk all the way back to report it?"

"I want to show you one more thing," I said. Using the stick, I worked the skull out of the bush. Pushing it with the stick I rolled it to Blackhawk's feet. "See anything?"

Jimmy choked out, "I don't."

I rolled the head onto its side and using the stick as a pointer, I pointed at the neat little hole that was right behind where the ear had been.

Blackhawk leaned down and studied it. Finally, he looked up at me, "22 short or long, can't tell which. Or maybe AR-15 shooting 556's."

"Probably an AR223. I don't know who would be hunting this far out here with just a .22 long."

"Have you looked for ID?" Jimmy asked.

"Waiting on you," I said.

"Waiting on me?" he said.

"Even if we find the torso, do you want to go through his pockets?" Blackhawk asked.

"Hell no," Jimmy said. "I'm about to gag as it is."

"What do we do?" Blackhawk asked.

"I've been thinking about that," I said.

"Bet you have," Blackhawk said.

"Probably immediate medical attention is going to do no good."

"What the hell do you mean?" Jimmy blurted. "The guy's dead."

Blackhawk smiled. "Jackson has a weird sense of humor. Stick with him here."

"Where's the nearest ranger station?" I asked Jimmy.

"Probably Payson. Or at least down that way."

"How much time to get back, report it, wait for the ranger and get back up here?" I didn't wait for the answer. "We'd lose a day and a half of our hunt. I've pinged the guy. I say we continue to hunt. Won't matter to this guy if he's discovered today, tomorrow or the next day."

"At least we need to scout around and collect his personal belongings, if he had any," Blackhawk said.

I looked at Blackhawk, "How long do you figure he's been dead?"

"I can't really be sure. With the body that mutilated, a couple of days to a couple of weeks."

"Let's scout around, see what we find. Sure is a strange place to be hunting by yourself."

Just like looking for tracks this morning, we began circling. After forty minutes we came in with nothing.

"This is damn strange," Jimmy said. "No camp, no clothes, no weapons, no I.D., out here blank as a rock."

"No clothes," I said.

"I said that," Jimmy said.

"Yeah, but think about it. Except for remnants of a shirt sleeve, no clothes. None. No jeans or underwear, no boots or socks. No warm clothes and it's been colder than hell. I found his pelvic and leg bones. I thought I saw a watch on his wrist when I first spotted him, but it was a tattoo on a strip of skin. A Marine insignia. Not much of the arm left. The tattoo had been gnawed on. What I thought had been shiny metal was really bone."

Jimmy looked a little green.

"What now?" Blackhawk said.

"Ping this place on your phone and we go back to hunting elk."

Jimmy and Blackhawk backed up a few steps. They pointed their phones at the body and pinged the location on their GPS.

"Makes me nervous," Jimmy said.

"What does?" Blackhawk said.

"Knowing there is a killer bear around that has a taste for human flesh."

"Yeah," I said. "Just remember, I don't have my running foot on."

# 15

By one thirty the next afternoon, Marianne couldn't wait any longer and she called Elena. Elena sounded like she had just awakened but she said no, she was up.

"I'm sorry, I should have called you sooner," Elena explained. "I talked to Rosie and she said Tiffany was back home and was in her room asleep. So it looks like you have nothing to worry about."

"My God," Marianne said. "That's a relief."

"Kids get a little rowdy at that age. Girls turn eighteen and can't wait to lose their virginity, if they haven't done it before. Any dick'll do."

"That's so sad. Makes me a little queasy."

"Yeah, but that's the way it is. You have a show tonight?"

"Yeah, you?"

"Always. Okay, see you later," she disconnected. Marianne went to the couch, lay down and took a nap.

At the El Patron she started her ten o'clock set with Billy Joel's Piano Man. Always a crowd favorite. Halfway through, there was a commotion at the front door and Tiffany and a gaggle of girls, all Tiffany's age, came piling into the club. They were all dressed for clubbing. In other words, showing as much skin as possible. Male attractor. Marianne could see Tiffany telling her friends I was her aunt, but she didn't bring any of them over. It was like pointing out a guy in the band you know. At that age anyone connected to a band was a celebrity.

Piano Man was always a good set starter because everyone knew the *la-la-de-da* parts to sing along with. The girls joined in with great gusto. It was obvious the girls had come to party. They kept ordering shots, and never left the dance floor. Marianne had the guys adjust the playlist to accommodate them. She usually did American standards, Sinatra music, but the gig she had before, at the casino, her repertoire was geared for the younger rowdy crowds. The music was more modern. Foo Fighter, Green Door, Imagine Dragons, Bad Bunny. Modern pop and rock and roll. Some hip hop. She was pleasantly pleased that her trio handled this music so well. Marianne noticed the girls all watched her with great interest, so she put a couple more watts into the smile and belted the songs. Just knowing Tiffany was okay lifted her spirits.

Toward the end of the set, another group of kids came boiling into the club. This group included boys. It was a rowdy reunion of kids from both groups that knew each other. Some of the girls went through the room collecting empty seats so they could all sit together. The waitresses, who weren't much older than the kids, were really hustling. Marianne signaled one of the senior waitresses. She leaned down so the waitress could hear her.

"Check all their ID's."

"On it," the girl said.

A minute after the second group had come in, two young men came in. Even with the activity, Marianne noticed them. They didn't look around for a place to sit. The other kids had kept two chairs for them. One was a pretty ordinary looking guy except bigger than normal. The other was Clyde Slick. He wore a shiny light blue suit like a magazine model. He was very good looking with dark hair slicked back behind his ears. He moved with a self-confidence that appeared to be natural. The other kids made room for him and periodically girls would come up to him to talk. He didn't show deference to any one girl. Almost inevitably he would take something from his pocket to give to them. Marianne had an urge to sing Sammy Davis Jr's Candy Man. She never saw money change hands.

Marianne noticed a small but steady erosion of regulars leaving. Jimmy had told her once to watch the women. He said the women were the ones that started the problems. Rick's American was not a beer and whiskey joint where booze flowed and tempers flared. But tonight, trouble started when two young men couldn't agree whose turn it was to dance with the tipsy blonde who couldn't dance without flipping her short dress up to show her panties. Which in the back was nonexistent. Luckily, Tiffany was sitting, talking with other girls. She was wearing a short skirt and a tank top, stressed to the limit. Marianne was happy to see Tiffany didn't appear to be drunk. And she was relieved that she had not seen Tiffany talking to the blue boy.

Inevitably one of the boys shoved another and Marianne crooked her finger at the same senior waitress she had talked to before. The girl came over. "Get Ben in here," she said, loud enough for the waitress's ear. Ben was manning the front door.

He was ex-cop with forty years on the Chicago force. Blackhawk had hired him when Elena had been taken. Not much he hadn't seen. He was a no-nonsense bouncer. He came in and Carla, the senior waitress pointed out the two troublemakers. Ben perfunctorily walked across the dance floor, grabbed one kid by the arm and shoved him toward an empty chair. The kid put up no fight.

Ben then moved to the other boy, and Marianne waved the band to silence. You could have heard a pin drop. Marianne expected Ben to put this kid in another chair, presumably on the other side of the room. But he didn't. He yanked the kid up and walked him to the door.

"You're eighty-sixed, kid. Don't come back for a month."

"Hey," the kid squealed. "Why me? Why not him?"

"I said eeny meeny miney moe," Ben said. "You lost."

Marianne leaned down and touched Carla on the shoulder. Carla looked up. "Follow them out and tell Ben to come see me when he gets rid of the kid."

"You got it," she said.

As soon as Ben and the kid cleared the door, Marianne signaled the band to play. She turned to the piano player. "Instrumentals," she said. "I want to speak to Ben." The piano player nodded. He turned and began Coldplay's Clocks.

She stepped off the bandstand and moved to the door. Before she got there, Ben came back in. "Yes ma'am?"

"You see the girl sitting with her back to the wall. The blonde?'

"Your niece?"

Marianne was surprised. "You know that?"

"Elena pointed her out to me. I think when you first brought her here."

"When she leaves, I want you to detain her, long enough for me to talk to her."

"You got it."

The fight and expulsion put a damper on the dancing fervor and the kids started leaving. The first to go was the blue boy. When Tiffany and her friends began to go, Marianne followed them out. Ben had stopped them.

Tiffany saw Marianne and didn't look happy. Marianne looked at the others and said "I want to speak to Tiffany for a minute. Just a minute. She'll be right with you." They moved off.

Tiffany said, "What?"

Marianne said. "Your mother and I love you very much. I want you to make good decisions."

"I always make good decisions."

"It wasn't a good decision to be out all night with strangers your first day in school."

"They aren't strangers."

"They were then. Look, I'm not trying to bust your ass. I just want you to be safe."

"I'm a grown up. I'm of legal age. I can take care of myself."

Ben was standing to the side, trying to be invisible. Marianne looked at him. "Ben, how long were you on the police force?"

"Forty-two years ma'am."

"What would you tell this girl?"

"Honestly?"

"Yeah, honestly."

Ben turned to the girl. "First of all, you are way too pretty. Without true friends around it can get you in trouble. And secondly, it is a proven scientific fact that the human brain isn't fully mature until the twenty fourth year. How old are you?"

Tiffany looked at him, then at Marianne, then turned and walked away. They stood there and watched her.

Ben said, "Well, you can tell a kid, you just can't tell'm much."

# 16

We spread out again. I forced myself to concentrate on elk instead of a skull with a hole in it and the face eaten off. No boots. No weapons. Who the hell was he and why was he alone in the deep woods.

When I was a kid, I loved to go into the woods. I always pretended I was a mountain man or an Indian. In my imagination I always found plenty of game and ate like a king. The Colonel's survival training taught me that was a fool's paradise. Unless he was well trained in the flora and fauna, even a good hunter would be hard pressed to find enough food to keep him from losing the thirty pounds I had lost during survival training. Hunting, especially big game, has a large amount of luck involved in being successful. Eating nothing but rose hips would give you the runs which would dehydrate you and kill you as soon as starvation. Worse yet, the nights were now freezing. Without shelter, it would be impossible to survive.

After a while I got a rhythm and glided along silently. I could tell my progress because when I had started I was pushing the small critters out away from me, but now I was coming up to them. Getting closer before they would spook. And, they didn't spook as hard.

My walkie-talkie clicked twice. I took a careful look around then clicked three times. Mine clicked again three times. All clear to talk.

It was Jimmy. "I'm up here on the edge of about a ten-acre meadow. I've got elk scat all over the place."

"Fresh?" Blackhawk said.

"Fresh enough," Jimmy said. "I see you guys are on either side about an eighth of a click back. Work toward the middle. I'll wait here. Be cautious. They could be in between us."

"Roger that," I said.

"Roger," Blackhawk said.

I clicked my walkie back on. "I've always wondered who Roger was," I said.

Jimmy clicked on. "Roger Von Steubens. Aide de camp to General Washington. Washington had so much information coming in he didn't know what to believe. He also couldn't remember Roger's name. So, when someone told him something he would turn to his aide de camp and say, "That true Rueben? And Roger would say, Roger Sir."

Both walkie-talkies were silent, then finally Blackhawk clicked on, "I wish Nacho were here. He'd have three or four follow up questions."

"Roger that," I said.

"Let's hunt," Jimmy said, his voice tinny over the walkie-talkie.

"I also wondered who Wilco was?" I said.

"Shut the fuck up. Let's hunt." Blackhawk said.

Above the canopy of the forest, it was a bright shiny day. The air temperature was in the mid-forties. I found a focal point that was a couple of steps off my center route, and slowly made my way forward. I thought about the primitive men that had hunted here before my kind had taken over the world. I had read the life expectancy 10,000 years ago was maybe 25 years. 25 years and you were the old guy. A hard cheese life.

I would move forward for maybe twenty, thirty yards, then stop and listen. Many times you hear the animal before you see it. I was in no hurry, and I sure didn't want to just walk by an opportunity.

It was a good forty minutes before I caught a glimpse of Jimmy's red hunting cap through the trees. Seconds later I saw Blackhawk moving in from the right. Blackhawk didn't wear a hunting cap. He wrapped a red bandanna around his forehead. Pure Cochise. I stopped for a brief moment and watched him move. He was like poetry. Gliding through the forest, pausing, moving, then pausing again. I'd been with Blackhawk for a number of years, and I knew that if he was going to injun up on me from behind, I'd never hear him.

Jimmy was sitting, his back to a dead pine whose branches were rubbed off by moose and elk to almost twelve feet off the ground. In front of him was the meadow he had spoken of. I unslung my pack and dropped it next to his and sat cross-legged on the pine needles. Blackhawk set his pack next to mine, then leaned down and rummaged until he brought out a zip lock of home-made trail mix. Elena had made it for him. She got the recipe from her nana who got it from her nana. Back in the old country when the family had a one mule farm, the papa's would

84

go to the field with a bag of it. Walnuts and hickory nuts and pecans and raisins and grapes when in season. They would spice it up with dried peppers and strips of smoked Gambel quail. Elena would use beef jerky instead of quail, and always included a handful of diced jalapeno, poblano and serrano peppers that melted your lips.

"You walked around this yet?" Blackhawk said shoving a handful of mix into his mouth. He handed me the bag of mix. Knowing I would regret it, I took a mouthful. I offered it to Jimmy but he wisely declined.

"Yeah, I went about halfway around. There was a helluva herd here. The ground is literally covered with elk scat," Jimmy said.

"You said it was fresh."

"Fresh enough. No more than a week. Been rained on, so still damp."

"What now?"

He stood. "You two go right, and I'll go left. Scout the edges and try to find which way the herd went when it left the meadow."

"Probably toward the Rim," I said.

"Then we'd be looking at it," Jimmy said.

"True that."

I stood and slung my pack on. Blackhawk followed me. We had the advantage because we could space one of us further out. It would be easier to tell if that indeed was where the herd had gone. The ground was tough and trampled so it was hard to tell. Fifteen minutes later our walkie-talkies clicked twice.

We didn't bother clicking back. Blackhawk said, "What's up?"

"You boys need to come across and see this."

"Where are you?"

"Oak tree, about midway, turning red and yellow."

"I got it," I said. We started across.

We saw it before we got to him. Big gut pile with the head of a bull elk on top of it. Gut piles don't last long in the forest. It was fresh.

"Nice kill," Blackhawk said.

"Nice sized bull," I said.

"Really fresh," Jimmy said. "Whoever did it knew how to dress it out. Scavengers haven't been on it much, yet. I found it because it had attracted some turkey buzzards." Jimmy was looking at the ground. There were tracks of four-wheel drive quads coming up to and leaving the gut pile.

Blackhawk looked at me then at Jimmy, "We're not alone in the forest." The three of us were looking around. Looking hard.

"You tell Bambi and I'll tell Thumper," I said.

# 17

Blackhawk and I walked back across the meadow to continue looking for the direction the herd had exited. We made our way into the timber looking for any sign that the mass of animals had turned. It was slow going. It didn't seem that we went very far when our walkie-talkies clicked. We clicked Jimmy back.

"It appears they turned southwest," Jimmy's tinny voice said. "I'm going to trail along. You guys can come across double time and catch me."

"Roger," Blackhawk said.

"And Wilco," I added.

Blackhawk didn't smile.

We cut left and began to hustle back across the meadow. It was rugged walking when you were trying to hurry. Especially with a prosthetic foot. The GPS showed Jimmy just ahead of us when his walkie-talkie came on. Not clicking to signal us, but, just on. We could hear other voices. Jimmy said, "Hey!" like he was alarmed. "What the…?" There was a commotion then a deep gruff voice came on, "Hey, who you talking to on this?"

Blackhawk looked at me and I shook my head. My GPS

showed Jimmy's phone as an eighth of a mile ahead. As I was looking at it, the phone signal disappeared. Behind the gruff voice Jimmy said, "What a pretty deep purple your face is."

The guy said, "Shaddup. What're you, queer?" There was a commotion then the walkie-talkie shut down.

The last time I had heard the words "*deep purple*" was when the Colonel's wife Martha had called to tell me the Colonel was missing. It was code words to indicate that a member of the team was taken or missing. Jimmy was familiar with the story.

Without unnecessary talk, Blackhawk and I checked the loads in our pistols. We made sure the bullet pouch on our belt was filled with cartridges. We made sure the Kbar knives strapped to our legs were secure.

"One click to talk," I said. "If I don't answer it means I'm in deep shit or I'm too close to someone I don't want to hear our conversation."

"Of course," Blackhawk said. We slung the backpacks across our shoulders and racked a round into our rifles. We looked at each other and simultaneously nodded. We started forward. I had memorized the spot on my phone map where Jimmy had been before the signal was lost. It wasn't very far ahead.

"Follow Jimmy and the herd or the ATV's?" Blackhawk said.

"We know the ATVs, or at least one of them, ended up with Jimmy."

"We have to be very careful. They spot us we not only lose the element of surprise, if they intend to hurt Jimmy, that's when they will do it."

"Let's straddle the tracks and try to catch up."

Blackhawk nodded and we started forward, then cut sideways to pick up the ATV tracks. It didn't take long. The big, ribbed tires were chewing up the forest floor. Tracking was pretty simple. It was fifteen minutes when we heard the ATV's idling in the distance.

"We'll have to move," I said, wishing I had a different foot on. Too late now. Just forget it and make the time you can. We picked up the pace to just under a jog. Now I was worried. If the ground was open and they decided to take Jimmy, they could move faster than us. We reached a flowing creek and as we jumped it, we spooked two elk. They burst from the underbrush and immediately blundered into the thickening forest. With our hearts in our throats, we stopped to listen. We could still hear the ATVs in the distance. We started again.

The terrain was becoming more rugged, and I realized that I wasn't in the shape I wished I was in. The muscles in my thighs began to burn and I realized the engine noise of the ATVs were becoming louder and louder, and then it stopped.

Blackhawk held up a hand to stop us. I was sucking in great gulps of cold mountain air. If it weren't for the tracks, I wasn't sure I could determine which direction the engine sound was coming from. There's a lot of stuff up here to deflect noise. We just had to be more careful. We both pulled our rifles off our shoulders.

We started again, one eye on the tracks, the other eye out in front. We restlessly swept the underbrush looking for tracks and trouble. The underbrush was getting much thicker and wetter. Even though they were waterproofed, my boots were almost soaked, and we were struggling to get through the head-high bramble. The branches clawed at me. If it wasn't for the heavy camo overshirt and the heavy pants my skin would have been ripped to shreds. Getting the rifle barrel through the young branches was a problem. I had to point it straight out in front of me to glide it through the openings and I had to pick openings large enough for my body to follow.

Blackhawk had taken the lead because of my foot. Suddenly he pulled up, raising a fist in the universal gesture to halt. I came up beside him. He pointed at his ear. I listened hard. Then I heard it. Very faint voices bouncing through the trees. The voices, though faint, weren't getting fainter. There was no engine noise.

Blackhawk and I split and moved cautiously forward. In a few minutes the voices became louder. I could hear Jimmy. He didn't sound stressed. Just the calm, modulated voice he always used with an unhappy customer. Blackhawk caught sight of them through the trees and he stopped us. He stood listening and I moved up beside him. Ahead, we could see their movement and Jimmy's red cap. We slowly squatted. I stuffed my hunting cap inside my coat. Blackhawk dropped the red bandana from around his forehead to around his neck. He tucked it in. We remained still.

"You make any of this out?" I said in the barest whisper. He shook his head. He held up two fingers.

I held up one and whispered, "Plus Jimmy." He nodded.

"Could be more. They're all bunched. Let's just walk up on them."

# 18

We came up on either side of the group. If you call three a group. Jimmy was standing beside a tree with a broken branch. His backpack was hooked up on the limb. His rifle leaned against one of the quads, a few steps away from him. Standing beside the quad was a tall, muscular young man with full camo's, including his cap. He had knee high rubber boots like he wanted to be ready to wade in the marsh. His outer jacket was zipped up and on its breast was an insignia patch. It looked like the revolutionary war flag of the snake, d*on't tread on me.* There was the same thing on his shoulder with some kind of stitched garland underneath it. He had long blond hair and a stubble beard. The other quad had a woman sitting on it. She wore the same thing even down to the patches. They both had rifles strapped across the gun racks that were built on the handlebars just for that purpose. They each had pistol holsters strapped to their legs and each held an automatic pistol in their right hands. Except the young man's pistol was pointed at Jimmy's face and the man had an ugly look on his face. The man's hands were bare. The woman had camo gloves. She was older than her companion. She appeared to be around forty. She looked fit and strong.

I didn't get what the man was saying to Jimmy, but it was strong and threatening. They turned, surprised, when Blackhawk and I stepped out. The man's pistol moved, pointed somewhere in the no man's land between me and Jimmy. The man's fly-boy sunglasses had our reflections in the lens.

We had barely made our move when we heard more quads and they were coming quickly. The young guy got a smug look on his face. Within seconds, three more quads came at us from the trees. They roared in on us skidding sideways to a stop. Their big tires were kicking dust and pine needles into the air. Making a statement. The last one hot-dogged it and skidded in a half circle, kicking up more dirt and dust than the others.

We had drawn our pistols before we stepped in. We had them pointed low until now. Blackhawk raised his pistol to cover the young guy and I covered the newcomers. The one that had kicked up the half circle was smaller than the others and long red hair flowed down from her helmet. The helmet had a protective mask on. She raised it and settled it on top of her head. Young and pretty. My guess was, she was the daughter of the woman. There was a resemblance. She had a quiver of arrows slung across her back and a bow fastened to her handlebars.

The threat was the young guy. The other two had strapped down pistols and their hands moved to the gun butts. They had no idea how quick I was. If they moved to lift their pistols, they would be dead. The two men were on either side of the girl. The man to my right pulled his helmet off to reveal salt and pepper hair with a matching mustache. He was the obvious leader of the pack. The young guy and the woman looked to him, waiting for him to speak. He surveyed all of us, taking his time. Our pistols didn't seem to bother him. All of them wore the same insignias on their shoulders. It all looked very military.

Finally, he looked to the older woman. "What happened here?" His voice was mild like asking her to pass the salt.

She nodded at Jimmy. "He said he and the other two are elk hunting."

"I want my wallet back," Jimmy said.

The leader looked at Jimmy then back to the woman, "What did you find?"

"Nothing," she said. "Student ID from ASU. Driver's license. Two hundred dollars cash, Visa card, American Express. Blood donor card."

"Give it back to him," I said. I put my pistol on the leader.

He looked at the pistol, then back at me. He didn't seem particularly worried. There was a long pause. He looked at the woman and nodded. She tossed Jimmy's wallet toward him. It landed short. Jimmy picked it up. He wiped it off and zipped it away.

"What are you doing here?" Diego said. He was looking at me.

"She just told you. We are elk hunting. We have two tags. Do you want to see them?"

The young man spoke, "Your bullshit paper is no good here. You motherfuckers are trespassing."

The leader held his hand up to silence him. "I'll handle this." He looked back at us, his eyes resting on me. "You motherfuckers are trespassing."

I couldn't help but laugh.

"This is national forest," Jimmy said. He wasn't amused. "BLM territory. Perfectly legal!"

"Everything north of the rim and for a hundred miles either way, east or west, is sovereign land of Free America. Those are the laws you must obey."

"I'll bet the White Mountain Apaches would love to hear about that," Jimmy said.

"Put your weapons away," he said.

I nodded toward the woman and the young man, "Them first." He turned and looked at them, then nodded his head. The woman holstered her weapon. The young man hesitated.

"Do it," the leader said, his voice firm. The man reluctantly holstered his weapon. The leader turned back to me. He said, "If you want to hunt, you have to pay for a permit. Each permit is good for one bull elk."

"How about the hunter that left a gut pile a way back?"

"Might be one of ours. If not and if we find such a person, they will have to produce a permit."

"Or what?"

"Or they'll have to appear before the magistrate."

"Who's the magistrate?"

He smiled. "I am," he said.

"What's the penalty for not having a permit?"

"Depends on the magistrate."

"Say it was us."

"Fifteen days in the stockade and a ten thousand dollar fine. Each."

"Expensive elk meat."

He shrugged, "Hunt below the rim."

"No elk there."

He shrugged again. "I can't tell elk where to be."

"What is the penalty for a felony crime out here?" Jimmy said.

"Poaching is a crime," the leader said.

"Say, a felony. A major crime? Say murder?"

"You know of one?"

The girl looked at the young man beside her, then at Jimmy.

I wondered if perjury was a felony out here, because we were on the verge of it. I took the rap. "No," I said before Jimmy could say anything.

"The bible says, *an eye for an eye*," the older woman said.

"I imagine people get lost up here all the time," Blackhawk said. "Come up here and never come back. You ever seen that happen?"

I was watching the girl. She ducked her head and stared down at her handlebars.

The leader started his engine. "You buy hunting permits up here and you get lost, I'll come looking to help you. If not," he took a moment to look at each of the three of us. "You are on your own. Go hunt below the rim. If I catch you up here again, I will assume you are poaching, and I will throw you in our stockade." He wheeled around and drove off. The others followed with the girl going last. She took another look at Jimmy, then goosed it to follow the others.

We watched them go.

Blackhawk said, "Now what?"

"Are we going to let them run us off?" Jimmy said with some heat in his voice.

Neither Blackhawk nor I said anything.

"Why didn't you ask them about the dead guy?" Jimmy asked me.

"Didn't seem right," Blackhawk answered for me. "Just didn't seem to be the time. And for all we know they're the ones that killed him."

I was watching them disappear into the forest. They were headed west. "Let's double time back to the quads and go east for a few miles. Put some space between us. We still have several days to hunt."

"Roger that," Blackhawk said.

"Don't say it," Jimmy said looking at me.

# 19

Marianne called Tiffany every afternoon for three days. She got no answer. Rosie said she hadn't seen her at home for at least three days. Marianne sat drinking coffee in her kitchen. She didn't know what to do. Maybe go out there again and hope she was home, see if she would listen. Her phone chimed.

"This is Marianne," she answered.

"Hi hon. It's Boyce. I have a day off which means I have time to think about things and I was thinking about you and your niece. How is that going?"

"I don't know," Marianne said. "Thanks for calling. A few days ago, she and a bunch of friends came to the club. When I saw her, I thought it was a gesture for us to get closer. Turned out to be the opposite."

Marianne told Boyce what had happened at the club. How the bouncer had to throw a guy out and how that pissed all the others, so they left, including Tiffany.

"Who's the bouncer?" Boyce asked.

"Guy named Ben."

"Ben's a good guy, retired cop," Boyce said. "I've known him for a while. If you have trouble, stay behind him. He has some hard bark on him."

"I liked the way he handled it. I thought he'd just separate them. Different sides of the room or something. But he just kicked the one kid out. Told him not to come back for 30 days, or something."

"Smart," Boyce said. "If he had left them be, they'd have been in a fist fight inside a half hour."

"I felt bad about the boy that got the boot. When the kid protested about being the one picked on, Ben said he had to pick one and he lost."

Boyce laughed. "Sounds like Ben. Don't feel sorry for the kid. There's a lot of bars to go get drunk at."

"What do you think I ought to do about Tiffany?"

"I've got time today. Let's drive out and see if she's made it home. If she hasn't, we'll go visit the ASU police. And we can check to see if she's been going to class. The police won't know where she is, unless she's hurt or in trouble. But they do know their campus so they might have ideas we don't."

"Think they'll talk to me?"

"Honey, I'm the lead detective in the Phoenix Gang's Division. I've dealt with the cops at ASU a lot. They know who I am. I'll come by and pick you up." She hung up.

She was true to her word. In a half hour she pulled up into the driveway. She tooted the horn like a teenaged date. Boyce's city ride was a souped-up boat. Big old six-year-old Chrysler 300. The motor rumbled so loud the dishes in the sink rattled. She cut the engine, and came in the back door.

She declined Marianne's offer of coffee. Marianne grabbed a

photo of Tiffany and they headed toward the University. The police station on campus was on Apache Boulevard, an impressive modern looking building with large letters proclaiming it was indeed the ASU Police Department. She pulled into the lot and parked in an official reserved spot that sported a sign reading *Authorized parking only, others will be towed.* She slid out and Marianne followed, thinking about how great it must be to not have to follow other people's rules.

Marianne followed her up to the double glass doors and followed her through. To the right was a counter. A uniformed policeman was behind it. He looked up from whatever he was doing.

"Hey Boyce. Long time no see."

Another policeman turned from a bulletin board he was looking at, "Hey Boyce," he called.

"Officers," she returned.

"You seem to be well known."

Boyce chuckled and walked to the counter. "Hey Rex," she said.

"You got something going on or you just can't stay away from me?" the policeman said. He was young, fit, and good looking. His uniform fit like a glove. Marianne could see Boyce coming out just to see this guy.

"How's the wife and kids?" Boyce said. The man's hands came up from below the counter. In his left hand was a sheaf of papers. Marianne saw the wedding band.

"Kids are into soccer and Kirby is teaching again this year."

"Second grade, right?"

"Third grade this time."

Boyce almost shuddered. She shook her head. "God love the teachers," she said. "I couldn't do it without murdering one of the little monsters. Present company excluded of course."

Rex smiled, "You and me both." He looked at Marianne. "Who's your beautiful friend?"

Marianne blushed. Boyce laughed, "Down boy. She's why we are here. Her niece enrolled from out of town and has seemed to have gone off the grid."

He looked at Marianne and she noticed his piercing blue eyes. "How long has she been gone?"

"Four days," Marianne said.

He shook his head. "Department policy dictates that we don't even start getting worried until they are gone at least a week." He looked at Boyce. "What about the city? What's its policy?"

Boyce smiled and nodded, "Yeah, about the same unless it's a minor, or we have reason to believe there has been foul play."

Rex looked at Marianne. "How old is your niece?"

Marianne dug the photo out and handed it to him. "She just turned 21."

Rex looked at it, then at Boyce. "You knew all of this. Why'd you bring her when you already knew what we'd say."

"She's my friend."

Rex nodded. He looked at Boyce and smiled. "Hang tight, I'll be right back." He turned and went across the room then disappeared down a hallway.

"He's probably right," Marianne said. "It doesn't stop me from worrying."

"It doesn't hurt for them to check."

It was a few minutes before Rex came back. Besides the photo Marianne had given him he carried another. He waved at them, beckoning them to follow him down the hall. They followed him into an anteroom. It had a long utility table with five chairs. He waved them to a chair. They sat. He sat across and handed Boyce the new photo. She studied it then handed it to Marianne. It was a head shot of a blond girl. Her face was badly beaten. One eye was swollen shut. Her lower lip was split and crusted with blood. The one open eye was diluted but wasn't dead.

"This happened the night before last," Rex said.

Marianne studied it closely, turning it to get good light on all of it. Finally, she set it down. "Not her," Marianne said. Her eyes were filled with tears.

"I didn't think so," Rex said. "I thought there were enough similarities to have you look."

Boyce was looking at it. She set it down. "What happened to her?"

"Beaten and raped in the basement level of the parking garage. Surveillance cameras got good images of the two guys that did it. One black, one white. They were stupid. We'll get them."

"Do you know anything about a real slick looking dude, drives a very expensive blue sports car. Wears a sharkskin blue suit. Hangs with the party kids."

"Blue Boy," he said. "First name is Salvatore. Sally for short, but his nickname is Blue Boy. He's the pipeline for the recreational drugs here, but you called him slick. He is. So slick we haven't got anything on him. Not even a speeding ticket. We ran the plates and the car is owned by an off shore corporation, which is owned by a corporation in Mexico City, which is rumored to be owned by the Dos Hermanos cartel. We have nothing but suspicion right now. He plays it close to the chest. He doles out the dirty work. You get anything on him, I want to know."

He scooted back, indicating the meeting was over. Marianne and Boyce stood. "What I'll do," he said, "is give a copy of your picture to all of our foot patrol. I'm pretty sure she'll show up. Freshmen are the worst. Especially if it is their first time on their own."

# 20

Tiffany was with five other girls in an apartment off of Apache Boulevard. They had been with some boys all night and had smoked some joints and done shots of Tequila. One of the boys had singled her out and they were in a corner making out. Somewhere along the line the boy decided Tiffany was high enough that he could do whatever he wanted. He was wrong. As soon as his hand found itself between her legs, she slapped him hard in the back of the head. He called her a bitch and she slapped him again. She struggled up and went down the hall to the back. One of the bedrooms was empty. She went in, blocking the door with an empty dresser that had a mirror attached. She looked at herself in the mirror and realized she was wasted. Too wasted to put up much of a fight to anyone. She crossed the room and fell on the bed.

When she awakened it was light outside. She wasn't sure she knew where she was. On her first night on her own, her new roommate, Elena's niece Rosie, had introduced her to a couple of girls at a party. They were fun. When Rosie had to leave one of the girls had offered her a ride home, so she stayed. One party led to another and one day led to another. Now Tiffany had lost track of how many days she had been away. She remembered going to her aunt Marianne's club but not much else. The girl that had befriended her was named Becky. When she came out of the bedroom, she could hear Becky's voice coming from the other part of the house. She felt sick and dirty. She detoured into a bathroom. She stayed in there until the nausea subsided. The taste in her mouth was vile. She washed her face and pulled her hair back into a ponytail. There was a bottle of mouthwash in the medicine cabinet. He rinsed her mouth three times. She opened the door and could hear Becky talking with someone. She felt relieved that Becky was there.

She tentatively went into the living room. Becky was there with two other girls. They were trading hits from what looked like a miniature porcelain pipe. A strange odor hung in the air. It had a hint of burnt rubber or even gasoline.

"There's the party girl," Becky said with a smile. "This is Michelle and Lindsey," she said, introducing the others.

"Hi," Tiffany said. "Is there anything to drink in the house?"

"I think there is some tequila left."

"Oh, no. I mean like water, or milk, something like that."

"This isn't my place," Becky said. "Look in the fridge."

Tiffany opened the fridge and there was very little in it, but there was half a quart of 2% milk. She pulled it out and smelled it. It smelled okay. She drank out of the carton and drained it. She belched and immediately felt better. She rinsed the carton and not knowing where the garbage can was, sat it on the sink.

"Have a seat," Becky said, pushing a kitchen chair out toward her with her foot. Tiffany sat.

"You disappeared in a hurry last night."

"I should never mix marijuana and tequila. Besides, that guy was a creep."

"I thought he was cute," Michelle said.

"They're all cute until you are drunk, and they try to force their hand down your pants."

"Least they could do is say please," Becky said, smiling. She offered the pipe to Tiffany. "Take a hit off of this."

Tiffany shook her head. "Hell, I just got up."

"And you feel like shit," Becky said. "One hit off of this and all that will go away."

Tiffany hesitated. Lindsey said, "If you're not going to hit that, I am."

Tiffany took the pipe from Becky and took a tentative hit. "Take a bigger hit," Becky said.

Tiffany took a bigger hit. It wasn't long before she was reluctant to give the pipe up. Four hours later Tiffany was back on the bed, sound asleep.

She woke up to Becky shaking her. The window showed that it was getting dark.

"Get up Tif," Becky was saying. "We're going to a party. Sally wants to meet you. He thinks you have potential."

"Potential for what?"

"To model. He runs an agency and can get the right girl modeling work. I made two thousand dollars last week."

"Holy crap, two thousand dollars?" She sat up. "I can't go like this. Can you take me to my place so I can shower and get better clothes?"

"We have to hurry. Sally doesn't like to be kept waiting."

"He's waiting now?"

"He just called."

"Why me?"

"Don't ask him questions. Just answer his."

# 21

Rosie wasn't home when they got there. Tiffany rushed through a shower and put on fresh clothes. The party was in a huge three-story home just a couple miles from the University and just inside the Scottsdale city limits. Becky had to park a half block down the street. As Tiffany started to get out, Becky said, "Hold on." She pulled a half smoked joint from her purse and lit it. She took two deep drags and handed it to Tiffany. Tiffany took a deep hit. She slowly exhaled.

"What's this for?"

"This will calm you down. You don't want to look nervous. You want to look confident."

"Where are Michelle and Lindsey?"

"They weren't invited." Becky opened her door to pinch off the joint. Making sure it was totally out, she put the roach into a tiny rubber pouch in her purse. "Let's do it," she said, climbing out.

Besides the fact that the room they entered from the foyer was huge, Tiffany noticed it was mostly girls. There were two guys talking to the girls. They looked like street toughs.

Bodyguards, she thought. This guy must be really rich.

In the corner of the large room was a bar. It had a female bartender in a white shirt and black vest.

"Let's get a drink," Becky said.

"I really don't feel like a drink right now."

"Look around," Becky said. "All the girls have a drink. You don't have to drink it, but if you are the only one without one, you will stand out."

"Jesus, what is this, like high school? We just have to fit in?"

"That's exactly what it is."

There were open seats on a long couch. They carried their drinks over and sat. Tiffany watched the people and wondered why the hell she was there. They had sat for about a half hour when the door opened, and the blue suited guy from her aunt's club came in. The one they called Blue Boy. There were five men with him. They were older, definitely not students. They were well dressed and looked like prosperous middle-aged businessmen.

Blue Boy led them to the bar and invited them to get whatever they wanted. As they gathered around, he turned to the girls. "Girls," he said. "These are friends of mine. Make them feel welcome."

The girls in the room moved over to talk to the men. Tiffany looked at Becky. "Just sit tight," Becky said in a low voice. Blue Boy disappeared up the stairs. After a while one of the bodyguard types came over and asked Becky to follow him. As she stood, she said in a low voice, "Just sit tight."

A few minutes later, the bodyguard type returned to the room and took up his position. A half hour later, Becky came through a different door and beckoned to Tiffany. She held the door and when Tiffany came through, Becky said "Follow me."

There was a different wide stairway that led to a landing. At the landing it turned and continued upward. At the top Becky led her down a hallway to some double doors. She rapped on a door and a male voice said "Come in."

Inside was a large room. There were two other rooms on each side of this one. Back against a wall with a huge window was a desk and chair. On the other side was a large, oversized couch. Against the third wall was a queen-sized bed complete with dress pillows and a comforter. There were three large photographer soft-box lights spaced around the room.

Behind the desk sat Blue Boy. For the first time, Tiffany studied him. He was very good looking. He had deep dark hair that was gelled and swept back. It reminded Tiffany of her aunt's boss, Blackhawk. He had a starched white shirt on, and his sharkskin jacket was hanging on a coat rack beside the door.

"Tiffany, this is Sally. He's the guy I told you about."

"Call me Salvatore," he said. He moved around the desk and took her hand. "It is a pleasure to finally meet you. I've seen you around."

For some inexplicable reason Tiffany felt she was blushing. Holding on to her hand, Salvatore pulled her to him and kissed her on the cheek. Not releasing her hand, he sat on the corner of his desk.

"Do you know why I wanted to meet you?"

Tiffany felt very self-conscious. "Becky said something about modeling."

"Yes," he said. "And up close and in person, I think my instincts were correct."

"Would you like me to go?" Becky said.

"No dear, I think Tiffany would be more comfortable if you stuck around a while. Why don't you sit on the bed." He released Tiffany's hand.

Becky dutifully went to the bed and sat.

"Would you be interested in modeling?" he said turning to Tiffany.

"I think so."

"Are you interested in money?"

She smiled. "Of course."

Salvatore looked at Becky. "Becky, hon, how much money did you make last week?"

Becky said, "Two thousand dollars."

"What's the most you have made in one week?"

"I guess, maybe five thousand dollars."

His voice took on an edge. "I don't want you to guess, how much?"

"Five thousand," she said.

"Does that interest you?" he said to Tiffany.

"Yes, it does," she said.

"Good," he said. He stood up. He reached across his desk and picked up a Go Pro camera. "To the naked eye, you look beautiful. But the camera isn't the naked eye. The camera doesn't lie. I'd like for you to go sit on the couch. I want to do some video with you."

Tiffany turned and went to the couch. She sat. She glanced at Becky, but Becky's face showed nothing.

Salvatore hit a switch and the soft boxes lit up. They put out a very soft, even glow of light. "Let's get you standing at first."

Tiffany stood. Salvatore fidgeted with the camera then pointed it at her. "Turn around slowly." Tiffany turned around. "Put your hands on your hips and keep turning." Tiffany complied. "Wonderful," he said. He lowered the camera. "I should ask you what kind of modeling you would like to do, but before you answer you might want to know more about the business. For instance you can do catalog modeling or still advertising. Swimsuits pay a lot more, but you have to have a particular kind of figure to do that. The same with runway, but even with the right figure, it is almost impossible to get into. It's nonexistent here in Phoenix. I recommend you take advantage of the attributes you've been given. I'd like for you to take off your blouse please."

Tiffany froze. She looked at Becky. Becky was just watching her.

"Tiffany hon," Salvatore said quietly. "You are not naïve. You know there is not a model in the world, at least none that make any money, that have not posed nude. You have my word that these videos are kept locked in my personal vault unless to show to potential clients."

Tiffany still didn't move.

Salvatore turned to look at Becky. "Becky hon, last week when you were paid two thousand dollars, did you have your top on?"

Becky shook her head, "No, I didn't."

"I think Tiffany, here, is a little nervous. Every woman has breasts, would you mind taking your top off so Tiffany isn't so nervous?"

Becky stood and quickly stripped her top off. She wasn't wearing a bra.

"You see, sweetheart," Salvatore said to Tiffany. "Becky has beautiful breasts. But I couldn't send her out to do work if I didn't know that. So, you need to decide. If you don't want to model for me, then we just wasted a little of each other's time. Then you can go on your way."

Tiffany made her decision. She began to unbutton her blouse. She dropped it on the couch. She reached behind and unfastened her bra. She indeed had beautiful breasts. Salvatore began to film again. "Slowly turn around please."

After a few minutes Salvatore said, "The big money is full body modeling. Would you please strip out of your jeans."

Tiffany stared at him. Salvatore turned to Becky, "Can you show her?"

Becky kicked her shoes off and stripped out of her jeans. Salvatore was filming. She was left with a red lacy thong. "That too," he said. She stripped it down and kicked it aside.

"Your turn," he said to Tiffany.

"It's okay," Becky said. "It really is no big deal."

Tiffany turned her back then worked her jeans off. Her underwear was a little more sensible. "That too," Salvatore said. Without turning, Tiffany worked them off. "Now turn around," he said.

She turned around but kept her hands modestly in front.

"Becky, you said you made five thousand dollars. What did you have to do?"

Becky was looking at Tiffany. Tiffany was staring at the ground. "It was girl on girl."

"Of all the videos out there, it is girl on girl that makes the most money," Salvatore said. "Have you ever made love to a girl?"

Tiffany shook her head. "Becky, why don't you tell Tiffany what it's like."

Becky walked over to Tiffany. "Girls are soft and smell good and are gentle and they know what a girl likes. I'm telling you true, honey. It is a lot better than some sweaty, horny college creep."

Becky put her arms around Tiffany and pulled her in close. Tiffany's hands automatically went to Becky's waist. Becky leaned back and looked at Tiffany then leaned in and kissed her. It wasn't a long kiss. She leaned back. "Tell me this isn't better that being pawed by that jackass last night." She leaned in again and this time it was a much longer kiss and Tiffany kissed her back. They continued like that for a long moment.

Salvatore said, "That's great. I think I need some more."

Tiffany looked at him. "What does that mean?"

"It means five hundred dollars if it's good."

# 22

We had moved through the forest about a mile from where we had the confrontation, when I came along side Blackhawk. "Drop out," I said. "I feel like someone is following us."

"You see anyone?"

"No, but you know how you just get that itch. I just want to make sure we're not followed. We'll wait up ahead."

Blackhawk turned and disappeared into the forest. Jimmy and I moved east again, working through the pine and brush. We moved quickly, not thinking about hunting. Just trying to get to a suitable spot. Finally, we found a stand of pine that formed an almost perfect square. Enough space inside for us to hunker down. We picked a trunk to lean against. We waited. We had been waiting for about a half hour when I heard something in the brush. Jimmy looked at me. We both listened, expecting it to be Blackhawk. When it moved again, we knew it wasn't Blackhawk. It was much larger. We both lay prone, facing the sound. It was moving even slower. Then its huge head poked through the underbrush as it munched the grass. It was an extra-large bull elk. It was nosing through the dead leaves and brown nettles. It was magnificent.

Jimmy slid up alongside me, looking expectantly at my face. I reluctantly shook my head. As low as I could whisper, I said. "You already know we can't risk it. A rifle shot can be heard for miles. If those yahoos hear us, I don't want to fight them for an elk carcass. I'm sure as hell not spending time in their stockade."

"Damn shame," Jimmy said out loud. "Beautiful animal."

The bull thew its head up and bolted through the brush. I heard Blackhawk laughing behind us. He came walking up.

"You know that'll be the only chance we'll ever get," he said, smiling.

I stood up, brushing the nettles from my chest and pants. "We'll probably end up regretting letting that get by us." I fetched a piece of jerky out of the backpack side pocket. I twisted off a bite.

"So, what now?" Jimmy said.

"Let's get to the skull. Take it with us."

"Thought we were going to hunt first," Jimmy said.

"And we still can. But I don't think we are far enough away from those militia asswipes."

"You think the sovereign nation of bullshit killed that guy?"

"The odds in Vegas would be saying yes. Far as we know they are the only ones out here," Blackhawk said.

"Except us," Jimmy said.

"Except us," I said. "I want to get back to where the bear mauled that guy and collect the skull bone. We get back to Payson, the sheriff could run DNA tests."

"We need to get our quads," Jimmy said.

"Once we get the quads, we can move east a few miles. Then

we can hunt," Blackhawk said. He looked at his phone. "According to my ping, it's about three miles dead east. But I'm about out of juice."

"Let's keep moving," I said.

We shouldered our packs and headed back into the forest, toward the body. The temperature was dropping but we were almost sweating. We weren't surprised. We were moving faster now than if we were hunting.

I was leading since I was the one that had found the body and I had the best idea how to find him now. It was a hard arduous hike and I ended up walking right by it. If I hadn't stopped to look around, and actually looked back the way we had come, I would have missed it. But there it was, fluttering in the breeze, the orange ribbon I had tied off. I went to the ribbon and turned to look at the ocotillo where I had placed the skull. It wasn't there. I walked over to the ocotillo. It wasn't there.

Blackhawk looked at me, I was bewildered. "You sure this is the place?" he said.

I looked carefully all around. "Absolutely."

"What about the rest of him," Blackhawk said. I nodded. We moved back to the spot where the skull had originally rested, and the bear had mauled the body. There was nothing. Stains of blood in the grass but that was all.

Jimmy said, "Look here." We walked over. He was pointing at a boot print beside a patch of snow, in the mud. The sole was worn and smooth, but the edge of the print looked fresh. The edges of the impression had not eroded with the snowfall. I pulled my phone and tried to take a picture. I didn't have enough juice. I leaned down to examine it and the branch above my head came away from the tree with a crack, immediately followed by the simultaneous bang of a high-powered rifle.

Already leaning I just kept going. In a flash Blackhawk dropped, grabbing Jimmy's arm and pulling him down. We immediately began to crab sideways, getting back into the bushes. It was one of those moments when you actually feel the tingling of a crosshair in the middle of your back. The way the branch had sheared off the tree told me the direction from where the shot had come. I got under a low pine and got lower and crawled backward, my belly never leaving the ground. The pines were thicker here. There was the smell of old mulch, wet nettles and old bird droppings. We all had rounds in the chamber. We all slipped the safeties off. I looked over my shoulder and Blackhawk was crabbing away from me. He was pointing to where he wanted Jimmy to crawl. I felt a pang of regret. I never thought a simple elk hunt would turn into a fire fight. I didn't think Jimmy was ready for this.

Now the forest was quiet. The gunshot had shut everything down. Staying flat, I began to crawl backwards, alternating looks over my shoulder and looks to where I thought the shot had come from. My rifle pointed in that direction, covering my escape. But there was nothing to be seen. I could hear Blackhawk and Jimmy off to the side. When I reached a large group of broad-leafed evergreens and had decent cover, I stood. Blackhawk came over to me and was fiddling with his phone. "I don't have juice or signal. But the last signal I had put the quads about two miles that way." He nodded east. "You guys have juice in your phones?"

We looked at our phones. "No," I said.

"No," Jimmy said. "We have to get the sheriff," Jimmy said.

"What are you going to tell him?" Blackhawk said. "We found a guy with a bullet hole in his head but he's no longer here. Someone is shooting at us? The evidence to that is a spent bullet out there somewhere. Let's get the quads and get out of here, then we can figure out what to do."

"Yeah, you are right."

I didn't wait. I hustled. Not to just get the quads and get out of there, but that crosshair on my back was really pushing me. I knew that shot was meant for me. That really pissed me off. Why me? We kept moving as fast as the terrain would allow.

By now the sun was so low in the west it wasn't visible behind the trees. We were all breathing heavily. Despite the temperature dropping rapidly, I could feel trickles of sweat running down my back. Finally, we caught a glimpse of sunlight glinting off metal up ahead. It was the quads. We cautiously came into the clearing. Something was wrong. The quads seemed to have sunk in the mud and were leaning sideways. The tires were slashed, all the gear we had left was gone or scattered. They had emptied the gas cans and the smell of gasoline was strong.

I felt vulnerable walking into the meadow. I squatted on the offside of one of the quads. Fifty-fifty chance it was the right side. Blackhawk squatted down beside me, watching me. He waved Jimmy down. Jimmy didn't need much persuasion.

I nodded at the far side of the clearing. There was a tall aspen. "Think you can get up that tree? See if you can see somebody?"

"Sure," Blackhawk said.

# 23

Blackhawk didn't wait, he took off.

We both aimed our rifles across the carcass of the quad. Covering Blackhawk. Jimmy picked up a rucksack that had been tossed aside and started looking through it. "They took everything of importance. You think it was that same group?"

"Unless there are others out here."

"What now?"

"Survival 101," I said. "Shelter first, then water, then food. In this environment shelter includes warmth. Luckily, we were planning on sleeping out a couple or three nights anyway. So we brought the heavy below-zero bags. And I don't want to stay close to these quads. We need to get some distance. Someplace they won't know where we are before we can have a fire. How much chow do we have?"

"If we ration, maybe a couple of days."

"That should give us time to find them. We may have to go old school and live off the land."

"Easier said than done." He looked at me and shook his head. "You want to find them? You know they are shooting at us. With real live bullets."

"You want to stay here and wait for us?"

He shook his head, "No, but don't want to get shot either."

I had been thinking about what we had to do. "There are enough creeks up here to keep us in water. Something about that young guy bothers me." I looked across at Blackhawk. He was up the tree. I raised my hand. He raised a hand then turned it thumbs down. Nothing to be seen.

"Yeah, me too. I've been thinking," Jimmy said.

"Uh-oh," I said.

"We are not that far from the Big Creek road. A few miles and it's downhill. Maybe we'll get lucky and the Forest Service might come by, or down closer our phones may have service."

"Then what? We tell our tale and talk the sheriff into coming up here?"

He shrugged. "They destroyed my quads. That's something."

"I know. And they shot at me." I looked at the horizon. "We are losing light. I don't want to travel down the mountain in the dark. The moon won't be brighter until late. But I'm not going down anyway."

"No?"

"At least Blackhawk and I aren't. We are going to work our way around and pay these assholes a visit. But maybe you should go on down."

"What the hell do you intend to do?"

I thought about it. "We are going to cause some problems. We are going to get our hands on that young girl. Get her to tell us who the dead guy was. Get her in front of the sheriff. Without evidence we need a witness."

"Why do this?" Jimmy asked, genuinely puzzled.

"You were there."

Jimmy continued to gather stuff. Finally, he said, "Because they shot at you?"

"They weren't just taking potshots. They tried to kill me. I take this personally. If I hadn't been moving, they would have killed me."

"Blackhawk know what you are planning?"

"Not yet."

"But he'll go along." He thought about it. "Yeah, he'll go along. You two stick together." Jimmy sat back on his heels. He stared at Jackson a long time. Finally, he said, "I never met anyone like you in my whole life." He thought some more. "You didn't even hesitate to jump off that three story boat. With one foot."

"Baby would have died."

"And this little teenage girl is more than a witness. You're worried about her. You think she's in trouble."

I looked at him. I always liked how he squinted when he was thinking smart thoughts.

# 24

Blackhawk had not seen anyone. We moved east at a good clip and found a perfect night shelter about a mile on. The closer we got to the edge of the actual Rim, the land dropped off. The more the ground slanted south, the granite outcroppings became more prevalent. We found one with a flat piece of granite that jutted straight out into the air for eight to ten feet. It formed a natural cave under it and was surrounded by scrub pine. The west side was closed in with thick brush, but the front and east were open. It would provide protection from the wind and rain, if it came to that. It also hid us from the view of pursuers. The thick brush would disperse the smoke from a small fire. It was filled with old pine nettles and old leaves. Something had used it before us. It had a musky, earthy animal smell. But it appeared nothing had been there for a long time.

We bunched up nettles and leaves to make our beds, and laid out our sleeping bags. Jimmy mixed up some cubed Spam in a can of beans and tore a bagel into thirds. As he heated it on a small smokeless fire, Blackhawk and I left the shelter and took a walk. We went several yards into the forest and hunkered down to listen. After a while Jimmy whistled. Good enough. It was too dark to see anything. The best we could do is listen for someone stumbling around in the dark. We'd have to be damned unlucky for them to stumble onto us. We were safe until daylight.

As we ate, we talked about the militia and what we wanted to do about it. I wanted to talk to the girl alone before we decided to do anything.

Blackhawk said, "What is it about the girl? Why so interested in her?"

I shook my head. "I don't know. Just a hunch. You and I are good at reading people. I got the impression that the woman with the young guy didn't like him much. I think the girl is her daughter."

"Now that you say it," Jimmy said.

We banked the fire and bedded down. It took a while to get warm in my bag. When I awoke, it was damp and foggy. It was too dark for me to see anything yet. It was freezing cold. My arm and hand were outside my sleeping bag. Even with my coat and glove it felt like they were frozen solid. I put my hand between my thighs. I closed my eyes and waited for light.

It seemed like I had just shut my eyes when a small noise brought me awake. It was Blackhawk working on a small fire. Blowing on old embers that might still be alive. I lay still and watched him. I was reluctant to leave my warm bed. It was finally the coffee boiling and a larger fire that seduced me out.

I rolled my bag up and sat it against the rock wall so I could lean against it. When I got my boots on, Blackhawk handed me a cup. We sat, alternately blowing and sipping and watching the sky brighten.

I looked at Jimmy slumbering. I looked at Blackhawk. He looked at me and smiled. "Just a kid," he said.

"Old enough," Jimmy said, his eyes still closed. I laughed.

"Old enough," I agreed.

Jimmy reluctantly climbed out and rolled his bag. He took over the breakfast chores. Powdered eggs with sliced salted sow belly Jimmy had brought in a zip lock bag. And the inevitable bagel. While he fixed the food, Blackhawk and I cleaned our weapons. Blackhawk cleaned Jimmy's. We packed the bags. Jimmy had to use the same pot to cook in as last night. He had swabbed it with handfuls of Gama grass. He let the meat sizzle until he had enough grease aided by a splash of water to constitute the eggs. When it was finished, we each got a fork and our own bagel. We shared the pot. Once finished, we stepped out away from the fire to pee. We slung our packs on and Jimmy said, "What now?" He was looking around. It was foggy and the light was dim. No one in their right mind would be out in it.

"Let's take a look at your map," Blackhawk said.

Jimmy pulled the map from his hip pocket and unfolded it. We gathered around and Jimmy pointed to a spot. "This is where we were," he said. "Where we found the body."

"I'm thinking we only saw a portion of the militia," Blackhawk said.

"Yeah, me too," I nodded. "They'll be in a winter camp close to water."

"Blue Ridge Reservoir is right up here," Jimmy tapped his finger.

"Too well known. Ranger heaven. Even in the winter they would send periodic drive throughs."

"Down here," he said, pointing, "there's an old, abandoned ranger station straight south of of the lake a few miles. Not far as the crow flies but a distance to trek through this terrain."

"Does it have water?"

"Rangers wouldn't have built it there if it didn't," Blackhawk said.

"Anyone have a better idea?"

"Let's go look for them at the ranger station. If we don't find them, then we decide what to do."

Jimmy said, "One thing I'm unclear on. You said you wanted to get the girl. Are we going there to grab the girl?"

"No reason to grab her or anyone until we talk to her. Get some answers on the dead guy and who would shoot at me."

"And who and why they destroyed my quads. The more I think about that, the more pissed I get. One of those wasn't even mine."

"Let's go," Blackhawk said. He led the way, moving cautiously at first because of visibility. As it got lighter, he picked up the pace. Optimally we wanted to find them before they got active. We were quite a distance from them, so I didn't know what the feasibility was for that. We put Jimmy in the middle and we both hustled behind Blackhawk. It was at or below freezing so the constant moving kept us warm.

We moved steadily for over an hour when we heard the distant rumble of a quad. Maybe two. We stopped and listened. I couldn't tell where the sound was coming from. I looked at Blackhawk. He shrugged.

"Let's keep moving," he said in a low voice.

# 25

Marianne just went through the motions that night. Her heart and her mind were not on her music, or her audience. Twice Carla, the senior waitress, stopped by between songs to inquire if she was all right. She couldn't get the photo of the beaten ASU student out of her mind. Twice the band bailed her out as she blanked on lyrics she knew like the back of her hand.

She was happy to get home. As she pulled into her garage, she had an irrational hope that Tiffany might be there. Of course, she wasn't. Inside, she double checked the door locks and poured a glass of blended red wine and took a long shower. Sipping her wine, she stood under the hot water until it was no longer hot. She slipped on a sleep gown, pulled the comforter and the under blanket back and climbed into bed under the cotton sheet. It took a long time for her to fall asleep.

She came awake and at first didn't know why. She looked at the illuminated clock. It was just past three thirty and no light showed between the cracks of her drawn blinds. She rolled over and closed her eyes. There it was again. A scraping sound and like a light tapping on a door, or window. She sat up and slipped her feet into her house slippers. Again, she heard it. It was coming from the back of the house. Jackson had left a small caliber pistol in her bedstand, but she didn't even think about it.

She moved through the house, slowly, listening. When she heard it again, she realized that someone or something was on her back porch. She cautiously peered through the blinds on the backdoor window and could see nothing. She didn't want to, but she forced herself to turn on the porch light. There was nothing out there. Then movement caught her eye, straight down. She realized someone was crumpled on the porch floor, leaning against the screen.

She slowly unlocked the door and opened it. Tiffany lay in a heap, moaning. The screen opened outward, and it wouldn't budge, with Tiffany's weight.

"Get up Tiffany. Get up honey. I can't open the door."

Tiffany slowly moved enough that Marianne could get the door open. She slipped out and wrestled Tiffany to her feet. The light of the porch showed the girl had been battered, her face a bloody mess. It took all of Marianne's strength to get her inside. She helped her into the bathroom. She sat her on the toilet lid. The girl began to cry. Not hard, just tears rolling, accompanied by a soft moaning.

Marianne ran water until it was hot, then put a clean washcloth under it. She gently began to swab the girl's face. The blood had come from her nose, her lower lip and a small, scraped area on her left cheekbone. The blood was all dry. Marianne studied her face and could see her pupils were constricted. She looked at the inside of her arms. Small red needle tracks told the tale. The girl was higher than a kite.

Once she had her cleaned up, she helped her into the spare bedroom. The one Marianne had made up for her. She sat her on the bed. She was going to help her undress, then stopped herself. She moved around to where they were face to face.

"Honey, have you been raped?"

Tiffany wouldn't look at her. Marianne took hold of her chin and raised her face so she would have to look at her. "Tell me now. Have you been raped? If you have, I'm taking you to the ER where they can do a rape kit. Get DNA. Get the son of a bitch that did it. Have you?"

Tiffany slowly shook her head. "I let him do it," she said in a voice Marianne could barely hear.

"You let him do it? Then he beat you up?"

"I let him do it, then he wanted to do things I've never done before. I tried to tell him no, but he knocked me down and beat me, then did it anyway."

"What did he do?" Marianne said, then wished she hadn't said it.

"He took me from the rear. In my rear." She hesitated and began to cry even harder. Then she said, "And he filmed it."

Marianne rocked back. "Oh my God," she said.

# 26

Marianne could barely sleep. She got up three times during the rest of the night to look in on the sleeping girl. A little after five she finally got up for good. She fixed tea and turned on the early local news and sat on the couch like a zombie. Tiffany had been so stoned she had passed out when her head hit the pillow. She slept until after noon. When she finally arose, she spent an hour in the bathroom. When she came out Marianne wanted to know more about the previous night, but Tiffany wouldn't talk about it.

Neither one of them had much to eat and the day dragged on until it was time for Marianne to go to work. She thought she should call Elena and take the night off, but when she mentioned it, Tiffany got very upset. She shouted at Marianne that she didn't want to talk about anything. She didn't want to think about anything. She wanted to forget the whole thing. It didn't happen. She said she just wanted to start over. Make everything normal again. Never mention it. Never think about it. It didn't happen!

Marianne gave her the space and she decided she'd rather go

to work than to sit here all night brooding. So, when the time came, Marianne locked all the doors, double checked the ground floor windows, made sure Tiffany had a cell phone with her number in it and went to the club.

Of course, the first thing Elena said was to ask if she'd heard from Tiffany. An hour, a thousand tears and enough self-incrimination to sink a battleship later, they had to go to work. Marianne had told Elena about the filming, but not about the anal sex. Elena knew a lot about the local porn industry and was very sympathetic. She didn't give names but she said she had nieces and daughters of cousins that had gotten sucked into it. She said they all were promised they were going to be modeling stars, be famous and make a lot of money. Ridiculous amounts of money. But once they had been filmed having sex, the pornographers had what they wanted and blackmailed them into doing even more outrageous things. Threatening to send the tapes to their parents or their bosses, or their spouses or fiancés or whoever they didn't want to know. Of course, at first, they had promised the tapes would remain private, but of course, as soon as they had the victim on tape it went out for sale.

Marianne made it through the night but again her heart wasn't completely in it. On her break she called Tiffany. Tiffany did answer but other than that, there wasn't much interaction. She sounded like she had been drinking and Marianne regretted she hadn't remembered the bottle of scotch Jackson had kept under the kitchen sink. She should have poured it out. She couldn't leave early. It wasn't fair to her band.

Driving home she convinced herself that when she got there, Tiffany would be passed out in bed. It wasn't to be. When she got there, the back door had been kicked in and Tiffany was gone. She stood in shock for a full minute. She went in but knew no one would be there. The scotch bottle still had an inch in it, sitting beside the sink. There was a drinking glass in the living room, smashed on the floor. Tiffany's bed looked the same as it had when she got out of it that morning.

Marianne called Elena and caught her before she went to bed. Elena said, "What's up honey?"

"My back door is smashed in, and Tiffany's gone."

Elena said, "Do you have a weapon?"

Now Marianne remembered the pistol Jackson had given her. "Yes," she said.

"Good. Get it. Go to your bedroom. Pull your dresser next to the closet and leave enough room for you to get behind it. You get small and point the gun at the door. Make sure it's loaded and cocked. If someone comes into the room and it isn't Nacho or me, or the police, you shoot them. You understand?"

"I don't think...."

"No, don't think! You shoot them. Do you understand?"

Silence.

"Do you understand me? Answer me."

"Yes, I understand."

"Good. A half hour or less." Elena hung up.

It was less. Nacho and Elena came in the broken back door calling Marianne's name. She was a mess. They bundled her up and took her to the club. They were convinced and they convinced her, there would be no finding Tiffany that night.

# 27

It began to rain. Light but saturating. It made the forest very cold. I had a below-zero parka with an attached hood. Over it I slipped on a rain slicker with another attached hood. Somehow the sneaky, insidious little freezing drops got in and ran down my neck under my shirt. The other guys didn't seem to notice. You're getting old and weak, I thought.

I had made sure to wrap the rifle with a piece of plastic I carried in my pack. Every time Blackhawk led us through a thicket, water rained down on us from the pooled leaves. There had been a time on maneuvers he would have done that on purpose, but not today.

The sound of the quads had become louder, but there still only seemed to be two of them. Finally, they sounded like they were close. The terrain had changed. Now it was a large expanse of pines as far as the eye could see. There was less brush. We had crossed a track where a number of quads had traveled. They had beaten down the dirt into a single two track path. I thought it showed discipline that everyone had stayed in the tracks. Much harder to tell how many there were. Indian war parties always traveled single file. Blackhawk led us off of it, deeper into the trees. We wanted no surprises.

Blackhawk slowed his pace and became careful. That many people, all it took was one out behind a tree taking a leak or hunting small game. He slowly led us through the tall pine and Douglas fir. Suddenly he squatted, holding up a fist. He signaled us up beside him.

"Where is the old ranger station?" he said in a very quiet voice. Jimmy pulled the map and studied it for a while. He pulled his glove off with his teeth and pointed to a spot on it. He tapped it. "The station is right here. I'm guessing we are close to here." He said pointing at another spot. "So, we are very close." He looked around then studied the map again. "There is a ridge along here. It overlooks the building. I'm thinking they will be using the building for something. I don't remember much about it. I think it had a good roof. It's too small to house them all but they'd be smart to use it to store perishables." He looked from Blackhawk to me and back. "I think we should use the cover of the rain to get up on the ridge where we could see everything down there."

"We'd have to be careful of their sentries. They'll surely have some up there." Blackhawk nodded.

"Jimmy's right. Let's move while it's raining," I said.

As if on cue it began to rain harder. Blackhawk waved Jimmy up front to lead. The boy didn't hesitate and led us off back the way we had come. After a while he turned us west. Occasionally he would stop and look at his map. For the first time I noticed it was covered in oilskin. Smart. Fair weather hunters wouldn't have that. Just as the rain began to lighten, the terrain began to climb. When we reached the top, Jimmy didn't seem to need his map anymore.

The three of us squatted behind some juniper. Two hundred yards ahead, and down the ridge there was the flash of green and blue tarps. The ranger building sat in the middle of a clearing. Linen colored tents surrounded the area. Each tent looked able to hold at least six men and there were eight tents.

"What d'ya think?" Blackhawk said to me.

I studied it for a moment. "Flat and open where they are. It will be difficult to get close going downhill."

'Have we seen any guards?"

"Too wet. They'll be figuring that, even if they expected someone, only an idiot would be out in weather like this."

"They'd be right."

"What else do we do?

"Hunker down till the rain stops."

"If the rain stops."

"Yeah, if. If it does, they'll probably be tent crazy and want to get out of camp. We can get closer then."

"I bet the first one antsy will be the girl. Never saw a teenage girl yet that could be cooped up for any length of time."

"Indigo was good at sitting still."

"Yeah, Indigo. When she was on mission she could be still for hours." He looked at Jimmy."You know we didn't have any other females."

We sat silent, watching the camp. Blackhawk started laughing. "She about killed Nacho."

"Just about," I said grinning.

"I caught them once in the back storeroom," Jimmy said.

"Well, not exactly caught them. I saw them before they saw me. I got the hell out of there."

The quads we had been listening to were located under a tarp. Two guys, bare chested except for their coveralls, were working on the engines. The cold didn't seem to affect them.

"Those suckers are hot blooded," Jimmy said.

"Like Nacho," Blackhawk said. We watched them while it rained. After a while they revved the motors until they were satisfied. They both took a piss out into the rain, then gathered their shirts and walked across the compound and disappeared into a tent, shaking the water from their hair.

I kept an eye on the sky and a half hour later I saw one of those Arizona phenomena where bright blue sky appears to the right and dark gray storm clouds are unloading on the left. It was soon after that, the rain stopped. It didn't take long for the girl to step out of the ranger cabin. She was followed by her mother. These two females seemed to get the high-end accommodations. They wore heavy parkas and warm ski stocking caps. They each carried a satchel over their shoulders. They went to the two quads the men had been working on.

"What do we do?" I said.

"We try to follow," Blackhawk said. "We may not get another chance at them."

We hesitated just enough to see which way the women were headed.

"They have a destination in mind. They're not out for just a joy ride. The entire forest is saturated."

As they started away from the cabin Jimmy said, "They're heading for the creek."

"The creek?" Blackhawk said.

"There's a creek?"

"I think it's called McClintock Creek."

"Get us there quick," I said just as the moving sunshine hit us.

# 28

We took off, scuffling back down the rise, the wet plants soaking our outer, supposedly waterproof clothes. When the world is water saturated as bad as this was, there was no escaping the wet and cold. Jimmy led the way, and we knew that tires and the internal combustion machines could out pace human legs anytime, so we kicked it in gear.

It appeared that Jimmy knew where he was. He set the pace and we followed. After a half hour of racing through the forest Jimmy brought us to a halt.

"It's close," he whispered. "I don't know which part of the creek they are going to."

"Why are they going to the creek. Too damn cold to bathe."

We stood listening. With the sunshine now hitting the tops of the trees, the birds began moving. We didn't hear anything human. Jimmy signaled us forward. Another five minutes and he held us up. We all listened hard. Then there it was. The lower range of human conversation. We began to move toward it and at the same time we smelled wood smoke. And there was something else in the air. We all recognized it. Marijuana.

We knew we were close when the female laughter became brighter and louder. We crept closer. We edged up through the brush. Finally, we could see through the leaves. They were taking a bath. Beside the creek was a small, galvanized cattle tank. The tank was propped up off the ground and they had a fire going underneath it. The water in the tank was steaming in the cold air. Beside it was a large stack of chopped wood that had been covered with a waterproof tarp. The tarp had been cast aside. The two women were in the warm water, each as naked as an egg. Their clothes, along with bath robes and towels, were draped across their quads. Their rifles were still in the handlebar racks.

They were sharing a joint, passing it back and forth. They were leaned back against the top edge of the tank. Their hair was wet and steaming. Our observation point was high enough to see down into the tank, all the way to the girl's knees. The younger woman's breasts were perky. Her areolas were light and pink and smooth while the older woman's were darker and wrinkled showing the experience of having nursed at least one baby. But her breasts were still firm and were not sagging like other women her age would be. She wasn't that old. My guess that she was the girl's mother was probably right. There was a distinct resemblance. If so, she probably had birthed the girl while in her teens. The younger girl's pubic area was shaved and hairless. The older one had a triangle of cropped hair with a point reaching down to between her legs.

"Is it Christmas yet?" Jimmy said, his breath catching.

I looked at Blackhawk. He was looking at me. I nodded. I stood and walked into the opening. The elder one immediately began to climb out of the tank, but it was no use. I moved between her and her rifle. I pulled the large beach towel and her white robe from the back of her quad and offered them to her. She took them but I distinctly got the impression she was going for the rifle, not the clothes. Jimmy pulled the young girl's towel and clothes in a big wad and offered it to her. She made no effort to reach for it. She made no effort to cover herself. She stood glaring defiantly at us.

Mom finished climbing out and I handed her the towel. She began to vigorously rub herself dry, ending with wrapping the towel around her hair. Like her daughter, she made no attempt at modesty. She casually took the robe and wrapped herself in it.

"Jesus it's cold," she said.

"You can't stay in there forever," Jimmy said to the girl.

"Lay my towel and robe on the ground and you all turn around." Now, all of a sudden, she was getting modest. Too late. We had already seen everything there was to see.

Jimmy lay the wadded towel and robe on the ground and turned. Blackhawk turned and I turned enough so I could still see Mom, but not the girl. I waited and when enough time had elapsed, I turned back. She had her hair wrapped in her towel, her bathrobe on and held a walkie talkie in her hand.

"Shit," Jimmy said.

The device crackled and we heard a man's voice on the other end, "This is Diego, come back."

The girl said, "Diego, we're at the bathtub. Those elk hunters are here. They're holding us."

Blackhawk stepped forward and with a lightning move took the talkie from her. He thumbed the talk button. "Mister, we are here with your girls, but we intend them no harm. By the time you and your group get here they will be dressed, warm and will have their weapons in their possession. We had no idea there was a bathtub here. We stumbled onto them by accident." He took his thumb off the button and waited. There was no response.

The girl said, "You can try to run but you can't get away from Diego. He is an expert tracker. And he's not the only one."

I reached down and stoked the fire with two more pieces of wood. "You girls need to get dressed. Get your feet warm before you get frostbitten."

They began to dress. Blackhawk nodded his head to the side and moved away a few feet. Jimmy and I followed him.

We stepped out of earshot, "No way we can get away from these guys," he said. "They are motorized, well equipped and I believe the girl when she says Diego, whoever he is, is a master tracker."

"If we had our quads working, we'd have a chance."

"But we don't," I said.

"So we just wait here and look innocent."

"We get on Mom's good side if we can. I think she could be an ally."

"That's your specialty."

"How old is the girl?" Jimmy said.

"Young," Blackhawk said.

"I thought mountain people got married young."

"Depends on what the laws of the United Brotherhood are in the land of bullshit."

"You want to get married," Blackhawk grinned at Jimmy.

"Not on Auntie Matilda's sweet ass," he said.

"That ain't the ass you need to be worrying about," I said. We could hear the quads approaching in the distance.

# 29

Just after we heard the quads, we heard another set of quads from a slightly different direction. I immediately thought they had two groups coming.

Madonna's walkie talkie crackled, then came to life.

"Madonna! Madonna!" Diego's voice was urgent. Blackhawk handed her the talkie.

"Yeah sir," the girl answered.

"Get the hell out of there. The Redcoats are coming. They know you are at the tub."

Mom and Madonna swung aboard their quads. Mom said urgently, "Two of you can get on with us. One of you is on his own."

Madonna looked at Jimmy. "You're with me, cutie."

Mom revved her engine. She looked at Blackhawk, then me. "If one of you don't get on, they might shoot you. Or, if you're lucky, throw you in their stockade. If one of you stays, they might spare you."

"I'll stay," I said. "What did he mean, *Redcoats?*"

She didn't answer.

Blackhawk swung up behind her. Jimmy jumped on behind Madonna and had to grab quickly as the girl ripped away. They disappeared into the forest. As the roaring sound of their quads faded, the sound was replaced by the sound of quads coming all around me. When we surprised the girls, Mom had dropped the joint they were sharing. I walked over and picked it up. It was still smoldering. I placed it between my lips and leaned against the warm tank as I leaned my rifle against it. My best defense was to bluff it as a dumb hunter separated and lost from his buddies: *Boy, am I glad to see you guys!*

Redcoats indeed. Through the trees, as the quad sounds became louder, I could see red colored parkas and maroon quilted winter coats. I pulled my lighter and relit the roach. I took a deep drag. The thing about dope smokers is that everything they do is deliberate. Slow and deliberate. Taking speed is just the opposite.

There were a dozen quads that came pouring into the bathtub clearing. A third of them were women. To their benefit, they all wore helmets. As the helmets came off the long hair was flying. All of these women were young. Not as young as Madonna but not as old as Mom. They all had rifles on their handlebars and side arms strapped to their legs. They each had a walkie talkie strapped to a bicep. These people looked serious.

I straightened up and took another drag on the joint. "Boy, am I glad to see you guys. My buddies left me here. They said they were going for help, but I think they must have got lost. I followed this creek for a while, but it meandered so much I didn't know where it was going. Then I found this tank and decided to wait here. The water was warm, so someone used it. I was hoping they would come back."

One of the men pulled forward. He had some kind of insignia on his red parka. He pulled off his helmet. "Where is your machine?" he asked.

I turned and looked over to the east. "Over that way someplace. We came across some elk tracks but couldn't follow on quads. We lost track of the elk and when we came back to where we left the quads, someone had trashed them. Cut wires and slashed tires and stole all our stuff. That was yesterday. We've been trying to find a way back ever since. Can you guys get me back to a ranger station? I think there's one on Houston Mesa Road."

One of the women laughed. They all smiled. The one that laughed said, "You sure as hell don't know where you are. Where's your phone?"

I took it out of my pocket. I looked at it ruefully. "Got no signal. Can I use one of yours?"

"There ain't no cell towers that reach up here, even if you did have a battery that would last," the leader said.

"Can somebody give me a ride to a trail or something that'll get me out of here?" I tried to sound pathetic.

"Yeah, we'll give you a ride," the man said. He turned to another man. "Get his rifle, his pistol and his backpack. Search him good." He looked back at me. "Gather up what you can carry." He turned to one of the women. "Helena Jean, get him up behind you. We'll head back to the compound."

"Jesus, Francis, why me?" the woman said. She looked to be a little older than me. She had streaked blond hair and she was as well armed as the rest of them.

"Because I told you."

Off into the faint distance there was a fusillade of gunfire. A pause then sporadic firing.

Francis didn't look surprised. He looked in that direction. He turned to one of the other men. An older guy. "Is that our patrol?" he asked.

"Might be," the guy answered.

"When we get back, send out someone to find them. Get them back to the compound." The guy nodded.

Helena Jean hitched forward. "Get on," she said, still not happy about it.

I hopped on and put my arms around her waist. Felt good to hold on to a real live woman. Marianne had been a while.

# 30

Nacho was sitting at the bar reading the newspaper. He insisted on subscribing to it and was usually the only one to read it. After he and Elena had brought Marianne back to the club, he had decided to spend the night. Nothing was said but he knew it made Marianne and Elena feel better.

This morning he had slept late. For his stayovers, he had made a space in the corner of the storeroom and kept a cot and a reading light. He washed up in the men's room and was usually the one that fixed the coffee. He always read the whole paper. He was only half-way through when Elena and Marianne came down the stairs. By now it was mid-morning. The new guy would open the bar in another hour.

Elena came over to him and said, "Come on. I want you with us."

He folded the paper and set it aside. "Where are we going?"

She told him. He sat a moment looking at her, then he slid off his stool and went behind the bar. He retrieved his Glock. He slipped it into the back of his belt. The girls were headed out the back. He hustled to catch up with them.

Elena drove, which made Nacho very nervous and scared Marianne. She attacked every stop sign and every stoplight with fierce aggression. Speeding until the last instant, then trusting her brakes to get her stopped. The instant the light turned green, she would roar away without hesitation.

She took I-10, then within minutes, exited onto Seventh Street north. If Marianne weren't so nervous, she might have enjoyed the trip through downtown. She usually was driving and didn't get the opportunity to look around.

Finally, Elena reached the restaurant she was seeking. She turned right off Seventh, then immediately pulled into a back parking lot behind the building. She parked in a handicapped spot and slid out. Nacho and Marianne followed. There was a lit sign on the back of the restaurant proclaiming it to be Milano's Italian Eatery. An ornate door led to a hallway that led to the bar. In the hallway there were doors on either side. The doors were closed.

It was too early for customers. But inside the bar there was a man sitting at the last table and another one sitting on the first stool next to the front door. They were both short brown men with shiny black hair and Hawaiian shirts. The shirts were unbuttoned, and underneath were ribbed wife beater undershirts. They were alike, with tattoos creeping up from their collars to their necks and almost to their ears. Their arms were sleeved with tattoos coming up out of their shirt sleeves. If you knew to look, you could see the slight bulge as their shirts lay across their pistols.

Elena didn't hesitate. She walked down the bar to where the bartender was washing glasses.

"Excuse me," she said.

He glanced up at her. He looked at Nacho, who had taken a neutral seat in the middle of the bar. He looked at Marianne and his look lingered on her.

"Yes ma'am," he said.

"Tell Emilio that Elena is here."

"I'm sorry, ma'am we're not open yet."

"I don't give a shit if you are open," Elena said. "Go tell your boss that Elena is here."

The guy looked at her blankly. "Elena who?" he said.

The guy at the table stood. Nacho swung slightly toward him, moving his hand to his thigh.

"Just go do it," the guy that had stood, said.

The bartender looked at him for a moment, then nodded, turned, and went around the bar and down the hallway.

"Sorry about that," the guy that had stood said. "He's new. He doesn't know who you are."

"Maybe next time he will," Nacho said.

"You may be assured, he will," the guy said. "How are you doing, Nacho?"

"Living the dream," Nacho said.

"Aren't we all."

The bartender came back in. "Mr. Garza will see you now," he said. "First door on your left."

Elena led the way. The guy at the table said to Nacho as he passed, "Give Blackhawk my best."

"Will do," Nacho said. He and Marianne followed Elena down the hall to the door. Elena rapped on it. It opened and man came out shutting the door behind him. He was only about five eight and thick with an aura of force and danger.

"May I see your purse, please," he said to Elena. She didn't hesitate. He opened it and looked in it. He didn't touch anything. He handed it back. He looked at Nacho. "Are you carrying?"

Nacho nodded. The man looked at Marianne.

She said, "You mean like a gun?"

The man said, "Yes, like a gun."

Marianne shook her head. "Oh God no."

The man said, "You two stay in the bar. Only Elena goes in. She will be safe."

Nacho didn't like this.

Elena looked at him and nodded. "It will be okay."

The guy opened the door and held it for Elena. She went in. The guy followed her and shut the door behind her leaving Nacho and Marianne in the hallway. Nacho turned and went back to the bar.

Following, Marianne asked his back, "She'll be okay?"

"None of these guys has a death wish."

"A death wish?"

"She's Blackhawk's woman." That was all he said.

She was silent until they had returned to the bar and took a booth. The bartender started toward them, but Nacho waved him away. "So, Blackhawk is dangerous?" Marianne said. "These guys seem dangerous. Blackhawk seems like a pussycat."

Nacho looked at her calmly. "You really don't know, do you?"

"I guess not. I don't even know who you are."

"I'm the pussycat," he said.

Marianne was silent. "Why are we here? These guys look like gangsters. Who is Emilio?"

Nacho leaned back and looked around. He turned back to her. "How many people do you know who would or could dive off a three-story boat to try to save a baby who was already twenty feet underwater?"

She shook her head. "I still can't get my head around Jackson doing that."

"Blackhawk."

"Beg pardon?"

"The only other person that would not only attempt it but carry it off is Blackhawk. It just turned out that Jackson was closer." He looked at her. He thought about it, then made a decision. "Emilio Garza is the Jefe of the Valdez drug cartel in Arizona. Actually, in all the Southwest."

"Jefe?"

"The big cheese. The Don. The head honcho."

"And Elena knows him?"

"If it weren't for Jackson and Blackhawk, he wouldn't be the honcho and he would probably be dead. "

She started to say something, but he held up a hand to stop her. He lowered his voice. "His Excellency, the Colombian Ambassador, is the international head of a conglomerate of drug cartels of which Valdez is one of the largest. A few years back a rival gang kidnapped his granddaughter, drugged her up with the intent to sell her to those that would use her to blackmail the Ambassador. Jackson and Blackhawk rescued her and returned her to her grandfather. He has held a debt of gratitude ever since."

"How in God's name did they get involved in that?"

"You've been out to Jackson's boat."

"Of course."

"You remember it is moored at the end of his dock. His is the last one."

"Yeah, so?"

"The rival gang tried to sell the girl, but something went wrong, and they panicked, so they decided to cut their losses and get out of the whole thing. They drugged her to the point of her being comatose. They wrapped her in painters' plastic. They weighed her down and tossed her off the end of Jackson's dock to get rid of the body. That's eighty feet of water there. Fortunately for her, Jackson happened to be sleeping on top of his boat, and they woke him up. When they dumped the girl and ran, Jackson realized what was going on and went off the top and swam down. Sound familiar? And he dragged the girl out of the water. It wasn't a three-story dive, but it was dark, deep and again he was lucky as only Jackson can be."

Marianne sat looking across the room, trying to get her mind around this. Elena came from the back and signaled them to follow her.

Nacho slid out of the booth, and Marianne automatically followed. Marianne said to no one in particular, "I don't know who any of you are."

# 31

Marianne climbed into the back seat and immediately began a string of questions, but Nacho held up a hand to shush her. She felt a flush of anger, then realized, as Elena pulled out of the parking lot, jumped the curb and went across two lanes of traffic, it wasn't the best time to distract the woman. It was all she could do to hold herself in until they got back to the club.

As soon as they were inside Elena gestured to Marianne to follow her and went up the stairs. Nacho helped the temporary bartender stock the bar and polish the mahogany wood of the bar top, until it gleamed. Blackhawk had a husband and wife cleaning team that came in at 3 AM to clean the El Patron. Elena had handpicked the couple for her main room and the apartment. There was another professional cleaning company that took care of the rest of the building. It was Nacho's habit to walk through the El Patron main bar to check the tabletops and adjust the chairs that weren't aligned to his eye.

Satisfied, he returned to his unfinished newspaper. A half hour later Marianne came down. She took the stool next to him.

"So, what happened?" he asked.

She looked discouraged. "Not much. Elena said the Garza guy assured her that he would find Tiffany."

"His people are all over the city," Nacho said.

"That's what she said. She said it probably wouldn't be until tomorrow before he might have an idea where she is."

"Are you working tonight?"

"Elena thinks I should."

"Elena's right."

"But what if Tiffany comes home and I'm not there?"

"How safe is home?" Nacho said. "Last time she was all locked in, safe and snug. Somebody kicked in the back door and took her. If she goes anywhere, it will be here. Lots of people around, and lots of people who would protect her."

"You're right," she said.

"Yes, I know."

It was late the next day before anything happened. A little after five Nacho moved behind the bar and began to slice limes. He had two bowls, one for thicker slices for drinks like gin or vodka tonics, or margaritas. Another bowl was for thinner slices for Daiquiris, Moscow Mules and Citrus Martini's.

The batwing doors opened and a slender, dark-haired woman in a beige suit came in. She came to the bar and slid up on a stool opposite of where Nacho was working.

"Hey, Nacho," she said.

"Detective Boyce," he said. "What brings you in?"

"Thought I'd check on Marianne and see if she's heard from her niece."

The door to the landing opened and as if planned, Marianne began descending the staircase. Jackson always said she looked like Loretta Young making an entrance, but Nacho had no idea who Loretta Young was, so that was lost on him.

"Your lips to God's ears," Nacho said. Boyce swiveled and watched. As she reached the bottom, she saw Boyce and came over. She slid up beside her. "Hey girl," she said. "Have you heard anything?"

"I came down to ask the same thing. Did you hear about the night before last?"

Boyce shook her head. "Nothing that I didn't know before. What happened the night before last?"

Nacho fixed Margarita's and sat one in front of each girl. Marianne picked hers up and took a large drink. She told Boyce about her door being kicked in and Tiffany taken.

Boyce said, "Did you call the police?"

"Better yet," Nacho said. "Elena went to see Emilio Garza yesterday."

Boyce gave him the dead eye cop look. "What did Garza do?"

The batwing doors opened again. Emilio Garza's main lieutenant came in and waited while his eyes adjusted. He spotted Nacho and moved over to him. He stood beside Marianne. He looked at Boyce but didn't say anything.

Nacho did the introductions. Looking at the man, he said, "Ladies, this man is Manuela. He's very close to Mr. Garza." He turned to the girls. "Manny, you saw this lady at Mr. Garza's. Her name is Marianne. It is her niece we are looking for." He turned more to Boyce. "And, this lady is….."

"Detective Boyce," Manny said before Nacho could finish. "Every cartel member in every gang in Maricopa County knows who Detective Boyce is."

"Just Maricopa County?" Boyce said.

Manny shrugged and grinned. He nodded his head. "Arizona," he said. "But she doesn't know where Blue Boy is, and I do." He looked at Nacho. "Mr. Garza has instructed me to help you in any way I can."

# 32

Marianne wanted to go with them, but neither Nacho nor Manny would go along with that. Manny was driving a two-year-old black Escalade. He had parked it toward the back of the parking lot. As Nacho and Boyce followed Manny, and as they came closer to the SUV, they could see someone sitting in the front passenger seat.

Nacho and Boyce climbed into the back seat. Manny started the engine and said, "This is Willy. He's the one that found your girl." Willy was darker than Manny with coal black hair, all slicked up like Elvis. He had a gold tooth in front.

"Where did you find her?" Boyce said.

Willy hitched around so he could look at her. She was behind Manny. Willy looked at her for a long moment, then at Manny.

"Who's she?" Willy asked.

"This is Detective Boyce," Manny said.

"Detective *First Grade* Boyce," Nacho said.

Willy looked at her for another long moment. "So, you are Boyce?"

"Where is she?" Boyce said.

"I don't know the address, but I can get us there. Dos Hermanos has a casino in an industrial warehouse in Tempe. I saw her in there."

"How did you know it was her?"

"I didn't until yesterday. Mr. Garza showed all of us a photo. I remembered seeing her at the casino a few days ago."

"You are sure it is her?"

"She is a beautiful girl. I don't forget beautiful girls."

"So what were you doing in a Dos Hermanos casino?"

"It's considered neutral territory," Manny said. Manny pulled out on the street. "So tell me where to go."

It turned out to be mostly highways. It didn't take long to get there. Once on highway 202 they went east and just past the ASU campus Willy instructed Manny to take the McClintock exit. A few blocks south, he had Manny turn back west and then they were in an industrial area. Hundreds of small businesses filled the warehouse-sized buildings.

Willy finally pointed at a nondescript warehouse with no signage. "That's it."

Manny took the turn in and circled around the parking lot until he found a parking spot that was closer to the entrance than the fifty that were empty. Like walking a little bit might kill him.

As they parked, Willy told them that unlike the Indian casinos, this one had metal detectors and guards at the entrance. No guns allowed. Manny and Nacho set their pieces on the floorboard. Boyce left hers in place, on her hip close to the badge. The badge wasn't enough. The guards made her show her city I.D. They reluctantly let her in and immediately went to their radio.

Like all casinos, once inside the place it was a cacophony of noise. Bells signifying jackpots. The jingle, jingle, jingle of the machines designed to draw you in. It was a weekday. The place was half empty. They followed Willy around. Four sets of eyes looking for a beautiful blonde girl. Nobody matched that description.

Finally, Nacho said, "Where did you see her and how long has that been?"

"Last week," he said. "She was up on the high stakes area," he nodded toward that area. There were four steps leading up to it, with a velvet rope across the entrance.

"What do they play up there?" Nacho said.

Manny said, "Baccarat."

"Never heard of it."

"Was she with somebody?" Boyce said.

"No one I knew. The only one I remember was a flashy little dude in a shiny blue suit. Had a stack of chips a foot high in front of him. I think he's the one they call Blue Boy. The one you're looking for."

"When was that?"

"Less than a week ago."

They continued to walk around the perimeter of the main floor. Nacho sidled up beside Boyce. "Do you see him?"

"Yeah, I got him," she said.

They had picked up a tail that had been following throughout the gambling floor. This was no surprise. In forty minutes, they had covered everywhere people were gambling. Willy had gotten bored and peeled off to a slot machine.

"Time to go," Boyce said. Nacho nodded. Willy had hit a couple of small jackpots and Manny was behind him, watching.

Nacho and Boyce came up behind him. Manny looked at them. "No luck?"

"No luck," Nacho said.

"I'll get this place watched," Boyce said.

"Isn't this illegal?" Nacho said.

"Technically," Boyce said. "But in city politics, there's illegal and there's illegal."

"Kickbacks?"

"And taxes," she said.

"You're a cop."

"I'm a Phoenix city cop. This is Tempe."

Manny said, "Ready to go?"

Nacho nodded.

"Willy's staying here," Manny said. "Thinks he's going to hit it big. He'll take an Uber."

As they walked to the car, Nacho said, "That was disappointing." Boyce nodded in agreement.

This time, after retrieving his pistol from the back floorboards, Nacho climbed into the front. More leg room for him. It was getting warm, so the first thing Manny did was fire up the A/C. The people that had designed the parking lot forced anyone leaving to circle counterclockwise. Manny cursed them as he drove all the way around the lot, back to within ten yards of where they had been parked, just to exit.

He pulled out onto the street and started back to the highway. Two blocks away they passed a van with its side door open. As they went by, two men with AR-15s stepped out and opened fire. There was the chatter of automatic fire and the simultaneous thwocking of bullets punching into the Escalade.

# 33

As his window shattered, Nacho instinctively dodged down on top of the center console. Manny yelped and the Escalade swung to the left, almost up on two wheels. Boyce, sitting behind Nacho, saw the two guys before Nacho did and was on her way to the floor when the bullets hit their vehicle.

Without realizing she had it, Boyce's pistol was in her hand. She lunged at her shattered window and screaming in rage at the top of her lungs, she was hanging halfway out and emptied her 9mm Colt Defender at the receding van. She knew, with the range of the pistol, she had little chance of hitting anything.

Rubber screeching, Manny brought the SUV to a sideways halt. Nacho fumbled his seatbelt open and kicking the door lever down, he tumbled out onto the ground. He fired three quick rounds in the direction of the van and crabbed around until he was behind the front passenger tire. It was flat. Laying prone, he fired at the moving van until he was empty. The two guys were nowhere in sight and the van was ripping backwards. It reached the corner and bounding over the curb and still going backwards, it disappeared.

Boyce had climbed back onto the backseat. Nacho heard her voice, "Nacho. Manny's been shot."

Nacho came up off the ground and went around the driver's side of the vehicle. Manny was leaned back in his seat holding his arm. Boyce climbed out and she and Nacho yanked the driver door open. Manny was looking at them sheepishly.

"I got shot." He almost sounded like a little boy saying he had a boo boo.

Blood was running down his arm and into his lap.

"No shit," Nacho said. He looked at Boyce. "We need to get him to a hospital."

Boyce gently nudged Nacho out of the way, "Let me see it."

She gently pulled the short sleeve out of the way and leaned in to look at the wound.

Manny was grimacing. "Beginning to throb," he said.

"Nearest hospital is all the way out to Power Road," Nacho said.

"Didn't hit an artery, let's wrap the wound. I want to take him to St. Joe's."

"Why St. Joe's?"

"Inner-city hospital. I'm an inner-city gang cop. I've been there so many times they know my name."

"First-Aid kit in the back," Manny said between gritted teeth.

"Let's start with that," Boyce said.

"I thought you were hit," Manny said. "You were screaming so loud."

Boyce chuckled. "Something a friend taught me. It could unnerve your opponent in a gunfight and give you an edge."

"Who told you that?" Nacho said.

"Your buddy, Jackson."

# 34

The Redcoat leader, Francis, led the way. I was determined to keep track of the path Francis would take but it didn't take much for me to get turned around. I knew I was turned around when fifteen minutes later, off to the side I caught a glimpse of the water tank bathing spot. It had to be the same one. They had to be purposely getting me confused. We followed the stream then turned off and went up a knoll. Then we followed higher ground before swinging down a deep ravine and staying at the bottom for five minutes. When we came up out of the gully and traveled the level ground, I saw what I thought I had seen before, but by now it all looked alike.

I leaned into the girl. I felt a little guilty. She was suffering the brunt of the wet forest. She was wearing sturdy canvas pants and boots and her worn red parka was waterproof, so she did have some protection. We drove along for quite a while. The best I could tell was that we were traveling north, then east, then north again. Finally, we settled into a straight eastern trajectory. At least it felt east. I could find no evidence of the sun.

It was a long forty minutes before we came to the edge of a

long sloping ravine with a valley below that was open and patched with snow. There still were small patches of green grass. It was filled with lodge pole structures and tents and here and there a teepee. There were a lot of people, more than I would have thought. Some had red or reddish orange parkas, just like Helena Jean's. A lot of them had ordinary store-bought parkas. They were all dressed for the cold. It could have been an Eskimo village.

As we reached the top of the hill two guards stepped out of hiding and I could hear them talking with Francis, but I couldn't tell what they said. Down below, in the compound, were two elk carcasses being stripped and cleaned. My stomach growled. There were several cookfires burning and the smell of smoke and roasting meat drifted up to us. I was hungry enough to join up then and there. We reached the bottom and the group scattered to their living quarters, which for the most part were log buildings. Most were one room. It didn't appear that everyone had quads. On the outside of the camp there was a steep red dirt cliff that bordered most of the east side.

Helena Jean wheeled over to where Francis had stopped. He had pulled up to a two-room cabin. Two young women came out to greet him. One was a little hefty with dirty blond braided hair. The other was younger. She also looked a little grimy around the edges. I never was good at guessing ages. She didn't look much older than a teenager. I would expect Jimmy or Nacho to check her ID at the bar. They each had a horse blanket across their shoulders.

Francis dismounted his quad and walked over to me.

"What's your name?"

"Jackson," I said.

"Jackson what?"

"Just Jackson."

He turned to Helena Jean, "Take him to nine, the empty. Get him some food. Stay with him until we can get him in front of the council."

"I have to stay with him? Can't we just put him in the stockade?"

"There's no heat there unless you want to chop the wood." He was right. I could see what appeared to be the stockade. It had been hastily built and there were spaces between the logs. She started to say the prisoner could chop the wood, but he said, "You take care of him." He turned on his heel and went inside.

I said to Helena Jean "Are those his daughters?"

"Two of his wives," she said. Neither of us had dismounted. She turned the key and the motor roared back to life. She kicked the gear and the quad jumped forward. I almost came off. I couldn't tell but it seemed to me it was intentional. I grabbed her tight and held on. She ripped around the edge of the compound and came to rest on the other side. She pulled up to a log cabin that looked relatively new. It had the number nine painted next to the door.

"Home sweet home," I said as I slid off. She looked at me sharply. "Count yourself lucky. This is better than many I've had to live in." She looked at me steadily. "We'll get along just fine, if you can keep your mouth shut."

"Yes ma'am," I said.

She pulled the log door open and indicated for me to enter. The door was made of pine poles with creek moss stuffed tightly between the poles for insulation. There was a cross board holding it all together. It looked sturdy with the moss designed to keep the warmth in and the cold out.

"When can I get my stuff back," I asked. "My rifle and handgun and my K Bar knife. I've had that knife since I was in the service." I ducked inside. She followed. It was dark and cold. She left the door open to let light in. It was cold enough to see our breath.

"The council will decide," she said.

I slid my pack off my shoulders and looked around. She carried her pack in and set it on one of the two sleeping pallets. It was the one closest to the cold fireplace. Each pallet had a horsehair blanket on it. There were odds and ends around. There was a bearskin that could serve as a rug or a robe. Shelves had been built next to the fireplace and a skillet and a cookpot sat on them. Close by her bed was a stack of firewood and next to it, a pile of kindling.

"You mind if I start a fire?" I said.

She pulled a box of matches from her bag and lit a kerosene lamp that sat beside the pots. Once lit, she advanced the wick to get the amount of light she wanted. She tossed me the box of matches. "Suit yourself." She reached back and made sure the door was secure. She sat on her pallet and crossed her legs on top of each other. She pulled the multicolored horse blanket up and around her shoulders.

I pulled some kindling off the pile and looked at her. "You have a knife?"

"You don't need a knife to light those."

"Don't need it, but easier with it."

She reached down and pulled a skinning knife from her boot. With a deft motion she tossed it toward the wood pile, and it stuck into the end of one of the five-inch logs. I took it and began shaving on the pine sticks. When I had a pile of shavings, I built a teepee of sticks around the shavings. I took the matches and lit the fire. It took just a few seconds before I could lay two larger logs on the flames.

She watched for a moment, then stood. "I'll go get us some food. Don't let that fire spark to the top and check the flue while I'm gone. I don't know who was in here last."

"Yes ma'am I'll be careful. If you have an axe, I can split more firewood."

She looked at him. "Axe is around at the back. So's the logs."

She left to get food. Evidently meat was cooked in several communal pots. She took our empty pot with her. I found the axe. The logs to split were in a communal pile and were a few yards away. There was not a lot of it. I dug into the work and was building a substantial pile of split logs when it began to snow. It started with flurries, then got more intense. By the time she was back, and I was finished, the falling snow was a full-blown white out. The wind was blowing and the temperature had dropped by twenty degrees. I was happy to get back inside with a warm fire and hot food.

# 35

Blackhawk and Jimmy sat in a single room cabin that was located fifty yards south of the old ranger station. There were other cabins between it and the open compound. They had been there a while, and the weather was turning. Blackhawk had asked several times about having their weapons and gear returned but he had been ignored. After an hour or so, Madonna came in and set a pot close to the fire.

She looked at Jimmy. "There is stacked firewood against the side of the cabin. It's supposed to get nasty tonight. I suggest you bring in enough to last the night. I'll be back with blankets."

"What about water," Blackhawk said.

"Once your food pot is empty, you can melt snow in it."

"What about going to the bathroom?" Jimmy said.

"Go outside," she said. "If you need to be a big boy, go to the latrine now," she pointed at the door. "It's straight out that way. Or you'll have to wait till morning. If you pee in that corner, or any other, I will personally shoot you."

"What was that gunfire we heard on our way here? Someone else pee in the wrong place?"

She ignored that. "One of our patrols taking target practice." She started to leave. "There are no guards. You decide to leave, you are on your own. There is nowhere to go. You would die before you got halfway down the mountain." She turned and went out the door.

Jimmy looked at Blackhawk. "You believe that? Target practice?"

"Probably not. Let's get the firewood," Blackhawk said. They went out and the wind was howling. Jimmy stood still as he dug out his hiker's compass. It was a good one it also had a thermometer. Blackhawk loaded his arms with wood. Jimmy used his foot to hold the door for him as he carried it in.

"Thirty below," Jimmy said putting the compass in his pocket. He gathered an armload and carried it in. They went back out for another load.

There were cups and tin plates and utensils laid out on a rough board cupboard that was nailed to the wall next to the fire. There were small cotton sacks of flour and sugar. The pot was simmering. It held chunks of elk, quartered potatoes and some carrots. The broth was elk fat and water. Blackhawk ladled some of the stew into two bowls. He handed one to Jimmy. He took another for himself. They sat next to the fireplace and blew on the hot food until it was edible. They each had a canteen, so they did have some water to drink.

They gobbled the stew, scraping the remnants from the pot. "Hope that wasn't supposed to be breakfast too."

"I hadn't thought of that," Jimmy said. Vittles had been scarce since they lost the quads. "Where do we sleep?" Jimmy said.

"On the ground, next to the fire. The girl said she would be bringing blankets. At least we have firewood. We are damned lucky to have this shelter on a night like this. I'd hate to spend the night out under that rock ledge."

"Like Jackson?"

Blackhawk shrugged. "Jackson was far and away the best woodsman in our unit. He can be very creative. The Colonel made him our tactician. When things would go wrong, and they inevitably did, Jackson was in charge of coming up with the solution. You can bet he's snuggled into a warm and protected shelter right this minute. '

"Anyone else help him? Or was it just him making new decisions?"

"Part of Jackson's genius was listening and picking the best thinking to help him form a strategy. Jackson will probably invent a new form of heat while he's out there."

"You have a lot of faith in him."

"No one I know can measure up to him."

Jimmy laughed. "It's a good thing he uses his superpowers for good. Nacho calls him Superboy."

Blackhawk shook his head. "My fault. I talk too much to Elena and Elena talks too much to Nacho."

Jimmy took a drink out of his canteen, then offered it to Blackhawk. Blackhawk shook his head. Jimmy put it away. "First time I realized Jackson was different was when that drunk football player came in with a bunch of them," Jimmy said. "Tried to push Jackson around and Jackson put him down with one punch."

"Butt end of a shot glass. If Jackson had hit him with the open end of the glass it would have sliced the guy's ear into a nice little circle. Guy went on to the Pros. Raiders, I think."

"Yeah," Jimmy said. "Bobby Helms. Still playing. Defensive lineman. Big son of a bitch."

"You know, he came back and thanked Jackson for putting him down. As it turned out, his buddies took him home and his coach pulled a surprise inspection. They weren't supposed to be out of their rooms. Had the Rose Bowl to play. He'd have been suspended if the coach didn't find him at home."

"Defensive player of the game. Probably got him the pros."

"You say he's still playing?"

"Far as I know."

The door opened and Madonna came in with a big armload of blankets. She kicked the door shut behind her. She piled the blankets on the floor.

"Thanks for the food," Jimmy said, putting that Jimmy personality forward.

"You're welcome," she said. She smiled at him. She turned to leave.

"Hey, I've got a question for you." She paused.

"My friend Blackhawk here and I have a difference of opinion. He says you are fifteen or sixteen years old. I think you are a lot older than that."

"I turned eighteen last Tuesday."

"How come you are out here in the middle of nowhere?"

"It ain't the middle of nowhere. Me and mom are here." She opened the door. "I'm tired. We get up early. You best get some rest." As she closed the door she said out loud, half to herself, "Who the hell is called Blackhawk?"

As the door closed, Jimmy grinned at Blackhawk.

"Last Tuesday, huh?" Blackhawk said.

# 36

I had a good fire going when Helena Jean came back. She was carrying a steaming pot of stew. As she came through the door, I caught a glimpse of what promised to be a raging storm. She sat the pot next to the fire. Staying in a log cabin can be fun if you aren't addicted to your easy chair. On her back was a large possible bag stitched together from the hides of smaller critters. Squirrel, rabbit, fox and marten stitched together to make a carry bag with shoulder straps.

Helena Jean dug into it and withdrew large tin coffee cups and forks and large spoons. She went back outside. Just a few moments and she was back with two buckets filled with snow. She set them close to the fire, keeping the handles away from the flames.

"It'll take a while but eventually we should have water for coffee."

"I appreciate your hospitality," I said. "To be honest I didn't expect it. I didn't know what to expect."

"Where are your other people?" Her eyes slid to me, frank and intelligent.

"I told you they left me by the tank."

She looked at the fire then turned back to me. It was a deep, probing look. "You can lie to us, or you can tell the truth. It will go better for you if you tell the truth."

I was thinking about what to say when she continued. "There were tracks all over the place we found you. We found where your quads had been vandalized and we saw where they were pulled away."

"And who did that?"

"It wasn't the Redcoats. I think you know who it was."

I looked at the bubbling pot. "Think that's about ready." She took one of the large tin cups and dipped it to almost overflowing. She wiped the excess with a spoon and handed them both to me. I blew across the top of the stew. I finally took a small amount in the spoon and tried to nibble it. It burned my lip. I dug a spoon full of snow out of a bucket and put it in the stew. The snow in the bucket showed no signs of melting.

"Our plan was to take the quads into the deep woods as far as we could," I said. "Then set up a base camp and then continue on foot and backpack it until we found the elk."

"You were already close."

"Yeah, well, before we could know that, we ran into some guys. Actually, some guys and a couple of gals."

"Probably Eileen and Madonna."

"Yes, the young one must be Madonna. Eileen is her mother? Who's the father? An older guy seemed to be in charge. Is it him?"

"That's Diego. That is who Eileen and Madonna live with, but he's not Madonna's father."

"Who is?"

She shrugged. "I wouldn't know. Her and Madonna were like a lot of us, living out of a tent, having to move every ten days, then they met Diego and he brought them out here."

"To be his concubines?"

Her face snapped around, her eyes were fierce. Then she turned away. "Nothing like that," she said.

"You said us?"

"My daughter. Evangeline. She's with friends while I have to babysit you."

"Is that a common story? Being homeless then being recruited to a commune?"

"It's why I'm here. Evangeline and I were living out of my van, bouncing around the campgrounds in and around Flagstaff, then Williams, then Payson. I met those two girls, you saw today, at a WalMart. They told me about Francis and the Redcoats. So I sold the van and we hitched a ride with them up here. They had a cabin available, and we moved in."

"How old is Evangeline?"

"She's sixteen," she said quietly.

I could see she didn't want to talk about Evangeline. "What's the name *Redcoats* about."

She smiled. "They try to make it about the Revolutionary War but in reality, a charity group that helps the homeless showed up in Payson with a semi full of winter parkas. They handed them out free and when the people up here heard about it, there was a mass exodus. Some people were too late. They were all red or orangey red and the manufacturer said they were imperfect's and they couldn't sell them. They decided to give

172

them away and write off the loss. It was a Godsend to most of us. I wasn't prepared for these deep wood's winters."

My food had cooled enough for me to actually eat it. "None of my business, but from what I've noticed, you appear to be living alone."

She took my cup and put more stew in it. "Yeah, I am. Francis wanted me to move in with him. I respectfully declined."

"Not your type?"

"Not even close. And I have no desire to be wife number four."

"I saw two."

"There is another. She was inside. She's young and still pretty. Francis favors her and she doesn't do anything to help the others. Trouble in paradise."

"How long will that last?"

"One of these days the others will get tired of her. She will disappear into the forest."

I don't shock easily, but that shocked me. "They'll take her out and kill her."

"Probably not kill her. Just lose her. She wouldn't last long all alone."

I thought about that. "That happen a lot out here?"

"I don't have firsthand knowledge, but I've heard some of the women talk."

"Where did you say your daughter is?"

"Staying with friends until it's been decided what to do with you."

I ate some more. It was delicious. "Speaking of women. That bath tank, where you guys found me. Does that belong to the other group or to you Redcoats?"

"The other group call themselves the Fremen. Deigo is a fan of Frank Herbert and his Dune books. In the book they all live in a wilderness, except it's desert. The desert dwellers are a tough bunch known as the Fremen."

"Tell me about the bath tank."

She finished her food and set her bowl aside. "A long time ago, a local rancher set it up below the Rim for his cattle and someone brought it up here. The women in both groups immediately saw the possibility, and a council was called with the two groups, and it was agreed that the tank would be no man's land and would be shared by all the women. First come, first served. One of our guys, Teddy, used to be a plumber until the pandemic killed his business. He figured out how to get water out of the creek and into the tank. If you use it, you're supposed to replenish the wood pile, but some assholes won't do it. Francis's little dumplin' third wife for instance."

"So, there are some things both groups can agree on?"

"Both groups of women. The men never agree on anything."

I put more wood on the fire. The snow in the buckets had melted and began to steam. Helena Jean filled the coffee pot. Once set up, she set it directly on the flames.

We sat and watched the fire. We were silent for a long time. I had other questions, but I didn't want to push too hard.

Finally I said, "How far away is the Fremen camp from here?"

"Five, ten miles. These are winter camps. In the summer it changes a lot more." She stood and went back into the shadows and brought two cloths back to the fire. One was short like a washcloth. The other like a bath towel.

"I always take a spit bath before I sleep. You can go outside or sit facing the door and if you turn around, I will shoot you. Understand?"

"Yes ma'am."

She poured steaming water into a tin bowl. I grabbed my pack and sat facing the door. I pulled my sleeping bag out. After a while she said, "Okay." I turned and she was in her pallet, piled high with blankets. "It'll be your job to keep the fire lit."

"Yes ma'am," I said. I put my bag by the fire and several small logs close to it. I took my boot and prosthetic off. She had left some water in the bowl. I used it to splash my face. I washed my stub, then put the prosthetic back on. I wanted to be ready. I turned off the kerosene lamp. As I climbed into my sleeping bag I said, "One last question."

She waited.

"Do you know if Madonna and Eileen are voluntarily staying with the Fremen?"

"Far as I know they are. It's not like we chat over the back picket fence."

The bag began to warm me, and I realized how tired I was.

I began to think of Blackhawk and Jimmy. I wondered how they were being treated. So far the Redcoats didn't seem too hard-core militant or anything. The crackling of the fire was putting me out and I was just drifting off when she said, "Did you peek at me?"

"Be a fool not too," I laughed. I rolled to my side and hunched my shoulders. I waited for the bullet.

# 37

It didn't happen often to Blackhawk, but this night when he woke up to put a couple more logs on the fire he had to pee. He pulled his boots on but didn't lace them. He stood by the door and listened to Jimmy breathe. The breathing was rhythmic and deep, the kid was down and out. The sleep of the innocent, he thought.

He quietly opened the door and stepped out. It had stopped snowing. He carefully moved away from the cabin into the deep snow and relieved himself against a tall pine. The air was crisp and cold. The new snow made it still. The moon wasn't completely full; it was high and bright. There must have been four feet of new snow, and it lay on the earth like a mother's blanket. The snow absorbed all sound, and the absolute silence was like a sound unto itself. It was so unnatural it made Blackhawk grin. He finished his business and despite the cold, stood and looked all around. It was a village. Each dwelling had a line of smoke coming from its chimney or the top opening if it was a teepee. There was no breeze, so the smoke rose in a straight line. There was nothing stirring, all manner of man and beasts were snuggled in against the cold. He wondered about the animals that lived here in the forest. He knew the elk usually moved south for the winter. They huddled up at night, usually in a stand of trees. They traveled up to 10 miles per day. Bears and mountain lions were in their winter dens. The bears would hibernate until the spring. Lions are active all winter. They usually needed a kill once a week to survive. The mama's didn't throw their litters until the spring. In the fall they shed their summer coat and replaced it with a double coat of fur so thick that moisture didn't penetrate to the skin. They also had unique blood vessels that pumped warm blood close to the major vital parts like the heart and lungs, keeping the cooler blood away next to the skin and in the extremities. He thought of Jackson. Jackson was the reader and the one that had told him all this.

Blackhawk looked across the compound and the surrounding trees. As soon as the sky began to lighten the lions would begin to stir to start their daily hunt. The deer would begin to forage and at some point, one of the lions and one of the deer would meet. The deer had two layers of fur also, and the thick underlayer of fur was hollow and stayed warm. It kept them so insulated that the snow that landed on the deer's back wouldn't melt.

The predator had a major advantage over the prey. The deer's hoofs were hard and narrow and sank into the deep snow, making their mobility slow. The lion had wide, padded paws that almost acted like snowshoes. It evened out because food was easier for deer, and they could survive all winter foraging for the stems, twigs, grasses and brush that was their natural food.

Blackhawk stood thinking about all that. He shivered and

went back into the warm cabin and climbed into his sleeping bag. He fell asleep thinking about deer instead of the militant gang that was sleeping all around him.

Jimmy was up first and lit the kerosene lamp. He stirred the ground coffee into the melted snow and put it on the fire. He added more logs to the fire. The cabin had cooled as the fire diminished during the night. Jimmy quietly went out the door to find a place to relieve himself. It was still dark. When he returned Blackhawk was up, sitting cross-legged on his pallet, the sleeping bag stretched across his shoulders. His tin coffee cup was sitting next to him anxiously awaiting the coffee to be ready.

Blackhawk took the now empty food pot and went out and gathered snow. Back inside he placed the pot directly on the flames. Jimmy was looking around the cabin. When he saw what he was looking for he got up and crossed the room. There was half a bag of flour sitting on an empty flour sack on a shelf that had been nailed to the wall. He took the empty sack and turned it inside out, fluffing it hard to dislodge the powdery residue. He poured the boiling coffee through the cloth and into the tin cups, capturing the grounds inside.

Blackhawk took his and blew on it, smart enough to not try to touch it yet. He set it aside and laced up his boots. "Let's go watch," he said.

He fastened his parka up and pulled the red bandanna down over his ears. Jimmy followed suit and they went outside. They carried their coffee with them. The sun wasn't up yet but the sky was beginning to lighten. There were people stirring, mostly cooking over open fires.

Fifty yards away were a group of young men doing calisthenics.

Some joggers were circling the camp. They had already been around more than once, and the new snow was trampled down into a path.

One of the cooks was Madonna. She was standing, watching a huge cast iron skillet. The scent of frying fatback wafted across the open ground. Blackhawk and Jimmy stood watching her move. Her hair had been recently washed and brushed and was held by a rawhide headband.

"You notice that?" Blackhawk said, gently sipping the steaming liquid.

"What?"

"Madonna's a redhead. I didn't notice before."

"More auburn than red. You just now noticed?"

"Guess so. You notice what else?"

Jimmy shook his head.

"This looks almost like an Indian village. Like an old time, mountain man rendezvous."

Jimmy looked around. "You're right."

Most of them had heavy buckskin and fur hats. Mountain man stuff. A lot, including Madonna, were wearing bearskin and elk hides. Madonna had on a bearskin vest with a white mink collar and buckskin leggings. She had fringed moccasins that went to her knee. There were unusual markings on the toes and the sides. The markings weren't beaded but painted on. She looked like a cross between an Indian princess and something out of Game of Thrones. She saw them watching and yelled. "Get a plate and a fork and come over." They did.

The cast iron skillet was loaded with sizzling slices of fat back. On one end were a dozen eggs cooking in the melted fat, sunny side up.

"You guys have chickens," Jimmy said.

Madonna shot him a look. "Can't keep anything from you," she said.

Blackhawk laughed. "Jimmy's the smart one of the outfit."

"Pity the outfit. Gimme your plates, I'll get you some breakfast."

The young man that had been with Madonna's mother when they accosted Jimmy came walking up. "You ain't giving them nothing." The guy was a little taller than Blackhawk, muscular with dirty blonde hair parted down the middle. He only wore a buckskin shirt and a vest. His biceps bulged against the shirt sleeves. Just like when he had stopped Jimmy, he exuded an arrogance that almost had an odor. He wore an emblem around his neck. It was handmade and Jimmy, who was closer, still couldn't make out what it was supposed to be.

"Since when did your dad die and leave you in charge," Madonna said, looking at him with steady eyes.

"Not yet," said an older man walking up from behind. It was Diego, their leader.

"They haven't earned breakfast," the young man said.

"They will, Deiter. They will." the man said. He turned to look at Blackhawk and Jimmy. He didn't offer a hand. "Name's Diego Murillo. I'm the Comandante of this Federation of Freedom Fighters. You call me Comandante." He turned to Madonna. "Give them food." He looked at his son. "Then they can earn it chopping wood. Bring them to me after they have finished." He turned and walked away. With a hard look at Blackhawk and Jimmy, his son followed.

"Could be worse, "Madonna said. "You could be digging a new latrine."

# 38

I was warm and toasty and sound asleep when Helena Jean climbed out of bed and thrust a couple more logs on the embers. In the dim early morning light coming through the plexiglass window, I peeked at her. She wore cream-colored long johns, from neck to ankle. Oh, dagnabit!

She quietly dressed for the cold. After the pleated pants and heavy parka, she sat on her bed and laced up her boots. Quietly as possible, she filled the camp style coffee pot and set it on the coals to heat. She turned and looked at me. I had my eyes closed and waited until I heard the door latch open before I looked again. She silently went through the door and pulled the latch shut. The prudent thing was to get more rest. I had no idea what the day would have in store for me. I closed my eyes and immediately went back to sleep. When I opened them again it was brighter, but not as bright as mid-morning. I looked at my watch and was surprised to see it was eight o'clock. Arizona doesn't do day-light saving time, so at certain times of the year it takes time to brighten up.

By now the coffee was hot and I poured a cup, then pulled

on my winter clothes. I stepped outside with the coffee steaming. The compound wasn't busy. I didn't see Helena Jean anywhere. Two cookfires were going. The snowstorm had put down about four feet and everything looked clean and bright. To my right was a guy scraping a hide that was pinned to a round frame. He was young and fit. He had stripped out of his heavy coat to keep from sweating. Biceps bulged against his shirt. It seemed all the guys here had biceps.

He looked at me and said, "You're new here, aren't you."

I nodded.

"You don't happen to have a cigarette, do you?"

"Sorry, I don't smoke," I said.

He nodded. "Nobody does any more," he said. "I love living up here, out of the clutches of so-called civilization and such, but no one has cigarettes. Guess I'm quitting whether I want to or not."

I reached a hand across. "I'm Jackson," I said.

"Jackson what?"

"Just Jackson."

"Robert Bruce," the young man said, taking my hand.

"Robert Bruce," I repeated. "Not Bob or Bobby."

"Only one person in the world is allowed to call me Bobby and you ain't her."

"Fine Scottish name. Robert the Bruce, one time king of Scotland. Direct descendant to Queen Elizabeth."

"Hey, no kidding. That's cool." He started scrapping again. "Your head full of odds and ends like that?"

"Full of useless information. Like you could grow your own tobacco."

He stopped scraping. "Here?"

"Well, maybe a little down the mountain, but it can be done. You have to be patient though. It can take up to three months for it to catch and mature."

"Damn," he said. Then "damn," again. "I need to figure that out."

Just then Helena Jean came walking up. "Good morning," she said to Robert. She looked at me. "Good morning sleepy head."

"Morning, darlin'."

Robert looked at me, "Darlin'? You sure do work fast."

"Don't misunderstand," I said. "Just a term of thanks for providing a warm pallet on the floor and a cabin to sleep in."

She looked at me. "Francis and the elders want to see you."

A woman in a red parka came up just as she said that. "They want to see you," she said to Helena Jean.

"I was told they wanted to see him." She bobbed her head at me.

The woman shrugged. "They said you first."

"Okey dokey," Helena Jean said and turned to follow the girl. She glanced back at me. "Stay close," she said.

"Okey dokey," I said.

Robert the Bruce watched them walk across the compound. I was curious. "I noticed you all don't wear the red parka's all the time."

"Some that's all they have. Others are on duty," he said. "Makes what they say official. Like a cop with a badge."

"What's that lady's duty?" I said, nodding at the woman walking beside Helena Jean.

"She patrols the camp. Looking for trouble. But right now, the council is meeting, so she stands guard."

"She must be tough if she's the peacekeeper. What's her name?"

"Sharon something. Don't know the last. She is tougher than a Norwegian boot."

I watched as Helena Jean went into the large cabin we had stopped at yesterday, the one where the Clampett girls had been waiting for Francis. I noticed a pile of sectioned logs just a few feet away. There was a large, round one, the top reaching two feet above the ground. The chopping block.

"Might as well split some logs while I wait."

Robert the Bruce slid me a look. "Not many people volunteer," he said. "This time of year, we always need firewood."

I picked up a log and balanced it on the base. I lifted the axe and felt the weight. I wiggled it a couple of times. I split two pieces and stripped my coat off. I had a sizeable pile going when a young rangy man came out of the cabin. He was tall with a mop of blond hair. He wore a shirt with the sleeves cut off to show off his biceps.

He looked across at me and yelled. He waved an arm. "We're ready for you."

I leaned the axe against the wood pile. I grabbed my coat and started across. As I passed Robert the Bruce, he said, "That guy's name is Jerry. Watch him. He's a backstabbing son of a bitch."

"Good to know," I said. Good to know that not all was peace and harmony in the group. I would have been shocked if it was.

# 39

The ER at St. Joe's was full. Nacho dropped Manny at the entrance, then went to hunt for a parking spot. He had to park way in the back and of course, because that's the way it goes, as he walked toward the line of parked cars closest to the entrance, a car backed out leaving a spot empty. He saw Boyce's car was parked in a no parking spot.

He found Manny sitting in the waiting room. His arm had been wrapped with gauze and a small spot of blood had seeped through. There was a seat open next to him. Probably because of the blood. Ninety percent of the people awaiting treatment were Hispanic.

"Where's Boyce?" Nacho said sitting next to him.

"She got me to the head of the line, then she went to file a report."

"What's she going to say?"

"She says she'll tell the truth. She says she will tell them that I gave her a lead on a missing girl that didn't pan out, and as we drove away two guys opened fire on us. We don't know why, but she says she'll give them a description of the van and they'll find it."

"Van's stolen," Nacho said.

"Yeah, she knows that, but that's the way she's going to play it."

"How long are you going to have to wait?"

"Nurse said it's not a consequential wound so those worse off will go first. Son of a bitch hurts like it is a consequential wound."

Nacho looked around at all the people. "Hours."

"Probably."

Nacho got up and found some magazines. An hour later Emilio Garza, Willy, Emilio's driver and another one that could have been Willy's twin came in. When Jackson, Blackhawk and Nacho had first met Emilio Garza he had been the number two man of the Valdez cartel. The Dos Hermanos cartel had kidnapped the young granddaughter of the Ambassador of Columbia, who was also the head of the Valdez cartel. They intended to use her to blackmail her grandfather. Jackson, Blackhawk, and Nacho had gotten her back. From then on, the ambassador thought Jackson could do no wrong. The Ambassador gave the reins of the cartel to Garza after the previous one got caught with his fingers in the till. No one ever knew what happened to that guy. His fingers were found in his desk drawer.

Garza wound his way over to Manny and Nacho moved so Garza could sit down.

"You okay?" Garza said as he sat next to Manny.

"Yeah, I'm fine. The bullet went through the muscle. It hit no bone. They just have to clean it out and bandage me up."

The place was filled with whole families, with the not-sick kids running around crazy like kids do when their parents aren't paying attention. "They just have a shitload of people tonight."

Across the room a baby was screaming. Garza grimaced as he looked over at it.

Nacho saw him looking. "These people have no insurance and no personal doctor so when the baby gets colicky the emergency room is their only form of health care," Nacho said. "I just wish they'd control their kids."

"We need to get out of here," Garza said. He pulled his phone from his pocket and hit a number that was on a speed dial. The noise was such that the other end couldn't be heard. He waited, then finally he said, "This is Garza. I need you to meet me at the restaurant. Bring your bag." He listened for a second then said, "Okay," and disconnected.

They left the ER. Manny rode with Garza. Garza's driver's name was Alvaro, which meant small or elf warrior. Somebody's idea of a joke. Alvaro was six foot four and weighed almost three hundred pounds. Nacho walked slowly back to his car. He was the last to leave the lot. He got in and started the motor, then texted Boyce to let her know they were headed to Garza's restaurant to have the cartel doctor look at Manny.

By the time Nacho arrived, the doctor was there. The doctor's name was Jose Vaqueiro. He was an illegal that had fled from Paraguay with his young family. He had been targeted by the ruthless gangs that had taken control of the country. Alvaro was there but Willie and the other soldier were not.

While the doctor patched Manny up, the office door opened and Emil walked in without knocking. Emil was a huge man. With him and Alvaro in the room there was little room left. Garza stood and offered Emil his chair. Emil waved him off. He nodded to Nacho.

"Long time no see," he said. "Where is our mutual friend tonight?"

"Believe it or not," Nacho said, "he's up above the Mogollon Rim elk hunting. Him and Blackhawk and Jimmy. Jimmy's our bartender."

"I know who Jimmy is," Emil smiled. "I know who everyone is. That's funny. I never saw Jackson as a mountain man, fur trapping, animal killer. He was always my poet, music lover, slayer of pan sized fish and connoisseur of good scotch. Unless of course he felt the need to beat the shit out of someone or blow them away from a thousand yards."

Emil was a specialist for his excellency the Ambassador. A man named Santiago Escalona was the Ambassador's personal attaché and had an office in Phoenix. This was where you usually found Emil, if he wanted to be found. The Ambassador usually stayed in L.A. Emil had no official capacity and you would not find his name on any piece of legal paper that had anything to do with Colombia. But if the Ambassador needed some really heavy lifting done, Emil did it. Emil had proved to be a very important part of getting the granddaughter back. Both Jackson and Emil were happy ghosts and neither wanted to become visible anywhere.

Emil looked at Manny. "Tell me your story, my friend. How and why did you find yourself in front of a speeding bullet."

Manny glanced at Garza. "Our friend Jackson has developed a relationship with a lady that sings at Rick's American at the El Patron. Her name is Marianne."

"Yes, I know," Emil said. "I've been to listen to her. I told you I know everyone. Go on."

"Marianne's sister's daughter has come from their hometown to go to school at ASU. Almost immediately, after arriving and after Elena gets her a nice, shared condo, she gets hooked-up with a party crowd. I mean a heavy party crowd and the girl disappears. There's a Dos Hermanos dealer that works the campus."

"Blue Boy," Emil said.

"Yeah. A punk with a blue sharkskin suit and drives a three hundred-thousand-dollar blue sports car. We know he was involved with her disappearance."

"Then?"

"Then Willy sees the girl at the Dos Hermanos casino in Tempe a couple of days ago. Nacho and I go out there and look around, but we don't see her. As we are driving away two guys open fire with automatic rifles and one of the rounds hits me in the arm."

"And that's it? I assume they got away?"

"Yeah, pretty much."

"You think Blue Boy was behind the shootings?"

Manny nodded. Emil was silent. He nodded. "Yeah, he was. Why do you think he wants that girl?"

"She's damn good looking and according to the aunt, she likes her drugs. She hooked up with a heavy party crowd. Those kids suck up to him like he's Jesus Christ. The boys suck up to sell the drugs and the girls suck up to take the drugs."

"And he runs a porno string," Emil said. "And that is probably why he's got her. Young, pretty, fresh from the Midwest. He could make a fortune with her."

"You already knew all this," Nacho said.

"I know everything. Including his connection to Dos Hermanos. He has a network of student dealers that take in a million a week. To the authorities, he justifies his lifestyle by saying he has inherited millions from his family. His money is channeled to companies in Mexico owned by Dos Hermanos."

"Not true?" Manny said.

"What's not true?

"The inherited money part."

"No, not true. The kids follow him like sheep. If they knew he was just another drug dealer he would not look so attractive. But the jet setting millionaire heir of an international fortune. Now, that's sexy."

The doctor finished patching Manny and packed his stuff. He gave Manny a bottle of pills to help with the pain. He said, "This blue boy you are talking about, I have treated girls that have worked for him. They are not treated well."

He nodded at Garza, turned to Manny and said, "Contact me if you think it is getting infected." He turned and left.

Emil said to Nacho, "Give me a day to find the asshole. When I find him, I will call. How long will Jackson and Blackhawk be gone?"

Nacho said, "I heard Jimmy say it was a ten-day hunt. But I don't know for sure."

Emil looked at Garza, then at Manny. "It would be easier if they were here, but this will be enough of us," he said. He turned to the door, then stopped. He turned back. "Oh, one more thing, did Detective Boyce get shot?" No one said a thing. "I sure hope not. I really like her." He opened the door and went out.

# 40

Blackhawk and Jimmy wolfed a plateful of food figuring, eat it while you got it. They didn't see Deiter again. Everyone tossed dirty plates and utensils into a steaming pot of suds.

"Might as well get on their good side," Blackhawk said. He selected a cloth from a pile next to the sudsy pot and began washing. Jimmy joined him, drying. It didn't take long till they had everything washed and hand dried. Much too cold to let them airdry.

Madonna and her mother followed by Deiter came marching across the compound. Deiter didn't look any more friendly than he had earlier.

"The Comandante wants to see you," Deiter said.

They followed Deiter and the girls back across the open compound to the old ranger cabin. The sun had been up long enough to start warming the air, but it was still bitterly cold. When they reached the cabin, Deiter held the heavy door. Blackhawk and Jimmy allowed the women to go first.

Inside it was warm with a fire roaring in the fireplace. The cabin was wide open, and the room was large, but it was set up to function as two separate rooms. There was a loft overhead. The main room was filled with roughhewn log chairs and a rugged picnic styled table with bench seating. Diego was seated there, whittling stakes. Madonna and Eileen slid their coats off and sat in the chairs. There were romance novels and People magazines piled on the table. Blackhawk smiled. In the middle of nowhere and some women were going to have their romance novels. Probably sent some women down to Payson periodically, to buy stuff the forest couldn't provide. Probably sold furs for money.

Diego was wielding a wicked looking knife, turning two and a half foot pieces of wood into wicked looking stakes. There was a pile on the table. Maybe a dozen finished and two dozen awaiting their turn. The finished ones were skinned of bark and trimmed down to a very wicked point.

"Spring spear trap," Blackhawk said to himself. Jimmy nodded. Deiter heard him.

"You know what these are?"

Blackhawk nodded.

"You ever used a spear trap?" Diego said.

"No, not personally. Always thought they were too cruel. I prefer to shoot my game. Of course that counts on having a firearm. Which we don't have at the moment." The two women looked up at him in surprise. Maybe this wasn't a good answer. "But I was taught to make and use them."

Diego smiled. "You don't always have a choice. You can't go around shooting deer and elk and such. It takes ammunition and the noise would have the forest cops down on you in an instant. Who taught you?"

"In the service."

"What branch were you in?"

"Navy."

Deiter laughed. "How many critters do you hunt on a boat?"

Blackhawk smiled, keeping it easy. "I never served on a boat. I had some specialized training and part of it was survival in the woods."

"SEALs," Diego said. "You were a SEAL?"

"In a time and place long, long ago."

Diego looked at him for a long moment then waved the knife at the table. He looked at Jimmy. "How about you. You a SEAL too?"

Jimmy shook his head, "Nope, not me. But, I've been hunting since I was twelve. My Dad taught me about spring spear traps."

"What did he teach you?"

"He taught me they were deadly, and you damned well better remember where you placed them."

Diego laughed. Diego looked back at Blackhawk. "Sit down. You can help me finish these up." He looked at Deiter. "Get him a sharp knife."

"What about our weapons?" Blackhawk said.

"In due time," Diego said. "We have to learn to trust you. Make sure you are who you say you are."

"Who would we be?"

"Could be anybody. We've had Forest Service and FBI up here spying on us before."

"You all doing something illegal?"

He shook his head. "Just living where they don't want us to live. Other than that, some moonshine, but always the legal limit per individual. Sometimes we have to shoot a critter out of their season. But that is to keep us from starving. The Feds just don't want us here."

"You're not hurting anybody." Blackhawk said. It was a statement.

He looked at Blackhawk for a long moment. "You're damned right we're not." He studied Blackhawk. "You look awfully young to be a retired SEAL."

Blackhawk sat on the bench and Deiter handed him a knife. Blackhawk instinctively thought about the five seconds it would take him to kill Diego and Deiter, and the women if they decided to fight.

"I was discharged. Conduct unbecoming," Blackhawk said. Jimmy was watching him. Jimmy knew this wasn't true.

"Why?"

"I guess they didn't like the idea that I didn't agree with their policies."

"Which ones?"

"Most of them." Watching this, Jimmy didn't smile but he felt like it. Madonna was watching him.

"What's your name?" Diego asked.

"Blackhawk," he said.

"What is that? A nickname?"

"It's what my squad name was."

"What's your birth name?"

Blackhawk started whittling, "I don't have one."

"Everyone has one," Deiter said irritated.

"I don't."

Diego gave him a straight look. "Explain," he said.

Blackhawk stopped whittling. "I don't like to explain myself," Blackhawk said. "But you are being hospitable. I'm an orphan. Sent to the orphanage at birth. I had no name. The orphanage gave me a Biblical name. That was their practice. I hated it, so I never used it."

"What name did you use to join the Navy?"

"I went to a judge in Arthur Illinois and changed it to Blackhawk. The Navy didn't give a damn if I was called Pocahontas as long as I had the papers."

"He did that? Just Blackhawk?"

"I accidently laid five one-hundred-dollar bills on his desk."

"Lucky accident for him."

Blackhawk picked up his stake and started again. He finished his stake before Diego. He picked up another.

"What do you do to live?"

"I own a nightclub. The El Patron."

"Hey, I've been in there," Deiter said. "It's like three bars under one roof. Good country music. You own that?"

Blackhawk nodded but didn't look at him.

Diego turned to Jimmy. What's your name?"

"Jimmy MacDonald."

"What do you do?"

"I bartend for him. Go to school part time. Hunt when I can."

Diego looked back at Blackhawk. "So, who else is with you up here. I'm told there was another man."

"Yeah, Jackson. The guy we were forced to leave back at the bathing hole. A friend of ours."

"Just one guy?"

"Yes, just one."

"Think he'll survive the storm?"

"Who are the Redcoats?"

Diego threw a hard look at his son. "Redcoats?"

Deiter caught the look. "We left the guy behind because we didn't have a ride for him. We knew the Redcoats were coming. I figured they were welcome to him."

"I'm surprised you didn't stay to fight them. You've been itching for a fight for months."

"You told me no fighting."

"And you obeyed my orders? Will wonders never cease."

He looked at Blackhawk. "Gather up some of this wood along with the spring stakes and take them back to your cabin and build some traps. You know how to do that?"

"Yessir," Blackhawk said. "Maybe I could help you take some out and place them."

"I thought you didn't like the spears," Eileen said. "Thought they were cruel."

"I don't have a gun," Blackhawk smiled, "stakes will have to do." Eileen chuckled. It wasn't that funny but maybe she just needed a laugh.

"By the way," Blackhawk said. "Is there any cellphone service up here?"

Diego shook his head. "No. Never has been. No need to build cell towers if there is no one to build them for. You'll have to wait until you get back down the mountain."

Madonna stood. "I want to go bow hunting. The new snow is just right for it. The bartender says he is a hunter. He can go with me. Earn his keep."

"He can chop wood," Deiter said.

"I don't want her out alone and I have things for you to do. No way he can run away without leaving tracks," Diego said. "He wouldn't make it anyway." He looked at Jimmy. "You behave with this girl, or I'll turn her loose on you. You know how to use a bow?"

"Yessir, I believe I do," Jimmy said.

# 41

As I walked into Francis's log cabin, I could smell the fresh cut wood of a new cabin. It was like the smell of a new car. Unmistakable. There was one large room with a storage loft at the back. A staircase with an attached rope to pull it down was fitted into the floor of the loft. The three wives were up in the loft. Their legs dangled over the edge. Two were reading paperback romance novels. The covers depicted long-haired, bare-chested, blond men with swooning women in their arms. The third one was engrossed in her knitting. The main room had three men in it sitting on chairs made of willow and wicker. The son of a bitch back-stabber Jerry held the door for me. He went to lean against the side wall. There was a chair in the middle facing the three men. Before it was offered, I sat in it. Just one of the guys by golly.

I studied Francis. He had long white hair slashed with grey, and a totally white beard. He could have been Moses's younger brother. He didn't look a thing like the fantasy stud the wives were lusting after. He wore a Paul Bunyan plaid shirt, and his feet were covered by heavy wool socks. His boots, along with two other pairs were by the fire.

All three men studied Jackson from top to bottom. "You don't look cold, did she feed you?" Francis said.

"Yessir, she did, and I appreciate it. Chopping wood will keep you warm. Gets the blood moving."

The man smiled. "My name is Francis." He turned to the man on his left. "And this fellow is Rudy and this one is Gilbert. They are my lieutenants. What is your name?"

"Jackson."

Francis waited a moment. "Jackson what?"

"Just Jackson."

"No first or middle?"

"No sir."

"Bullshit!" This from Jerry, still leaning against the wall.

I ignored him. So did the other men.

I decided to give them stock answer number five. The one Blackhawk and I always used when someone got nosy. "I was an orphan. Orphan from birth. The orphanage gave me a biblical name. I hated it. Soon as I was old enough, I named myself after a great-grand daddy. He was a moonshiner. Far as I could find he was known as Pappy Jackson. I thought I was a little young to be Pappy, so I stuck with Jackson." Okay, so mine deviated slightly from Blackhawk's.

"You a moonshiner?"

"No sir. Under different circumstances of life, I might have been. I live on a houseboat on Pleasant Lake, north of Phoenix. I'm retired military. I fish guide during the seasons."

Gilbert said, "If I called the lake, would they know who you are?"

"If you talk to one of the school kids they hire, probably not.

If you talk to Maureen the marina manager, then yes. But it doesn't matter. Everyone tells me there is no phone service up here. I know I sure don't have any."

"They tell you correctly," Francis said. "Which is okay with me. I came up here to escape all that down there." He studied Jackson some more. "We live simple lives up here, Mr. Jackson."

"Just Jackson."

He nodded. "No credit cards, no cash, no taxes. No insurance, no retirement funds, no computers, no stupid federal laws. Nothing. Just a simple life, like God intended."

"No drugs, no alcohol."

"Don't be stupid," Jerry said.

"Even prehistoric man figured out how to brew alcoholic beverages," Francis said. "Jesus famously drank wine."

"Good thing to know. You know I've been wondering about something."

"Pray tell," Francis said.

"I see that you have quite a few people here and most of them have snow machines. How do they keep them filled with gas, way out here in the middle of nowhere."

"They don't," Francis said. "They keep them filled with propane."

I smiled. "Propane? That's brilliant. I didn't know you could do such a thing." I thought about it. "But, I guess there's the same question. Where do they get the propane?"

"We have a guy, down below, that is in sympathy with our beliefs. He has an 1800-gallon Blueline MX Bobtail." This last he said proudly.

"I have no idea what that is."

"Most people don't. It's a large, versatile tank truck designed for propane. We have a thousand-gallon portable tank in a reachable area north of here. He fills it when needed. One of our machines can go a hundred miles on a tank of propane."

He seemed very proud of this, but I could tell his lieutenants thought he had gone too far.

"How do you pay for it? Does the guy take marten and fox fur?"

The third guy, Rudy, had not said a thing. Now he said, "Are you being a smart ass, Mr. Jackson?"

"Yes, I'm sorry. I suppose I am. It just seems it must be a very difficult task keeping the machines running all winter, way up here in the middle of the forest. What brought you up here to begin with?" I changed the subject.

The guy said, "Not too many years ago the United States was taken over by an elitist dictatorship. There were a few of us that weren't fooled by the barrage of lies the news media was forcing down our throats. There was no way to fight the government. They could reach out and take everything you had. They had the police forces, the Army and the IRS. They used the IRS as a militant arm to take our property and lock down our money. We decided we needed to be free. So, we established the Redcoats and came up here where we could live free. The Forest Service bugs us once in a while, but they are gnats compared to the IRS."

"They ever send the FBI or someone like that?"

"We know how to take care of our enemies," Francis said. "Tell me Mr. Jackson, what are you doing up here? Most of the elk are heading south, down the mountain to warmer weather. Didn't you check anything, the weather forecast for instance?"

"We checked everything we could, but you have to get drawn to hunt. And you have to hunt in the sections you are drawn for. Our sections were way up here. Yes, we did check the weather but if there is one thing I've noticed up here, is that the weather can change on a dime."

Gilbert spoke for the first time. "Fucking government."

Francis studied me for a minute. They were all silent. Finally, he said, "Is Helena Jean treating you well?"

"She has been very hospitable. She did threaten to shoot me if I got out of line."

Even Jerry smiled at that.

"While you are our guest, you will do anything she asks," Francis said firmly.

"Yessir. You all took my rifle, my handgun and I'm told you have my snow machine. Can I get those back? I can hunt and I'm willing to share the meat."

"That's mighty nice of you, seeing's how we can keep all the meat to pay for your room and board anyway."

"I still have a week on my elk tag. I can hunt every day, and you can have the meat. Maybe leave me some to take home."

Francis looked from Rudy to Gilbert. He smiled. "We will take that into consideration."

"Where are my two friends? Another group took off with them. I'm worried about them."

"The other group call themselves the Fremen," Francis said. "I'm told their leader is a big fan of the science fiction book Dune. I don't remember who wrote it."

"Frank Herbert," I said.

He frowned at me. "Are you a fan of the Fremen, Mr. Jackson?"

"Oh, no sir. My head is just filled with all kinds of useless trivia."

"Who saved the Continental Army at New York?" Mr. Gilbert said.

Jackson looked at him. The man looked smug.

"That's a trick question, Mr. Gilbert. It wasn't a who but a what. A lingering fog, that lasted longer than usual hid Washington's retreat across the river and saved the army from absolute disaster."

Francis laughed out loud. "He got you, Gilbert. Anyway, we have no idea where they, the Fremen, are. It's a big forest. In the meantime," he stood to indicate the meeting was over, "Jerry will take you back to Helena Jean's. Jerry, you tell her to keep an eye on him. Send him out to take down some dead trees." He looked at me. "You can do that?" I nodded. "In the meantime, like I said, you are our guest, not our prisoner. This weather has made us all prisoners. If I hear anything about your friends, I will let you know."

Jerry stepped away from the wall. He went to the front door and opened it. "Come on buckeroo," he said.

I went outside. It was still colder than ice, just not as cold as during the night. The compound was busy. I actually saw some kids playing in the snow. It hadn't crossed my mind the Redcoats would have children with them. I started across to Helena Jean's. She was standing several yards away from her cabin talking to a young girl beside one of the few teepees. Jerry came up behind me and grabbed my shoulder.

"Chainsaw's around back," he barked.

"I'll need my heavy boots and gloves." I started toward Helena Jean's again and he grabbed me again. I reached over and grabbed his gloved little finger and yanked it sideways. I heard it pop. I slid my shoulder under his arm and threw him to the ground. Hard. It knocked the breath out of him. I walked to the cabin and Helena Jean reached it the same time I did.

"That's going to cause you trouble," she said.

"Francis said I was a guest. I just want my heavy boots and gloves, then I will go chop his trees."

I looked over at Jerry and he was on his feet and was walking toward me. He wasn't happy. Francis had come out his front door. He had seen the whole thing. I expected Jerry to come charging at me, but before he could, Francis yelled, "Jerry!"

Jerry stopped.

"Let him do his job," Francis said in a firm voice.

Everyone stood for a moment, then I turned and went inside. When I came back out, I was expecting an ambush. Jerry was standing a few paces away and as I opened the door, I heard Helena Jean giving him hell. I couldn't tell what she was saying. She stopped as I stepped out.

She was holding her hand out. He reluctantly put his injured hand in hers. She gently pulled his glove off. The finger was at an angle. She took his finger and popped it back in place.

To his credit he didn't make a sound.

"Take him out and put him to work. Don't harass him. If you do, I'll go get Francis," she said.

He was rubbing his finger joint, surprised it didn't hurt anymore than it did. He looked at me with a scowl.

"I want no trouble," I said.

He stared at me, still riled. Finally, he turned. "Come with me," he said over his shoulder.

# 42

Elena decided not to perform tonight. As customers came in, Guy and Nacho informed them that Elena wasn't well and they would be closing at ten o'clock. If a customer showed a more than normal amount of disappointment, they offered a free drink and informed them the honkytonk bar would have the usual hours.

Marianne performed. Elena's band welcomed the night off, but Marianne's band had families and needed the income. Marianne normally performed from nine till one but tonight she performed from eight till eleven. At nine Emil came in and took a small table in the back. He sat with his back to the wall. He ordered a rum and soda tall and sipped it for the next hour. As usual he was immaculately dressed in an off-white suit, with vest and white shoes, which Jackson referred to as his ice cream suit.

Because it would be a short night Marianne didn't take any breaks. Twice she went to the piano and did a fifteen-minute solo to give her guys a break. When she finished, she received a large round of applause. As the crowd filed out, she came back to Emil.

He stood and held her chair. Carla brought her a very light scotch and soda tall. Emil watched her as she twirled the swizzle stick.

Finally, she said, "I guess if you had good news, you'd be telling me."

"The same with bad news, little one. And what that says is, I have no news at all." She looked disappointed. "Yet," he said. "I will find her."

Nacho came in and looked around. He saw them and came back. "You want to get together in here, or in El Patron?" he said. "Everyone else is already in there."

"Let's go in there," Marianne said.

Guy, the part time bartender, had left. Elena, Emilio Garza and Manny were at the bar. Only the bar lights were on, along with the dim overhead lights that were left on all night. The room had a dark secretive look.

As Emil and Marianne joined the rest at the bar, Nacho went behind. "How's your arm?" Elena asked Manny.

"It's funny," Manny said. "When I was shot, there was hardly any pain at all. A day later it hurt like a son of a bitch."

"What are we drinking?" Nacho said.

"Usual," Elena said.

"Water," Marianne said.

"I'll take a Modelo," Emil said. "Thank you."

Nacho hadn't had a Modelo in a while, so he pulled one for himself. As he did, the double doors opened, and Detective Boyce came into the room.

"Oh good," Elena said. "Come sit by me," she called to Boyce. "Get her a margarita," Elena said to Nacho.

"Coming right up," Nacho said as he set Elena's tequila and soda in front of her.

Boyce came and they all shifted so she could sit beside Elena. As she sat, she looked at Emil. "I hear I'm one of your favorite people."

He raised his Modelo in salute.,"Always have been."

"Good to know," she said, taking the margarita from Nacho's hands.

"Anyone have anything new on Tiffany since last night?" Emil asked.

They all looked at each other. No one said anything.

"I've had inquiries out all day," Emil said. "What I've got for it is a better feel for how I'm going to find the little son of a bitch. He has fled his normal hacienda, which means he knows we're looking, which means he was responsible for the shooting of Manny here." He took a drink. "He apparently has taken the girl with him. Maybe for protection or as a bargaining chip. Whatever, I don't know. What I do know is it won't work. I have people looking for him, but better, I have his people looking for him. He's been under the protection of Dos Hermanos for so long, he had started taking it for granted. It will take time, but the word will go out, and someone will come to us with the information we want."

"Like where he is," Boyce said.

"Like where he is," Emil said.

"So I can arrest him?" Boyce said.

"Indeed," Emil said. Then he paused and said, "If he survives the encounter."

"What if he finds out? What if he hurts her?" Marianne said.

Emil leaned over to look straight at her. "A man that does what he does to these girls is a coward. This guy is a coward. This guy knows that Emilio and Manny and I are looking for him. He knows if he hurts this girl, *this girl in particular*, we will kill him."

Marianne shuddered.

Boyce drained her margarita and stood up. "I can't hear this," she said. "In fact, I didn't hear this." She looked at Elena. "Stay in touch." She walked out.

"I promise you this," Emil continued, watching Boyce leave. "I will find the girl, but you must be prepared for it to take a few days. Three, four, five, I don't know. He's running now and it will take time. But no matter the time, I will get him."

# 43

I was thinking that the effort of taking trees down and sawing them into firewood was good for me. I could put my muscle to it and shut my mind off. Jerry pointed at the saw and then at the tree line. "Only take down the dead ones." He spun on his heel and stalked away. I picked up the chainsaw and it started on the first pull.

As I worked, I felt the weather beginning to change. The sun was warming the air. It felt good. As I worked, the tactician in me began to move. The cabins and the occasional teepee were arranged in a haphazard jumble. While the group had chosen this place to winter in, there was very little here. Just an open space. The cabins were poorly constructed and built next to the tree stumps of the trees they had felled to build them. That meant it would be hell to defend from a force like the Fremen or a phalanx of game wardens and sheriff's deputies. I would fell more trees and jumble them all around the complex. Not exactly a stockade wall, but it would make it difficult to be charged. Not my problem.

After a long hard day of gathering wood, the sun moved

behind the nearest trees and the air started cooling. Helena Jean came and got me.

"You need to come get some food while it's warm."

She had brought the food to the cabin. It appeared elk stew was the only thing on the menu, although she did surprise me with fresh baked bread. She also surprised me by having the young girl I had seen her with earlier follow her in the door. The girl had a red bandanna wrapped around her forehead to keep her ears warm. She pulled her heavy snow jacket off. She was dressed in military camos.

Without being told, the girl helped her get the food ready.

Helena Jean put the cook pot on the edge of the fire and stirred it to warm it. "This is Jackson," she said to the girl. "He is a guest of Francis." The girl looked at me but didn't speak.

Sometime during the day two more roughly made chairs had appeared. I had no clue as to where they came from. I pulled one over to the table and took a seat. She set a bowl of stew and two slices of bread in front of me.

"I can't tell you how grateful I am for the food," I said. "All I had with me was some jerky."

"You earned it," she said. "This is my daughter, Evangeline. She is staying with a friend while you are here."

The girl looked at me. She looked like her mother, fair, slender, and pretty. But she also looked sturdy. She took the food her mom handed her and sat. She didn't pull her chair to the table, but rather sat against the wall next to the fire. The outer corners of the cabin were always hard to heat. Helena Jean came and sat across from me at the table. We ate in silence. It could have been swamp rat stew as far as I was concerned. I was

210

starving. I saved the last slice of bread and used it to wipe the bowl clean.

"I'm sorry I don't have any more," Helena Jean said. "There are already some folks out there that begrudge you for being another mouth to feed."

"This is plenty," I said. "I'm grateful for it."

I looked at Helena Jean, then at Evangeline. The Colonel had taught us that we'd never find out if we didn't ask. So I asked. "So, Evangeline, I know it is none of my business, but since they've put your mama in charge of the prisoner, and I have noticed that she doesn't wear any rings, where is your father?"

Evangeline glared at me. "You're right. It isn't any of your damned business."

Helena Jean said, "Evangeline is right it isn't any of your business. But I will tell you that when Evangeline's father found out I was pregnant, he split and neither of us has seen him since."

"Sorry to bring it up."

Evangeline looked at her mother. "I thought you said he was a guest of Francis. Why is he here?"

Helena Jean didn't answer right away. I said, "Do you think I waited until there was ten feet of snow then I just dropped in to say hi? My friends and I came out here elk hunting and ran into the other outfit. The Fremen. They left me, then your mom and her group grabbed me."

Helena Jean said, "I remember you grabbing me."

"I didn't want to fall off." I yawned. I stood picking up my bowl. "Can I help clean up?"

Helena Jean said, "Evangeline and I will take care of it."

"Thank you. And thank you for the meal. I feel like I smell like a goat. Is there any way I could wash down before I hit the rack?"

Without being told, Evangeline stood and gathered my bowl, her mother's and her own and put them in a half bucket of water that had been sitting close to the fire. She began to wash them and set them on the table to dry.

Helena Jean said, "I'll walk Evangeline back, and you can wash up. Water is at a premium, so you'll have use the water that's in the bucket."

"You have another place?"

"I told you that. Does this look like a place two women would live?"

I laughed. "Yeah, I wondered about that."

As they were leaving, Evangeline didn't say goodbye and just as she shut the door, Helena Jean looked back and said, "I'll give you twenty minutes. Make sure you are finished by then."

"Yes, ma'am," I said.

I used my insulated undershirt to wash and dry with. I was finished and in the sleeping bag before she came back. I had left the lantern on and was already asleep when she came in the door. I awakened and watched her through half-closed eyes until I could tell she was ready to undress. I hated to miss out on that sexy set of long johns, but I rolled over and faced the wall to give her privacy. I immediately fell asleep again.

I don't know how long I'd been asleep when I awakened to the soft slippery sound of her climbing out of her bed. I put my wrist with the watch on it deep under the cover and pushed the stem to illuminate it. It read 1:50 in the morning. I lay quiet as she dressed. She put her heavy boots on, and her parka with the hood.

She stood silently, staring at me, then moved to the door and opened it so slowly I knew she was trying not to wake me. She pulled it quietly closed. I waited thirty seconds, then dressed quickly. Heavy coat and boots. I pulled the watch cap on and went out the door. I didn't have to be as quiet as she had been.

At first, she was nowhere in sight. Luckily no one else was either. The moon was just above the treetops and full. I caught movement across the compound. There she was, moving purposefully to the timberline. She disappeared into the trees, and I hustled after her. You wonder why I followed her? It's because I am naturally nosy. I like information. I may not use it but I like having it. Maybe she just had a sudden urge to go to the bathroom. But that wasn't it. It was late and cold. No one was stirring. If they were and spotted me, I planned to divert and take a leak. It wasn't necessary, no one was there. I moved across the open compound and followed her tracks into the forest. Thank God for the moonlight. I could see tracks of her fairly well and I was moving fast enough that I eventually caught sight of her ahead of me. She kept moving with the confidence of someone who knew where they were going. Of course, I had one troubling thought in my mind. She would no doubt see my tracks if she came back the same way. She seemed to know the forest well enough to not stumble over dead fall. As long as I stayed on her tracks, I was okay, but my footprints were obvious. She finally reached a very small clearing. In the center was a small two-man tent. Inside was the glow of a very small light. Probably from a small tent stove.

She stopped on the edge and stood studying the clearing and the tent. She stood very still and studied all the surroundings.

She began to turn, and I stepped behind a pine, frozen in place. The easiest thing to spot is movement. I didn't move.

When she was satisfied, she let out a low whistle. Someone rustled in the tent and the door flap snapped back. Diego of the Fremen climbed out. She moved to him and they embraced. It was a very long and passionate kiss. She jumped up and put her legs around his waist. He held her by her rear. Finally he let her down. He helped her strip out of her heavy coat and he tossed it inside. He leaned down and followed it in. She went to her knees in the entrance then turned and sat, half inside. She untied her boot laces, pulled them off then set them outside. She climbed in and closed and fastened the door. The small light inside cast shadows on the tent walls but they were vague and jumbled. Good. I felt like a voyeur already. From the shadows I could tell they were both lying prone. I didn't want to hear the moaning that I was sure to come. I turned and made my way back to camp. It had begun to snow. There you go. Come down heavy snow. Cover dem tracks.

# 44

Earlier Diego had said to Blackhawk, "Take these stakes back to your cabin and finish trimming them and make a half dozen notched trip sticks. I'll be by later and we can go set some traps."

"It's our cabin now?"

"It is empty. Guy that built it couldn't stand his freedom and went back to the Valley."

"Is there a sharp knife in the cabin?"

"Should be. Should be a whet stone and everything. The guy left in a hurry with just what he could carry. Here, put them in this basket and I'll be by later."

Blackhawk headed across the compound toward the cabin and saw Jimmy and Madonna on the other side. They were dressed for the cold, and both carried a bow and quiver of arrows. Jimmy saw him and waved. Blackhawk raised a hand in acknowledgement. The cabin was cold, so the first thing Blackhawk did was build a fire. He and Jimmy had searched the cabin the night before but now he really searched. They had already found a skinning knife and a utility, thick kitchen knife. They had hidden them. He poured the stakes out on the table and as soon as he got the fire going, he sat down and began to whittle.

It was two hours before Diego showed up. Blackhawk had long ago finished the stakes. He had been taught how to manage down time when on an op. He stretched out and slept. You never knew how much rest you were going to need.

Diego didn't knock, he just came in. Blackhawk sat up. Diego was dressed for the forest. The stakes were bundled and strapped to his back.

"Get dressed," he said. "We're going on a hike."

Ten minutes later they were heading into the forest. Diego had given Blackhawk a small backpack to carry. Blackhawk assumed it carried provisions. He had also given him a canteen. Diego had a pistol strapped on but didn't carry a rifle. He also had a canteen.

The day was bright. There had been a heavy shower of snow during the night but now the weather was changing. It was cold but not as cold. Blackhawk followed Diego as he followed a worn trail. Probably a game trail at first, but the Fremen had been using it for a while. The snow in the forest was fresh but with the temperature change, it was melting and it made everything wet. There were scattered patches of the forest floor showing through.

Diego didn't hesitate, wait, or look to check on Blackhawk. He forged forward. They worked their way through the dense forest for an hour. The movement felt good to Blackhawk. He hadn't been to the gym for a while and the only exercise he had lately was the hiking they had done the two previous days. He had always envied Jackson for the ability to swim every day. Usually ten laps to the buoy located a hundred yards off his moored houseboat. He even did it in the winter.

Once they moved off the trail, the going got tougher. Struggling over and around deadfalls, but Diego kept moving. Blackhawk figured the man had a specific destination. It turned out he did. They came to an open meadow. It still was covered with snow, but the snow was trampled with the tracks of an elk herd and the occasional small holes of deer tracks.

Diego stopped and surveyed the meadow. He pointed off to the right. "There," he said. "See that narrow area, opening into the meadow?"

Blackhawk nodded. "Yes, I see, animals coming into the meadow from that direction would have to funnel through there or come all the way around. Perfect place for a trap. Not big enough for bull elk or moose but perfect for mule deer."

"I found it while out hunting with Eileen and Madonna."

"Good choice," Blackhawk said.

"Let's go build a trap."

Diego headed across the meadow to the narrow opening. They both worked their way around the area looking for the right set-up. Blackhawk found it. Two saplings growing out of the same base. The idea was to take down a slender, flexible sapling and tie its base between the other two. It could then be pulled back bending like a bowstring being drawn. Two large and very sharp stakes were fastened to the flexible sapling at the same height as the animal's vital organs. Diego pulled cordage from his pack and tied it to the end of the spring sapling. Blackhawk cut another sapling about five feet high and then after sharpening the end, he pounded the sharp end into the ground across the trail, so the animal would walk between the spring

217

sapling and this one. They took the cordage tied to the staked sapling and wrapped it around the double tree trunk, then pulled the tip of the deadly sapling until it was bent in half. There was an awful lot of tension on the sapling, much like on a drawn bowstring.

While Blackhawk kept tension on the cordage, Diego stretched it across the path to the stake that they had put in place, and using some five-inch pegs with whittled notches he fashioned a trigger that very carefully held the cordage and kept the tension on the stake pole. He gently got them set. He cautiously moved his hands away. They held.

"Well done," Blackhawk said.

Diego reached into his pocket and pulled a length of bright red ribbon. He cut off three two-foot lengths then tied them head high onto two trees where they could be plainly seen.

"Smart," Blackhawk said.

"These traps are deadly," Diego said. "They are made to kill large animals and that means men too. We lost a guy a year ago. I have told my people that the ribbons must be placed on any medium to large game trap."

"What about at night?"

"No one is allowed in the forest at night."

"I'm sweating," Blackhawk said. "I believe it's warming up."

"Let's get back and get something to eat."

Blackhawk followed Diego. He was thinking that he could begin to like this guy. His son, not so much.

# 45

Jimmy had never hunted with a woman before. Madonna proved herself to be a pretty good huntress. Better than he expected, and in fact as good as he was. At least in doing what was necessary in the forest. She wore camo pants tucked into thigh high elk-skin boots with rabbit fur stitched into the top. She wore a coat made of raccoon with intertwined martin and mink furs made into a furry hood. She wore the hood down on her back, with a red bandanna around her forehead and covering her ears. She looked a cross between one of Robin Hood's merry men and a Ogalala warrior. She had a quiver of arrows slung across her back and carried a bow. She had given Jimmy the same.

He followed her. It was obvious to Jimmy the girl knew this part of the woods like the back of her hand. She had made it clear that they were after mule deer or elk. They weren't going to fool with small game. She moved decisively through the woods. Jimmy worked to keep up. At first, they followed a game trail made easy to use because the Fremen had used it often. Once the camp was no longer in sight and could no longer be heard, the going got better for hunting. Madonna moved off the trail and

Jimmy followed without question. She knew where she wanted to go. Some of the snow in the forest was beginning to melt and Jimmy was glad his coat was waterproof. Madonna's rabbit skin was more waterproof than Jimmy's artificial fabric coat. An hour into the forest they came to a deep ravine. It was fifty yards across.

Madonna stopped them. She stood silently. She looked all around, listening. She said, "Let's split. I'll go to the other side, and you continue along here. The ravine will peter out in thirty or forty yards. When it does, you turn north for a hundred yards and then turn back east to parallel me." She looked at him. "You know which way north is, don't you?"

Jimmy smiled and pointed.

"Good. You come across something, whistle. You know how to whistle don'tcha, Jimmy?"

"Just put your lips together and blow," Jimmy said in his best Lauren Bacall.

It was lost on her. She turned and moved down into the ravine, then up the other side. When she got there, she waved at Jimmy. Jimmy started off alongside the ravine, really hunting for the first time. It was moments like this that Jimmy lived for. This was when Jimmy felt alive. In the forest, actually at one with the forest, and searching for game. Not for trophies but for red protein meat. Substance. To fill empty bellies. In time, as Madonna had said, the ravine gradually became less deep until it was level ground. Madonna was nowhere in sight.

Jimmy turned north. He slowed to a smooth, silent walk. His senses were alive. It was the perfect time for deer. After a night in the forest, they would be up and foraging. When he felt that he had gone a hundred yards, he turned east again. This was when he saw his first sign. A young sapling had its low hanging limbs stripped of bark. He stopped and stood without moving. He slowly turned his head and studied the forest. He looked for movement. If deer were alarmed, they could stand immobile for a long time. Finally satisfied, he slowly started moving again. A few yards away he saw the fresh tracks in the melting snow. Again, he stopped and surveyed. The track was heading northwest. He followed, slowly. The tracks disappeared but the tracks were fresh. He knew the deer was there. He kept moving. After a while he was in a zone. An old W.C. Fields movie came into his head. "Inch by inch, step by step, slowly I turned…." He moved slowly. Step by sliding step, hesitate, look, listen, then move again.

He saw the movement. Off to the side, fifty feet away. He froze. There it was. It was a doe. And right behind was a fawn. Happily following mom, munching on the leaves and bark.

Where there was family, maybe there was the man of the house. The doe suddenly went on alert, her head turned to look directly at Jimmy. She must have gotten a scent. She bolted, bounding through the underbrush with the fawn on her heels. In a second, she was out of sight.

Jimmy's heart was pounding. Dagnab it. Couldn't shoot her anyway. Illegal to kill a momma.

Jimmy started moving again. The sun was getting higher and the air warmer. Probably up to a balmy 35 degrees. Jimmy got back into his pattern. Step, look, listen, another step. Time was moving slowly. He heard no Madonna whistle.

Then a slender, bare branch he was looking at moved slightly and turned into the antler of a buck deer. Again, he froze. It was a large animal. It was stripping bark, and luckily was facing away from him. He softly notched an arrow and slowly raised it. He pulled it full back and took aim. The animal was turned sideways with its rump toward Jimmy. If Jimmy shot, he knew that there was a good chance the arrow would hit a rib and bounce under the skin without doing any severe damage. Jimmy stood like that as the animal fed himself. Jimmy's shoulder began to tighten up. At long last the buck moved to attack another slender branch. This swung him around broadside and Jimmy released the arrow. It struck the buck where Jimmy was aiming. Just behind his shoulder. It went deep. The buck bound away in two giant leaps, then collapsed onto the forest floor.

Jimmy pulled his long, supersharp, Green River hunting knife Madonna had given back to him. He rushed to the animal. He was certain it was dead, but not taking any chances he touched the eye of the beast with the tip of his knife. There was no reaction. He lifted the head by an antler and quickly slit its throat. This served two purposes. One was to ensure the deer was dead and the other was to allow the blood to drain from the body. If the blood stayed, it could spoil the meat.

His heart was pounding. He started to whistle but his mouth was dry. He pulled the canteen and took a deep drink, then rinsed his mouth. When he finally could manage a whistle, it was a weak effort. He had always been a pathetic whistler. He had always been jealous of those that could stuff two fingers into their mouths and issue a long, loud, piercing whistle. His was so pathetic Madonna had to be just a few yards away to hear it.

The best thing for him to do was to start dressing the deer.

Neither one of them had brought a large knapsack, so he knew he would have to improvise. He turned the deer onto its back. There had to be six hundred pounds of meat on this critter. He started at the anus and began edging the knife blade up, slicing the belly skin. He was very careful. If he punctured the stomach lining the bile would spoil the meat. If you did that, you would have to get it in running water as soon as possible, and even if you managed that you would still lose a lot of meat. Unfortunately, there was no running water. He had not seen any on this entire hunt.

He was concentrating so hard that Madonna startled him when she materialized out of the forest. "You call that a whistle?"

"You heard it from way over there?"

"Hell, no. I was coming to look for you. Diego would be pissed if I took you out in the woods and lost you."

Jimmy didn't look at her. He smiled. "Get your knife out and start on the legs. Leave the hoofs on. Leave the legs attached to the body. Do you want the head and antlers?"

"No, I don't want them."

"Good. I don't want to carry it. We want to gut it and leave the skin on for the time being. We want all the blood out of it."

"This ain't my first rodeo," Madonna said, kneeling down beside him.

And hour later Jimmy was a bloody mess, but he was finished. "Do you have some portage line?"

She dug into her small bag and pulled out a wrapped-up ball of nylon portage line. Jimmy cut a length.

"Help me with this," he said. He situated the deer carcass on its back and pulled the four ankles together. "Hold this," he said.

Madonna took the feet and held them together. Jimmy tied the feet together.

"Can you carry my bow and quiver?"

Madonna picked them up and Jimmy hefted the carcass and slid it across his shoulders like a backpack.

"That's cool," Madonna said.

"Learned it from my uncle. We need to get this meat on ice."

"You need a bath. You reek." She looked around. "I know where we can accomplish both. Follow me." She turned and started off into the forest. Jimmy hesitated, then followed.

# 46

Deiter came hurrying out of the tree line to find his father. Diego was sitting with two other men beside the dying embers of a cook fire. It would be resurrected for the evening meal.

Coming up to the three men, Deiter said, "Hey, Dad. I need to talk to you."

Diego looked up at him, "Go ahead and talk."

"In private," Deiter said. Diego looked at the other two with a look that said, *kids, what are you going to do with them?*

Deiter moved out of earshot of the two men and Diego followed.

"What's up, boy?"

Deiter glanced around. No one was within earshot. "I know you told me you didn't like me setting spring spear traps by myself. But I accidentally came on the perfect site for one. Rather than come all the way back for you, I went ahead and built one while I was out there."

"You know better than that."

"I knew that is what you would say, but I did it and, Dad, I got the biggest bull elk I have ever seen. I need you to help me field dress him and carry him back to camp. I swear Dad, this guy is at least twelve hundred pounds. The spear hit him just perfect, right in the heart."

"I've never seen a bull that big. Not up here."

"I swear to God. Get your stuff and I'll show you."

"Should we get help?"

"No. I just want you and me to get the credit."

"Alright. I'll meet you at the tree line."

Fifteen minutes later Diego met up with his son. He brought two skinning knives, a small hatchet, and a length of portage chord. He figured they would build a travois to cart the carcass back to camp.

Deiter led the way and Diego kept close behind. About a mile and a half into the deepest part of the forest Deiter held up a hand.

"He's just ahead." He pointed through the thick brush. "You can see the ribbons I put out."

He patted his dad on the shoulder. "You go first, I want you to see this sucker."

Diego looked at the ribbons and calculated where the carcass would be laying. He wasn't surprised he couldn't see it. The grass and shrubs were thick and high. He was thinking that he was glad that he had taught the boy to put out warning ribbons. The last thing he saw was the trip wire when he felt it pull against his ankle. The last thing he heard was the sound of the spring stake releasing with the force of five-hundred-pounds.

# 47

Just enough time had passed that Jimmy was beginning to worry about the meat spoiling. He caught a glimpse of sunshine on metal through the trees. A couple of minutes later he heard the rush of spring water and they stepped into the opening where the galvanized tank was sitting. Just as they had left it. He dropped the deer and worked his shoulders to get the kinks out.

Madonna leaned their bows and quivers against a nearby tree. She picked up a slender, fallen limb that was about six feet long and began poking the dead coals under the tank. Some of the logs that were left were half burned to charcoal. She moved them around to give space for new ones. Jimmy walked down by the creek and saw what he wanted. On the near bank was a sharp drop that higher water had fashioned into an almost cave. It was filled with snow. The snow was in the shade and wasn't melting. There was a short stick nearby, so he began digging in the snow until he had a hole big enough to put the carcass in. By the time he finished burying the deer meat, Madonna had gotten a fire started and stacked more firewood close by. Using her bare hands, she splashed the debris off the surface of the water. The tank was less than half full.

Madonna reached underneath and pulled a hose out. It was actually two hoses, connected in the middle by a siphon bellows. She put one end of the hose into the creek and the other into the tank. She began to work the bellows. Once water started coming out, she quit, and the siphon effect took over. Jimmy threw two more logs on the fire and added an armful of small branches to speed the fire along.

Madonna came over and squatted down to warm her hands on the fire.

"I don't think I want to bloody the water," Jimmy said. "I'm going to rinse my hands and arms in the creek."

She went with him. When they came back, he squatted down and warmed his, now freezing hands next to the fire. Madonna had done the same. "Whose idea was this tank anyway?"

Madonna said, "The tank belonged to a rancher down the hill. He had a lot of free-range cattle and he put it up for them to have water. Pretty silly since there are a hundred creeks down there. My mom hated not having a full bath, so she talked Diego into getting several guys to lug it up here. Guy named Harry figured out the siphon system and everyone up here agreed that it was such a good idea that it would be neutral territory."

"Didn't seem neutral when I was here last."

"You can thank Deiter. God's gift to women. He thought he'd take a swing at the Redcoat guy, Francis', wives. So, when they were up here, he surprised them, got all naked and jumped in with them. What he didn't know was Francis always sent his enforcer, a guy named Jerry, with them. He'd stay out of eyesight but in hearing distance. When they raised a ruckus Jerry came and beat the shit out of Deiter. Damned near killed him. That started the war."

She stood up. The water was beginning to steam. She trailed her fingers in. "Just right," she said. She took the pole and knocked the logs apart so the flames wouldn't get hotter.

She turned and looked at Jimmy. Then with a mischievous look in her eye, she pulled off the rabbit skin coat and pulled her long-sleeved winter top off. There was nothing underneath. She worked her way out of her boots and took her pants off. Again, there was nothing underneath. She dropped the pants to the side and looked at Jimmy. She took her bandanna off and now she was completely naked. The cold air gave her goosebumps and made her nipples stand up.

"Do you have a girlfriend, Jimmy?"

He couldn't trust himself to talk. He shook his head.

"Are you going to stand there like a dummy?" She climbed the makeshift ladder and swung her legs into the water. Jimmy began to undress. As he got his boots off and then his pants, he stood in his underwear, completely aware that he wasn't sure how long he had been wearing the same pair. He stood there feeling helpless as she slid in, then turned and put her arms on the metal rim. She laid her head on her hands. She was smiling at him. "Don't quit now," she said.

Jimmy was completely aware of what his body was doing and as he pulled the underwear off, he knew she knew also.

As he hurried up the ladder she said, "Aren't you going to ask the question that's on your mind?"

"What question?"

"You want to know if I have a boyfriend."

He was so fixated on the condition of his own body, he had no idea how to respond to that. When he reached the edge of the tank and began to climb in, she said, "Well, I don't, and I don't want one."

Feeling extremely exposed, he pushed off the tank with his foot, slipped and fell in face first. When he came up, she was howling with laughter.

She slid to one end of the tank, and he retreated to the other. "You look uncomfortable, Jimmy."

"I'm not sure we should be doing this."

She cocked her head at him, "Why not?"

"The guys think you're too young for me."

"How old do you think I am?"

"You said you had turned eighteen last week."

"Which makes me of age. I can do what I want. How old are you?"

"I'm twenty-six," Jimmy said. "Well, twenty-six next month."

She laughed. "That's not too old. A lot of the couples in camp have some age difference between them."

The waves Jimmy had made were dissipating and the ripples that were left made Madonna's body appear to shimmer. Jimmy couldn't take his eyes off of it. Madonna was looking frankly at Jimmy as she floated her body back and forth, opening and closing her legs.

Madonna came across the tank and put her arms around Jimmy's neck. Her eyes were just an inch from his and they stared at each other. Jimmy felt like he was falling into them. She kissed him. A gentle sweet kiss that didn't last nearly long enough. The next one did, and this time Jimmy gave as good as he got. The kisses became more passionate, and they became more urgent. Madonna began to softly moan. Everything was in slow motion. The urgency was building in Jimmy until he thought he would explode. After a long soul sharing kiss Madonna pulled back. She reached deep into the water and took Jimmy in her hand. Not taking her eyes from his, she moved slightly and slipped him inside of her. At first there was resistance and she groaned slightly. She moved to push him deeper inside. They were completely joined and didn't move, looking into each other's eyes. They were feeling that one sensation that only a man and a woman can have. A feeling that can never be replicated by anything else. Tears came to Madonna's eyes and began to roll down her cheeks.

"A second ago, I was a virgin," she said in almost a whisper. He kissed her tears. Slowly she began to thrust herself, striving to get him deeper and deeper into her. Jimmy felt like his whole body, and all of his soul, was sliding into her and he didn't want to quit until every bit of him was inside. They began to move together, and now the urgency was taking over. It grew stronger and stronger. Jimmy heard a guttural growl and then realized it was him. Madonna's head was back, her mouth wide open and a low-grade scream began building. Their passion kept growing and from deep within, a spark became a flame, and then the flame was a roaring inferno. Madonna's head was back, her mouth wide open and she was making a sound she had never made before. Jimmy got to the edge of the cliff and threw himself off, and down and down he went until he felt like his entire body had turned to liquid fire and poured itself into this girl.

A longtime later when they got their breath, Jimmy looked deep into her eyes and said, "I think you have a boyfriend now."

# 48

They were sitting by a large fire trying to get their hair dry. Jimmy had cut a strip of meat off the deer and impaled it on a sturdy stick and had propped it close to the edge of the fire so it would roast.

"How did you and your mom come to live up here in the forest?" Jimmy asked.

Madonna reached over and turned the meat slightly. "Mom had me when she was sixteen. She dropped out of school. They had been living up by Clint's Well. She was an only child. Her dad, my grandpa, had a heart attack and died when he was in his forties. Her mom worked as a waitress at a gas stop restaurant, and they lived in a broken-down Sliver Stream camper the owner let them keep behind his buildings. Grandma decided to move to Payson to get a better job. She never did. By the time they could move, my mom was pregnant with me and Grandma had lung cancer. She died when I was four. I don't remember her at all. My mom wasn't lucky with guys at all. The only ones that came around were assholes. Finally, we were living campground to campground up on the rim when Diego found us. He painted this picture of a forest paradise where we could live as a community and be free from what he called "the man." So, we moved up there with him. He let me and Eileen move in with him, which was okay, except for his son, Deiter, who was a prick."

"I got that impression," Jimmy said.

"You ain't seen the half of it. Luckily, Deiter is about your age and Diego didn't like him messing with me when I was little. I know young girls like older guys but that wasn't the way it worked with me. I couldn't stand him. And then, I saw him coming on to Mom and that did it for me. Mom shut him down and made me promise to never tell Diego."

"Looks like the meat is done," Jimmy said. Jimmy stood, and with his knife stripped two slabs of bark from a nearby tree. He placed the hot meat on the larger of the two and divided it. He put a chunk on the other bark, sat down and cut off a strip, stabbed it and put it in his mouth.

"Hot," Madonna said chewing. Steam came from her mouth as her breath hit the cold air. They found they were starving and wolfed the meat down.

"I could eat more, but we have to get back. I have to be back before dark or Diego and Mom go batshit."

There was enough water left in the siphon hose for Jimmy to douse the fire with. It wasn't a good time of year for forest fires, but good habits are good habits. Madonna gathered the bows and quivers, and Jimmy dug the carcass out of the snow and slung it across his shoulders. He tried to not let on how damned heavy it was. He got it balanced higher up so it wouldn't put as much pressure on his lower back. Madonna started off with Jimmy following.

Heading back seemed easier, even with the carcass. The meat was cold on Jimmy's shoulders, but he was soon sweating. He spent a good amount of time on the trek back admiring Madonna. Not just her cute butt, but the way she moved through the trees and brush. How she could quickly choose a path and was never wrong. The bandanna held her hair in place and kept the cold off her ears. Her hair was just enough red that it caught flashes of sunlight as it flowed behind her. She followed a path off the four-wheel trail. Jimmy figured she wanted to keep their footprints hidden. She probably didn't want anyone to know they had gone to the wash tank.

It took the better part of an hour to reach the knoll overlooking the camp compound. Before they could see it, they could hear it. There were a lot of voices raised in anger. Madonna stopped. "Something is up."

"Let's take a look before we go blundering in there," Jimmy said. He set the carcass down and they moved slowly and stealthily to the edge of the forest that overlooked the camp.

It looked like all the people from the camp were gathered in the compound. Jimmy unhooked his binoculars from his belt and scanned it. The naked body of Diego lay on a roughhewn picnic table. Two women were working on the body, apparently readying the body for burial. Eileen, Madonna's mom, was sitting on the bench, hunched over, her face in her hands. A few yards away Blackhawk was tethered to one of the posts used for skinning deer and elk. He was bare chested and even from this far away, Jimmy could see marks where he had been badly beaten.

Madonna said, "Let me see." She took the binoculars from

Jimmy's reluctant hands. When she got it focused, she let out a gasp and a low moan. She kept staring at the group below. Finally, she pulled the binoculars from her eyes and turned to look at Jimmy. There were tears in her eyes.

"Diego's dead. What the hell is going on?"

"Did you see the marks in the side of Diego's chest?" She nodded. "Spear traps. He must have walked into a spear trap. He was going to take Blackhawk out to set some up. I don't know if they went, I assume so. You and I had gone hunting."

She shook her head, "The only one in camp that used traps like that were Deiter and Diego. And Diego only used them for a family that couldn't hunt. And that was when Diego didn't have time to hunt for them."

"Deiter didn't hunt?"

"I told you he was an asshole. He didn't care. Deiter only hunted for himself. I think he liked the spear traps because he liked things to suffer."

"Nobody likes him?"

"Not nobody. There are about ten guys his age that all hang together. I can't say they like him, but because he's Diego's son he's the leader of that bunch. They call themselves "the wolf pack." They get together and drink moonshine and talk about the revolution they are going to start. Why is Blackhawk tied up?"

"Tied up and beaten. I figure Deiter is blaming Blackhawk for Diego's death. Diego was going to take him out and show him how he set traps."

"Do you think Blackhawk killed him?"

Jimmy laughed. "Hell no. He could kill Diego with his bare

hands. They must've caught Blackhawk by surprise. You cut Blackhawk loose and he could kill any five men standing close by."

"Nobody can do that."

"Blackhawk can. He and our friend Jackson are two of most dangerous men alive. I saw Jackson take down a drunk 350-pound All-State lineman with one blow."

"That little skinny guy?"

"That little skinny guy."

They could hear Deiter ranting at the other Fremen in the distance. They couldn't understand what he was saying. He would gesture at Blackhawk and the crowd reciprocated with ugly roars.

"We have to get Blackhawk out of there before they kill him. Do you know where I could steal a couple of quads?"

"Better yet I know where your quads are. I have a friend that does repairs on all the quads."

"Do you know where my and Blackhawk's guns are?"

"Yeah, I do. They are in Diego's house."

Jimmy thought for a minute. "Okay, here's what we do. You take the deer and go down there. You think you can carry it?"

"I made you howl at the moon. I think I can carry a deer."

"Very funny. You go down. They are going to want to know where I am. You shot the deer and while you were dressing it, I ran away. And you are pissed because I took one of your favorite bows and a quiver full of arrows. If they ask, you didn't chase me because you'd rather come back with the meat than with me."

"Then what?"

"You take your mom back to your place. You are consoling her. When you get there, you tell her we're leaving. Pack very light. Warm, but light. Get my and Blackhawk's pistols and sneak them to me. Where would be a good place for that?"

"At the latrines. If I had to go, no man would stay around, and no woman would question me."

"I'll meet you and your mom there. You lead me to where the quads are. You bring our rifles and ammo."

"What are you going to do?"

"I'm going to race into that gang down there like the cowboy from hell. I'll be firing off both pistols with my knife in my teeth. I'll be screaming like crazy. That should scatter them enough for me to cut Blackhawk loose and get us out of there."

"Could you shoot Deiter while you're at it?"

"I can try."

"That sounds all well and good, but what then?"

"We take you and your mom and Blackhawk and head out to find the Redcoats."

"Do you know where they are?"

"No, but maybe we'll get lucky."

"You already did." He started to grin. "No, I don't mean that," she continued. "What I mean is my friend the mechanic, his name is Robert Bruce, has such valuable skills that he is allowed to travel between groups to keep the machines running. Fortunately for us, he hates Deiter and with Diego gone, he won't want to stay here."

"Gimme the bow and quiver, I'll take them with me." He turned back to the carcass he had dumped on the ground. He went to his knees and reached into the body and covered his hands with what blood was left. Then he rubbed blood all over his face.

"What are you doing?" Madonna said.

"Putting on my cowboy from hell costume."

# 49

After helping Madonna get the carcass on her shoulders Jimmy took her by the arms and kissed her. Then kissed her again and if circumstances were different, he would have taken her right there on the forest floor. Instead, he wiped the splotch of blood he had left on her chin with his sleeve. "See you at the latrines," he said and turned and headed off into the forest.

Madonna watched him go, then stood a long moment and went through what she was about to do in her mind. Taking a deep breath, she started down the slope. As she got to the flat Deiter stopped in mid rant and stared at her. Those that had not seen her turned to stare.

Eyes wide and mouth twisted in grief, she walked past Deiter to where her mom sat beside the body of Diego Murillo.

"What happened, Mom? What happened?"

Her mom was crying. Madonna dropped the carcass and sat beside her mom and put her arms around her.

Deiter shouted, "I'll tell you what happened. This murderous son of a bitch," he said pointing at Blackhawk, "tricked my dad into walking into a spear trap." He turned to the crowd and shouted, "And he's going to pay for it!" The crowd roared.

"Is that true, Mom," Madonna said in a voice that only her mom could hear.

Eileen looked at her daughter, her face streaked with dirt and tears, "I don't know," she said.

"Come on," Madonna said. "I'll take you home. Get you cleaned up. You don't need to watch this." She pulled on her mom's arm and Eileen stood up to follow her.

"Where the hell are you going?" Deiter said.

"I'm taking Mom home to clean her up, then we have a funeral to plan."

"Where's that other little son of a bitch? This guy's buddy."

Madonna turned and looked him in the eye. "You were the one that said he had nowhere to escape to. While I was dressing my kill, when I wasn't paying attention, he slipped away. At first, I thought he had gone out hunting but he never came back. I figured you would want 200 pounds of meat rather than him. The bastard took one of my best bows and a quiver of arrows with him." She turned to the crowd. "Whoever finds my bow, I will give my next deer to. I'll dress it and butcher it for you." There was a positive murmur from the crowd.

She took her mom's arm and led her to the cabin they had shared with Diego. Once inside she outlined Jimmy's plan. She poured a pan of water and washed her face and hands. Eileen dug under Diego's bed and brought out Blackhawk and Jimmy's pistols. There were two boxes of cartridges. Then she dug out the rifles. Madonna put on her heaviest below-zero coat. She put the pistols and cartridges in her deep pockets. There wasn't room for the holsters. Eileen had a wolf skin coat that had belonged to a much bigger woman. Eileen had barely used it. It was the warmest coat she had. They got it out, then strapped the rifles stock butt up, onto Eileen's back. The coat was bulky enough to cover them.

"Is this going to be okay with you?" Madonna said,

Eileen said, "I've known all along this moment would come. The only thing between me and going back to my old life, was Diego. He really treated me well. After Deiter and a couple of his boys came into camp carrying Diego's body, I was devastated. Deiter came to me and pretending to console me, he hugged me and at the same time grabbed my ass. He said something to the effect that now he was in charge. He said he would be moving in with you and me. Then he would marry us both." She turned around. "How does it look?"

The thought of Deiter made Madonna want to gag. "It looks good. Here's what I need you to do. You go find Robert Bruce."

"He was there when they brought Diego's body in."

"Good. He's a loner. He'll probably be at his cabin. He lives alone. You find him and tell him to meet me by the latrines. We are going to need Jimmy and Blackhawk's quads."

"What about mine?"

"How much propane do you have?"

"Not much."

"Jimmy said both of their quads were full of gas. So, Robert will take us to them. Jimmy will meet us at the latrines, we will get the gasoline quads and Jimmy will go rescue Blackhawk."

"By himself?"

Madonna looked at her mom. "He is a lot more capable than I thought. I think he can do this. He will meet us at the creek crossing. So you and I will be on a quad, and Jimmy and Blackhawk will be on a quad, and Robert will have his own if he decides to go with us. He will lead us to the Redcoats."

"You think Robert will do this for us? You think he'll go?"

"He hates Deiter. Can you imagine life here with Deiter in charge?"

"Ugh! What's Blackhawk going to wear?"

"Good thinking. What do we have?"

Eileen went through a pile of clothes and pulled an insulated long sleeve shirt and a quilted parka.

"That'll do," Madonna said. "I'll take them. If someone asks, I'll make something up. Now go ahead and don't clank. If anyone stops you, tell them you have to hurry because you have diarrhea."

Eileen almost smiled. "That'll keep them away."

As they moved out the door, the last thing Madonna did was strap on her quiver of arrows and sling her bow across her shoulders.

# 50

It was farther and longer to get around the camp without being too close than Jimmy estimated. He kept himself far enough in the tree line to stay out of sight of the camp. He was on high alert, but with the spectacle in camp he didn't expect anyone to be out here. Finally, he came up behind the latrines. He found a place to hunker into that kept him out of sight. After what seemed like a long wait, he caught movement in the trees toward the camp. Then Madonna came into the clearing. He waited a minute to ensure no one followed, then he stepped out. She came into his arms, and they held a long passionate kiss.

"You made it."

"I did," she said.

"Let's get out of sight just in case someone has to go to the bathroom." They stepped back into the brush. Madonna pulled the pistols out of her deep pockets. Jimmy took them, checked the loads and put them in his belt. She gave him the boxes of bullets and he put those in his coat pockets.

"Mom should be on her way with Robert Bruce. Then we'll go to where he has hidden your quads."

"He hid them?"

"Everyone runs on propane, so no one wanted them. He fixed them up and hid them, not sure what to do with them." Jimmy put his arm around her and held her tight.

Five minutes later they heard a quad. They saw Eileen and a man coming through the trees on a quad. They worked their way through the underbrush and came to a stop when Jimmy and Madonna stepped into the open. Eileen got off and Madonna hugged her mom. While she helped her mom get the big bulky coat off, she said, "Jimmy, this is Robert Bruce. Robert, Jimmy."

Jimmy held his hand out and they shook hands. "Robert the Bruce," Jimmy said.

Robert laughed. "That's exactly what that guy Jackson said."

"Jackson? Is he okay?"

"Last I saw he was fine. We have to hurry, follow me to your quads."

Jimmy took one of the rifles and Madonna took the other. They slung their bows and quivers over their shoulders and carried the rifles in the crook of their elbows. Eileen climbed back on the quad and she and Robert got out ahead. Jimmy and Madonna had to hustle to catch up. They were virtually running when Robert came to a halt. Robert had chosen a good hiding place. They were right on top of the machines before they saw them. They were in a stand of pines that had low flowing branches. Robert dismounted, then pushed his way through the limbs and climbed on one of the machines. He pulled the rope and it started right away. He pulled it out of its hiding spot, left it running and went back in for the other.

Jimmy unloaded the bow and quiver and handed them to

Eileen. He made sure the pistols were easily accessible.

"You know where to meet us?" Madonna said.

"At the creek crossing," Jimmy said.

"You know how to get there from the compound?"

"Yeah, I'm pretty sure."

"Pretty sure? You know if you don't show up, we can't run around the forest yelling 'hey Jimmy where are you?'"

"I'll find you."

"Where are you going?" Robert said.

"I'm going to go get Blackhawk."

"Jesus! Deiter and those guys will kill you."

"I'm not leaving him."

Jimmy took his knife and nicked his high forehead in two places. The blood began to flow down his face. It was a trick he had seen in a documentary about professional wrestling. The wrestler's handler would have a razor secreted in his towel and as he mopped the wrestlers face he would nick him. Usually right at the bell.

He wiped the blade on his leg and slid the knife back into the thigh-high sheath. Again, he checked each pistol to ensure they were loaded and there was a round in the chamber. He swung aboard the quad and revved the motor.

Madonna came over to him and kissed him. "You be careful."

Eileen began to grin. "Really?"

"See you soon," Jimmy said. He put the quad in gear and pulled away.

# 51

When Jimmy heard the Fremen crowd above the roar of the engine, he stopped and turned the motor off. He cautiously worked his way the twenty yards to the edge of the forest. Deiter was working the crowd up. Calling for a war against the Redcoats and making the forest one utopian group. He was egged on by a group of young guys. Must be his wolf pack. He was tormenting Blackhawk with a switch. Each time he made a point for war, he swatted Blackhawk. Blackhawk was covered with welts and the crowd roared. Blackhawk's body language showed he was beaten. He hung on the straps, leaning against the pole. Deiter was getting cocky, and he got too close. Blackhawk pushed against the post and swung his lower body out and kicked Deiter in the chest. Deiter flew backwards and landed hard on his back. Jimmy raced back to the quad, started it and kicked it in gear. He had a pistol in his left hand and his knife in his teeth. He was steering and throttling with one hand. He went charging into the compound, screaming at the top of his lungs. The wheels kicked up huge cloud of dust. He guided with his knees as he pulled the other pistol and began firing both.

People were screaming and running for cover, especially Deiter's wolf pack. Deiter had already set the tone. They all thought they were being attacked by the Redcoats. Jimmy looked hideous, blood flowing down his face. He indeed looked like a demon cowboy. He screeched up to Blackhawk. Deiter had scrambled to his feet, but he had no weapon except the switch. He stood dumbfounded and Jimmy shot him in the foot. Deiter screamed and fell on his back and grabbed his foot. Jimmy took the knife from his teeth and slashed the leather line that held Blackhawk to the post. He slashed the knot that held Blackhawk's hands behind his back. Blackhawk jumped up behind Jimmy, and Jimmy, in one motion, handed him a pistol and goosed the throttle. Clutching Jimmy, Blackhawk began firing rapidly, forcing even the bravest to dive for cover. He wasn't trying to kill anyone, but he accomplished what he wanted. He scared the hell out of them. They raced out of the camp, but not toward the creek crossing. Jimmy took the path that was forty-five degrees from the creek crossing. When they were out of sight, Jimmy wheeled and turned for the crossing. He finally got on the path that led to the crossing, but the going was getting rougher. He had to slow down. Jimmy heard something above the engine. He couldn't identify it. Then finally he did. Blackhawk was laughing. Blackhawk leaned forward and put his head on Jimmy's shoulder, his mouth next to Jimmy's ear.

"Goddam that was fun," Blackhawk said. Jimmy was working to get his heart out of his throat and back down in his chest.

It took twenty minutes to get to the crossing. Robert Bruce,

246

Eileen and Madonna were waiting. Robert was on his own quad. Eileen and Madonna sat on the other one. When she heard the quad approaching, Eileen pulled out the shirt and coat she had brought for Blackhawk. Blackhawk gratefully shrugged into it.

"I appreciate it," Blackhawk said. He held his hand out, "I'm Blackhawk."

Robert took the hand and said, "Robert Bruce."

"Robert the Bruce," Blackhawk said.

"You guys are consistent," Robert said.

"God, you look awful," Madonna said to Jimmy.

"Scared the hell out of them," Blackhawk said.

"Are you hurt?" Eileen asked Blackhawk.

"It stings, but no serious damage. They are going to be howling on our trail, we better get moving."

"You take Eileen, I'll take Madonna," Jimmy said.

"You know the way to the Redcoat camp," Madonna said to Robert. "You lead the way." In the distance they could hear the sound of quads.

Robert fired up his quad and led off.

# 52

I went immediately to sleep when I returned from spying on Helena Jean. I awoke when she came in. I waited for her to come over and accuse me of following her, but she didn't. I closed my eyes. When next I opened my eyes, she was gone and this time I hadn't heard her leave. According to my watch it was almost noon. I guess I had needed my sleep. This time no one had left me food. There was a bucket of water by the fireplace whose fire was down to embers. I wedged another log on and wondered if the habit was to keep the fire going during the day while people weren't home, or maybe to just bank it to keep some coals alive.

I poured water into a wash tin, stripped down, and scrubbed myself the best I could without the benefit of soap and running water. You forget how much you enjoy a good shower until you don't have one. Satisfied I had done what I could do, I dried off with a piece of rag that was hanging on a peg and got back into the same clothes. I thought about what I was supposed to do today. No one had given me instructions.

I dressed for the cold and stepped outside. It wasn't as cold as yesterday. The sky was clear. I looked around and everyone in sight was busy doing something. I began to wander. I wandered around the camp for a good while. No one paid a bit of attention to me. Finally, I got bored. I could always chop wood. I went back to the wood pile and started splitting wood. I worked solidly into the afternoon. I finally could take no more and I was at the beginning of a blister. I stopped and leaned on the axe. I had not seen Helena Jean or her daughter Evangeline. In fact, I hadn't seen Francis or his guy Jerry or even Robert the Bruce. Well, I thought, when in doubt, take the bull by the tail and face the situation.

I decided to go to Francis's cabin and demand my rifle back. It was an expensive weapon and I had been nothing but cooperative. Halfway across the compound I heard a rifle shot. I froze, listening. Then there was another, then another. I started toward the sound. It sounded purposeful and rhythmic like target practice. There were no game animals this close to camp. I followed the sound to the south end of the encampment. There I found Gilbert and Jerry standing beside a kneeling Francis who had my rifle propped on a block of wood and was shooting at a paper target a good hundred and fifty yards away.

Jerry had a pair of binoculars and was studying the target. "It's pulling an inch to the right," he said.

I came up behind them and they didn't notice me.

"It's not pulling," I said. "*He's* pulling it to the right."

They looked at me. "I'm not pulling it," Francis said. He jacked another shell into the chamber. He aimed again. He took a long time doing it. Finally, the rifle exploded. It was too far for me to see where it hit. Jerry said, "It's still to the right."

"Godammit," Francis said. "I'm not pulling. It's the godamned rifle."

249

"Try this," I said. I took the bandanna from my neck and approached Francis.

Francis put a hand on my wrist. "What are you doing?"

"Just give it a try," I said. Gently so as to not spook him, I tied the bandanna around Francis's head leaving the right eye uncovered. "You are blinking as you pull the trigger."

"The fuck I am," Francis said. He leaned down and sighted again. The rifle exploded and I was watching Jerry. Jerry grinned. "Bullseye," he said.

Francis looked at me. He had hit the bullseye, but I wasn't sure he liked it. I held my hand out. "I'd like my rifle."

He stood but didn't relinquish the rifle.

"I was an expert marksman in the service and went to sniper school. May I show you?" I still had my hand out. Reluctantly he handed it to me. It normally held three rounds. Four if I jacked one into the chamber and replaced it from the cartridge box. Gilbert was holding the box of shells.

I looked at him, "May I have the ammo?" He looked at Francis. Francis nodded. He handed me the box. I loaded the gun, then without using the log, I remained standing. I wrapped the shoulder strap around my forearm and took aim. I got into my shooters stance and slowly let my breath out. Jerry had his binoculars on the target. I fired, jacked in a new cartridge and fired again, then did it two more times. They were looking from the target then back to Jerry.

"I can't tell if he even hit the thing," Jerry said.

"Go get it," I said.

He just looked at me. "Go get it," Francis said. Jerry reluctantly turned and walked toward the target. "Hurry the fuck up," Francis said. Jerry started jogging. He pulled the target off the plyboard it had been taped to. He looked at it, then held it to the sky. We could hear him say, "fuck!"

He came back to us, holding the target, shaking his head. "I don't believe this." He handed the target to Francis. "He tore the bullseye out of the target."

"I don't believe it," Francis said. "I probably knocked most of that out myself."

"Put a fresh target up," I said. I began loading the rifle again. Jerry hustled a new target down to where they had the last one and fastened it the way the previous one had been fastened. Jerry swung wide and came back. I waited until he was behind me. I got in my shooter's stance and fired four more times. Jerry retrieved the target. They were all in the bullseye, but one had leaked about a millimeter on the line.

Francis took the paper from Jerry and studied it. "I'll be damned," he said. He put his hand out to me. "Gimme the rifle."

I shook my head. "This is a Proof Tundra, it's my rifle bought and paid for. I want my Kahr back too."

Jerry was giving me that hard look that probably scared children. There was a commotion on the edge of camp. It was fifty yards away. It was the roar of several quads racing into the camp. Even from the distance, I recognized Blackhawk and Jimmy. They each had a female on the quads behind them. I recognized the girls. They were the bathers that started this whole thing.

Francis forgot about the rifle and headed for the noise with the rest of us following.

# 53

"Well son, I'm sure glad you were there," I said to Robert the Bruce. A crowd had gathered in the center of the Redcoat compound. Madonna and her mother had taken the narrative and told everyone that Diego Murillo had been killed. Killed by the spear traps he himself used. No one knew who had placed the traps that had killed Diego.

Blackhawk said simply, "Deiter."

The narrative put Eileen in tears as she told the crowd that Deiter had blamed Blackhawk and had whipped him badly. Blackhawk was sitting to the side with Diego's coat off. Helena Jean and her daughter Evangeline were gently applying ointment to the red welts on his body. I had watched Helena Jean when the news hit about Diego's death, and she had turned her body away from the crowd and I could see her shoulders shaking. When she turned back and began helping tend to Blackhawk, she had wiped the back of her hand across her face. Evangeline hugged her.

"You okay, Mom?" Evangeline said. Helena Jean nodded. Eileen was watching Helena Jean with an odd look on her face.

"What happens now?" a lady in the crowd asked Francis.

Francis turned to Blackhawk, "What happens now? Is that son of a bitch coming after you?"

"You know Deiter better than I do, but I bet he's coming."

"I didn't even know Diego," a man said.

Francis looked at Blackhawk. "Were you followed?"

Robert Bruce answered, "When we first got out of there, I could hear quads, but they were pretty far behind. We stopped twice to listen, and I didn't hear anything." He looked at Blackhawk, "You?"

Blackhawk shook his head. He looked at Eileen and Madonna. They both shook their heads.

"They will be coming," I said. "Deiter is an asshole."

"This ain't my fight," a middle-aged man said. Several others agreed. Another one said, "We didn't come here to fight somebody. We just want to be left alone."

Eileen said, "Deiter has at least ten guys that will do whatever he wants. Deiter has always wanted to be in charge. I think Deiter killed his own father so he could take over."

"If they attack you," Jimmy said to the crowd, "Will you protect yourselves?"

"What will happen to my daughter?" Helena Jean said. "She can't protect herself."

"I'll tell you what will happen if we don't fight," Madonna spoke up. "Deiter will take her and me and what other woman is unprotected and we won't get a choice."

"The thought of it makes me sick," Evangeline said softly.

Blackhawk was looking at me. He spoke, his voice projecting so all could hear. "What you all don't know is that Jackson, here, was a soldier and a tactician for the U.S. government. That means his job was to assess and plan for any contingency that came along. I'm going to ask him what to do."

It seemed as if every eye was on me. I looked out above the trees. I had already thought about it. "The sun is going down. Deiter and his gang have been living out here a long time. If they can help it, they don't want to be out in the forest overnight. Not when they can spend the night in their own cabins with their own fire. It will be below freezing. They will come in the morning after the sun is up. If there is no resistance, no one should get hurt. He doesn't want you people. He wants Blackhawk and the women. I think the reason you didn't hear them following was because when he found that Robert was with you, he knew where you were going. Where else would you go?"

The man that had spoken up said, "He's right."

"So," I continued, "We have till morning to get ready. By morning my friends Blackhawk and Jimmy and whoever else wants to go, will be gone. We have quads that will take us to our truck which is stashed a few miles from here. We will leave and not look back."

"What should we do?" Francis said.

"Be prepared." I pointed at four buildings that were located toward the middle of the open compound. "Those buildings can be defended. I suggest we down as many trees as we can in the next hours and drag them to surround those four buildings. Don't trim them, just make as impassable a helter-skelter of trees as you can. The idea is to make it so the Fremen can't charge the buildings without getting slowed enough to become easy targets. If you are armed and ready for them, they will hesitate to attack.

254

I'll bet they'll be willing to negotiate."

"You said *we*?" Francis said.

"Blackhawk, Jimmy and I will help. But once we have you fortified, we are going to load up and get out of here before dawn. The moon is up, so we could make good time before they make it here."

"Me and Evangeline are going too," Helena Jean said.

"So are me and Mom," Madonna said.

"For my own health, I better go with you," Robert said.

"Yes, you should go with us," Evangeline said.

Jerry said, "Wait a minute." He turned to me, "You guys get down there and you tell the sheriff that we are up here, then they come and roust us till we are all scattered and we don't have homes anymore."

"That's a good point," Jimmy said. "I think you can handle Deiter. I'm told you have done it once before."

I said, "If we are compelled to, we tell the sheriff about the Fremen camp."

"We don't say a word about the Redcoats," Blackhawk said. "We probably won't even see a deputy."

"Just think about this," I said for all to hear. "You can bet the Fremen are coming in the morning. It's up to you to be ready."

# 54

With the help of all the men and some of the women in camp, we made a mess of downed trees surrounding the four cabins. Under my instructions Jerry and a buddy stacked firewood all along a wall inside each cabin. People carried bedding, water and food into each cabin, getting ready for a siege. Francis assigned who would be in which cabin. He returned my pistol.

It was after two in the morning when Blackhawk, Jimmy, Robert, Eileen, Madonna, Helena Jean and Evangeline were in Helena Jean's cabin. We packed four duffle bags with canned food, elk jerky, some rice and beans. Plus a cook pot and skillet, whatever we could think of for the run down the hill. We laid our sleeping bags out on the floor. Helena Jean and Eileen took the two pallets Helena Jean and I had been using.

"I knew I was on short time," Helena Jean said aloud. "What no one but Evangeline knew was that I had a relationship with Diego."

"I knew about it," Eileen said.

Helena Jean said, "It didn't bother you?"

"Not really," Eileen said. "He and I didn't have that kind of relationship. He let me and Madonna live there to take care of him. No one knew but he had diabetes. He wouldn't show it, but it debilitated him pretty badly. He was happy to have live-in care-givers. And he was the one that brought me up here in the first place. He was the only one Madonna and I could trust. But his boy was just awful. Dirty talking Madonna whenever he was alone with her. And he was after me all the time to sleep with him. I couldn't take it anymore. Without Diego it is just a matter of time before that monster would hurt my girl."

"I'd rather die than let that son of a bitch touch me," Madonna said.

"God knows, he tried," Eileen said. "He would even get after me. While Diego's body was still warm the little bastard told me he was going to take both of us. Ugh!"

"Lights out, let's get some sleep," Blackhawk said. He looked over to me and I nodded. We were going to have a very early day. No one disagreed and five minutes later we were all in our bags.

It was still pitch black when I opened my eyes. From the light of the fireplace coals, I could tell Blackhawk was sitting up. I got up and went to the door and opened it as quietly as I could. The moon was bright and high, the air crisp and cold. There was no movement in the camp. I shut the door. Eileen and Helena Jean were up. Eileen stoked the fire and Helena Jean started preparing something they had laid out last night to eat, and something to take with us. Now everyone was up. Madonna and Evangeline began rolling bedrolls. They talked between themselves very quietly.

We began carrying everything outside. We needed a minimum

of four quads. They had brought three and Francis gave us a spare
he kept in reserve. We had parked them, along with the spare, in
front of Helena Jean's cabin. Robert checked them over. Checking
oil, propane, air pressure, that kind of thing. Blackhawk and I
began loading them. Robert moved some things from his so he
could carry Evangeline, then he joined Jimmy inside. They studied
Jimmy's map in the light of the lamp. Jimmy had placed a circle
on the map where we had left the truck. Robert showed him where
we currently were, and Jimmy marked that. I came up behind
them and looked at the map.

"Ten to twelve miles as the crow flies," Jimmy said to me.

"What if you are not a crow?"

Robert said, "Very rough country between here and there.
Ten to twelve miles if you are a crow. Fifty if you are not."

"Damned rough," Madonna said. "We're ready if you guys
are." She was carrying her bow and a quiver of arrows.

Helena Jean took a last look around the cabin. I watched her.
I wondered if she was saying goodbye or good riddance. Francis,
Jerry and a few others were outside, waiting to see us off.

"Good luck to you," Francis said. "It's going to be rough out
there."

"We'll make it," I said. "You guys fort up. When they get here,
make sure they know that we've gone. They'll leave you alone."

"Sure you don't want to leave that rifle behind," he said with
a grin.

"Pretty sure," I said.

Robert fired up his machine. Evangeline got up behind him
and wrapped her arms around him and laid her head on his back.
Oh, so that's the way it is, I thought. Madonna got behind

Jimmy without being told who she was riding with. Eileen got behind Blackhawk and Helena Jean got up behind me. She held on but didn't lay her head on my back. Dang it.

The Redcoats were silent as we pulled out of the clearing. Robert and Evangeline led the way with Jimmy and Madonna behind them. Blackhawk and Eileen followed with Helena Jean and me holding up the rear. The moon was bright, and the quads had headlights, so it made our way through the brush and into the forest a little easier. It was still slow going and would be until the sun came up.

# 55

Soon after we started, we found we had to cover our faces with bandannas and scarves. Even with the headlights, unseen low hanging branches would slash across our faces. It stung like the devil. Covering our faces helped. The girls hanging on behind had it better. I had my pistol on my hip and my rifle, with the chamber empty, but three bullets in the magazine.

I had to hand it to Robert. He was an expert in the woods and without a discernible path to follow he was doing a good job of picking a way through the trees. I had an easy job. I just followed everyone else. It seemed to take forever before the sky began to lighten. Even then it took forever before there was enough light to make a difference.

Finally, the sun was above the horizon and Robert got us onto an elk trail that made life easier. After a long four hours of riding, Robert signaled a stop. We all pulled up to him.

"Evangeline needs a bathroom break. Anyone else?"

"Me too," Madonna said. We dismounted.

Eileen said, "Boys can go over there," she said, waving toward the right. "Girls over here."

"Anyone bring any tissue?" Madonna said. We all just looked at each other.

"I've got something you can use," I said. I dug into my pack and found my rifle cleaning kit. Inside were cotton patches that were just big enough. I handed them out.

"My hero," Eileen said. The girls took the swabs and went into the brush. We started over to our designated bathroom.

"I really don't have to go," Jimmy said.

"It's a long way to your truck," Robert said.

"We can't stop all of us later, just for you. You better try," Blackhawk said. You'd think he was Jimmy's dad.

It felt good to be off the quads and we had a chance to stretch while we waited for the girls. When it comes to bathroom activity, men are always waiting for girls. But in their defense, they can't just unzip, pee, zip up. While we waited, Blackhawk and I walked back down our trail to listen. All we heard were the girls chattering.

Reluctantly we mounted the quads, and we were moving again. Before long we came to the bank of a creek. The water was high and rushing due to the melting snow. We stood on the bank and stared at it.

"These creeks can change course if the rainfall is heavy enough," Robert said. "We'll just have to keep following it until we find a place to cross."

We saddled up and began following the creek. It wasn't easy. The trees and brush were down to the water, and we had to detour several times. We traveled a mile along the bank before we found a place to cross. Even so, we had to lift our feet high as we crossed to keep our feet dry. It wasn't any easier on the other side. We pushed on.

Periodically Robert would signal a stop so we could listen. Nothing but the birds. After being locked in by the freezing temperatures, they were active. Maybe Deiter and his goons weren't following. Knowing that jackass, that was unlikely.

After an eternity the sun was almost straight up. You don't realize how much work it is to drive a quad over rough terrain. We came to a clearing where we could take a break. Eileen and Helena Jean dug some food out and we all had something to eat. It was corncakes and fried fatback. It tasted good to me.

"As I understood it," Robert said around a half a mouthful. "You guys came as far as you could on the quads, then stashed them and continued on foot."

Jimmy said, "It got extremely hilly and thick with brush. And the machines made too much noise. They would spook the elk anyway, so we decided to walk."

"Think you could find where we left the quads on your map?" Blackhawk said.

"I marked it," Jimmy said.

"That's smart," I said.

"Oh, Jimmy. You are so smart," Madonna said with a grin and a twinkle. Jimmy's bandanna was down. His face flushed so deeply he looked sunburned. If you weren't aware of their relationship before, you knew what it was now.

Jimmy dug his map out and unfolded it. He spread it out on the front of his quad. We crowded around to look. He put his finger on it. "Here's where we left the quads." He moved his finger. "Here's where we left the truck."

Robert leaned in to get a better look. He put his finger on the map. "Here's the creek we just crossed. My best guess is that we're about here." His finger was quite a way from the truck. The topography looked rough.

"How long in time?" I said.

"God, I'd hate to guess. Four hours maybe. Maybe longer. We have other creeks to cross. One of them is a son of a bitch."

"I'm cold," Evangeline said. Robert wrapped his arms around her. "I have a ground blanket. We can wrap you in that when we move again."

"I think the rest of us ladies could use something like that," Eileen said.

We all had a ground blanket we carried with our sleeping bags, in case we got stuck overnight. We dug them out and handed one to each of the girls.

"Time to go," I said.

For the next few hours, the only blessing was that the air began to warm. By warm, I mean it got into the low thirties. The next creek was not as problematic as the first and we all got across safely. An hour later we pulled into a clearing and I recognized it as where we had stashed the quads and continued hunting on foot. The truck couldn't be too far. Once we had the truck we were out of here. Out of the woods, so to speak. The only thing that worried me was the time. By now it was mid-afternoon. That meant we probably wouldn't get to the truck until dusk which left us to drive out in the dark. And not all of us would fit in the cab. Someone would have to ride in the bed and freeze. I had a guess as to who that someone would be.

# 56

I was remembering we had hunted on the quads for about three hours before we stashed them. Keeping in mind we were *hunting*. So we were moving slower then than we were now. We should get to the truck in about half that time.

Every once in a while, I could hear the girls, Evangeline and Madonna, talking to Robert and Jimmy. Eileen and Helena Jean were quiet. I'm sure they were just wondering what the future would have for them and their girls now. I wondered the same thing. They had left the camp with literally just the clothes on their backs. If they had money, it couldn't be much.

My butt was getting sore. The ride had not been gentle. Robert called a halt. He and Jimmy consulted the map again while the rest of us stretched our backs and rubbed our butts.

"You doing okay?" I asked Helena Jean.

She nodded. "Just really tired. You think we are about there?"

"I'll find out."

I started away and she said, "Do you think we are safe now?"

I turned and looked at her. I came over and gave her a hug. She squeezed me as hard as she could. "The way I figure it," I

264

said into her shoulder. "Deiter and his thugs are young and reckless. They will be traveling a lot faster than we are. I think they should have caught us by now."

"Do you think they quit?"

"No."

"So we are not safe?"

I ruefully shook my head. "Not till we are down the hill. We need to get to a phone."

"Who will you call? The cops?"

"A guy named Nacho. We can't get everything in Jimmy's truck. Nacho will rent a van and quad trailer and come get us, and we will caravan it back to Phoenix."

I pulled away and went to Jimmy and Robert. Jimmy looked up at me. "Probably about an hour away," he said.

"Just hope the truck will start," I said.

He frowned at me, "It'll start. If not, I carry a spare battery behind the back seat."

"Oh, Jimmy. You are so smart," I said mimicking Madonna. He took a swipe at me. Laughing, I went back to Helena Jean.

We all mounted up and started out. I could tell that spirits were higher. This time Helena Jean leaned against my back. We were close to the truck. Forty minutes later Jimmy signaled a halt. There was room for all of us to pull up beside each other. Up ahead I could see white patches through the foliage. A white truck stands out. Nothing in nature is perfectly round, perfectly straight or perfectly white.

This time Jimmy led the way. Evangeline was fussing with her ground blanket, so Robert had to wait until she settled. He pulled in behind me. We rode single file into the clearing, all of us happy to see the truck. Jimmy swung around the empty quad trailers and pulled up on the passenger side. He cut his engine. We bunched up around him.

As Robert pulled up behind us a shot rang out and Robert yelped and went off the side of his quad. It tipped as he went. Evangeline screamed as she rolled across the ground. There was an explosion of gunfire from the tree line. The bullets raked the truck and Robert's quad. Evangeline crawled to the truck's flat rear tire. She huddled behind it. Her mouth was wide open like she was still screaming, but no sound came out.

The same instant the shot rang out; I yanked Helena Jean off our quad and pushed her to the ground. "Lie flat!" I yelled, pushing the palm of my left hand into the middle of her back. I held her against the ground. I pulled my pistol. By now Blackhawk and Eileen and Jimmy and Madonna were all lying on the ground. In just that short length of time another volley of gunfire erupted from the forest. The sound of the rounds slamming into the truck were loud and obscene. All the glass shattered, and all the tires had slumped flat. Lucky for us they had set the ambush on the driver's side of the truck and Jimmy had led us to the passenger side.

Blackhawk had his pistol out and Jimmy was jacking a round into his rifle. When the gunfire paused, I yelled "Now!" The three of us rose up and started raking the forest edge. None of us had a target but this gave Robert the cover to crawl to Evangeline. He was dragging his right leg and blood oozed out of his thigh. There seemed to be something wrong with his left arm. His quad was lying on its side and was chewed up with bullet holes from one end to the other.

I emptied my clip. As I ducked down, I grabbed my rifle from its clip. I felt very exposed. I jumped back against the truck. I jacked a cartridge into the chamber. I tugged on Helena Jean. She rose up and sat beside me behind the front tire. I handed her the rifle. She looked very frightened.

"Hold on to this," I said. Blackhawk was on the other side of me with Eileen next to him. Jimmy and Madonna were next to her. All of us were huddled up along the truck. With the tires flat, the truck body made a good shelter. Evangeline had stopped panicking. She was holding Robert.

"Cover me," I said to Blackhawk and Jimmy. They rose as one and began firing into the tree line. I heard someone yelp. I came to my knees and grabbed my pack off my quad. Again, I jumped back to the shelter of the truck.

"Here's the plan," I said, digging into my backpack.

"Oh, hell. They don't have a chance now," Blackhawk said.

"They don't?" Madonna said. For the first time I noticed the pistol in her hand.

Blackhawk laughed.

I ignored all that. I took out my oversized medic kit. I had always been the medic on our team in the field. I handed the pack to Jimmy. "You take this, it has a pretty extensive first aid kit." I looked at Eileen. "Take Blackhawk's rifle." I was reloading my pistol. Blackhawk was reloading his. We stuffed all the boxes of shells into our coat pockets. "Blackhawk and I are going to lay down a field of fire. Jimmy, you get Robert and the girls into the trees back behind us, deep enough to be safe. Who has first aid training?"

"Mom does," Madonna said.

"Anyone got hurt in camp, they usually brought them to me," Eileen said.

"Great," I said. "He has blood on both sides of his leg so I'm guessing the bullet went all the way through. If the blood is pulsating, he will need a tourniquet. Otherwise, you wrap it real tight. There is a big gauze pad in the kit. We need to stop the bleeding. I turned to Robert, "What's wrong with your arm?" I said.

"I think I just sprained it."

"Who can shoot?"

"All of us," Madonna said. Jimmy nodded.

"Okay, when you get into the tree cover, while Eileen is working on Robert, you shooters work your way back toward the truck but stay under cover. When Blackhawk and I give a signal, we are going to empty our weapons then yippie skippy right back to you. You shooters provide cover for us. Don't shoot us."

"Yippie skippy?" Jimmy said. He looked at Blackhawk. "Does he always talk funny when he's about to get himself killed?"

"Every time," Blackhawk said.

# 57

Eileen didn't wait to get into the trees to start working on Robert. She took his hunting knife and cut the leg of his hunting pants at the wound. Blackhawk and I waited. We wanted Deiter and his inexperienced boys to send another volley our way. We figured they would empty their weapons into Jimmy's truck. Then before they could reload, we would make our move.

The truck was already looking like the Bonnie and Clyde car. Eileen poured a packet of sulfur into Robert's wound and began to wrap it. When she was finished Robert's face was pale and shiny with sweat. That's when the volley of shots began again. We all scrunched down and made ourselves as small as possible. I don't care how tough you are, or how tough you think you are, being shot at is unnerving. Especially when the bullets are slamming into the metal of the truck just inches away. Some of them went through the already broken glass and out the other side to whack into the foliage on our side. Scary stuff.

I leaned low and spoke to Robert. "Think you can make it inside the tree line?"

"Or die trying," he said with a grimace.

"That's not funny," Evangeline said, her voice shaking.

"Evangeline and I will be his crutches," Helena Jean said.

The volley faded out. "Go!" I yelled. Blackhawk and I stood up and I began emptying my pistol across the clearing. Blackhawk waited until I was empty. I saw two guys, who didn't duck fast enough. The girls, Jimmy and Robert began to scramble to our tree line. Robert had Helena Jean on one side and Evangeline on the other.

When I fired my last round, Blackhawk began firing as fast as he could. There wasn't a space between us. I didn't know a better shot than him. Some of those guys had to have been hit. Lessons had been learned during the Revolutionary War when whole lines of soldiers would march at each other, then open fire at the same time. The smart ones wouldn't fire. While the ones that fired were reloading, the smart ones would run them over. I glanced behind me. They all had made the tree line and were disappearing into the trees. I shoved another clip into the Kahr and began firing, this time choosing my targets. While I was firing, Blackhawk grabbed Jimmy and Madonna's backpacks off their quads, and a duffle pack off his quad.

If I saw movement, I shot at it. He reloaded and yelled "Okay!" I dropped down beside him. I reloaded, then we both shouldered a backpack and waited. Now it was up to Jimmy and the girls to give us some cover fire. It was twenty minutes until I saw movement on our side. I gave it another minute, then reached up over the hood and fired blindly. It was a signal more than anything. Gunfire erupted from our tree line. Jimmy was smart enough to have moved them a few yards north so that Blackhawk and I weren't between them and their targets.

Blackhawk and I popped up and began to fire, heavy enough to keep them down. We grabbed what we could and ran like a striped ass ape to the tree line. We burst into the foliage like runners coming through the tape. We got in far enough and collapsed. We looked at each other and began laughing.

"We having fun yet?" I said.

"Almost as much as being tied to a post and switched."

"Sounds sexy."

In the dim canopied light, through the foliage, we could see the truck. Nothing was moving. "Maybe we can make them pay for that," I said.

"You can count on it."

The rest of the group came up from behind us. "You guys okay?" Jimmy said.

"We're good," Blackhawk said. "How about you?"

"We all made it. Robert's back there with Evangeline. What now?"

"We need to get our quads back," I said. "They weren't very smart. They should have spent some of their rounds disabling all our quads. Let's go bring Robert the Bruce up here with us. If they attack, we have good cover here. Once it gets darker, Blackhawk and I are going on a hunt. We'll circle wide, then flush them back the way they came. That will give you time to load the quads and get out of here. Sorry about your truck," I said to Jimmy.

"I loved that truck," he said.

"You are going to need the quads. I just hope Deiter's foot is so sore he doesn't think to disable them."

"Shit, I didn't think of that."

"You talk about going after them like you are going bird hunting. Those guys are killers," Helena Jean said.

Eileen said, "Madonna and I know who these guys are. They would just as soon shoot all of us and leave us out here for the bears."

Jimmy said, "After Jackson and Blackhawk go on their bird hunt, I'll tell you guys who they are."

"I wish you wouldn't," Blackhawk said.

"They deserve to know who they are in the boat with," Jimmy said.

Blackhawk shrugged.

"You say they're killers," I said to Eileen. "Before you guys took us, we stumbled across a human skull with a bullet hole in it. It wasn't far from here. It had to be a few months old. Do you know anything about that? Did you have anyone in your camp just show up missing?"

Madonna said, "Guy named Roy. Just came up missing one day but his stuff was still there. Deiter and his assholes went looking for him. When they got back, I heard Deiter bragging about getting his limit of FBI agents. He was always bragging about something. I didn't believe he would shoot an FBI agent. None of us had any reason to believe Roy was an FBI agent. I tried not to think anything about it."

I looked at the packs. I said to Blackhawk, "We'll need water and ammo and our knives and rifles and of course our pistols. We'll also need our below zero sleeping bags in case we are stuck out overnight which we probably will be." I looked at Jimmy. "Keep your ears open. I will fire three successive shots, then I will fire three more. That will be the signal that it is clear to load up the quads and start down the mountain. We will catch up."

Eileen said, "I never finished high school but according to my math, we don't have enough vehicles to leave you guys one."

"Blackhawk and I will make it on foot. Don't wait for us until you get to Washington Park at the top of the Rim. If we aren't there by midday tomorrow, go on towards Payson." I looked at Jimmy, "As soon as you get service call Nacho."

"Who's Nacho?" Madonna said.

"A friend," Jimmy said. "A friend we can trust."

I looked at them all, "Now listen to me. If you end up talking to a sheriff's deputy, either together or separately, you were all members of the Fremen. The Redcoats don't exist. When they brought Jimmy in as a captive you all decided to help him escape. They chased you to Jimmy's truck, which they had already shot to pieces. Remember, the Fremen camp is the only camp up here that you know about. When we leave and before you leave, all of you clean your weapons so they show no sign of having been fired."

"You don't think they'll believe us?" Helena Jean said.

"Cops don't believe anybody," Eileen said.

"They'll have to, if you stick together. All it takes is one loudmouth saying the wrong thing. None of you are that loudmouth." I looked at Blackhawk. "Let's load up." We unloaded our packs of all non-essentials, then loaded them with essentials. Ammo, extra water, heavy clothes we didn't currently have on. We strapped our sleeping bags to the top of the packs and slid them on. I took a can of camo grease and marked up Blackhawk's face. He did the same to me.

We were ready. "Clean your weapons. When you hear my

signal, it will be safe to load the quads and get out of here."

Helena Jean was looking at me. "I don't like this a bit," she said. "You guys be careful."

Madonna said "Duh."

I looked at Jimmy. "Get them down the mountain. Don't wait for us."

There wasn't anything else to say. We turned and disappeared into the darkening forest, staying parallel to the meadow.

# 58

When the sun was gone it was pitch black. It was getting colder. Eileen had them all huddle in together as close as possible. They wrapped the ground blankets around them all. A fire was out of the question. Jimmy had found a package of ibuprofen in Jackson's medical kit and fed three of them to Robert. They were sitting so that they could watch toward the truck even though they could no longer see it. They were silent a long time.

Finally, Evangeline said, "What if Jackson doesn't give us a signal? What if we don't hear anything?"

"Then we go to plan B," Jimmy said.

"What's plan B?"

"I don't know yet," Jimmy said. "But it probably entails us taking the risk of going out there to get the quads."

No one had anything to say to that. After another long silence Madonna said, "You said you would tell us who Jackson and Blackhawk are. Like it is some kind of big dark secret or something."

"They would prefer it be. They don't like to be talked about," Jimmy said his voice just above a whisper. He thought about how he was going to tell this.

"To tell it right, I'm going to start at the beginning. Both of them are orphans. Not just orphans but they have no family at all. Blackhawk had a brother, but he died in prison."

"None?" Madonna said.

"None. They both lost their parents when they were very young and were in orphanages or some kind of boys' home until they graduated from high school. They both joined the Navy. They both tried out for the Navy SEAL program and made it. They both were at the top of their class. When they officially were made SEALs and before they got orders, they were told to sit tight until someone came for them."

"Were they together?"

"No, not until the SEALs, they had no idea the other one existed. Finally, after all of the fellow successful SEALs were transferred out to new assignments, a man came to see them. One at a time."

"Who was he?" Helena Jean asked.

"He was an American secret. He was introduced as the Colonel. That's all they ever addressed him as. They are still in touch, and they still just call him the Colonel. At any rate, he told them they had been selected for a special, ultra secret team of operatives that worked for the government. So secret no one had ever heard of it. So secret that from that moment on the identity they had before no longer existed. All records were expunged. There were no records of them in the Navy, no records in their old high schools, no records with the IRS. No records at the orphanage. It wasn't like they disappeared, they just had never existed."

"Was it like SEAL team six?" Evangeline asked.

"Everyone's heard of SEAL team six. No-one ever heard of Black Mamba."

"Black Mamba? Sounds like something the movies would make up. What is Black Mamba?"

"I'm getting there," Jimmy said. "If I tell you this story, I have to tell you all of it so you will understand."

"Go ahead," Eileen said.

"The Colonel oversaw this covert group and Blackhawk said that he wasn't sure there were other groups. He doesn't believe so. So now, the Colonel starts a new phase of training and this one is way more intense than SEALs. Not just physically, but mentally. They were tested in many ways. Like they would drop them alone and naked in the deep woods and they had to survive there for twenty days before they could come out. And they had to find their own way out. They were trained in hand-to-hand combat. They were trained to use even the most mundane objects as weapons. Like a pack of matches or a rolled-up magazine. We had an unruly drunken three hundred and fifty pound All Pro lineman causing trouble in the bar and Jackson knocked him out with a shot glass."

"My lord," Helena Jean said.

Jimmy continued, "They were taught to kill a man with whatever was handy to them. They were tossed into a blacked-out room with a blindfold on and their hands tied behind them. In the room was a guy with a knife without a blindfold. They were taught to use their other senses besides sight and only their legs to subdue the guy. If they didn't, they got cut. They were given statistical problems, logistical problems and taught how to solve them under intense pressure."

"Oh my, that just doesn't seem real," Eileen said softly.

"Oh, it was real enough. There were ten members of the team. They all were given code names, in order of the alphabet. Blackhawk was second so his name started with B. Jackson was last, so he was J. Only one of them was a woman. She was number nine and they called her Indigo."

"Did you meet her?" Madonna said.

"Yeah, I did. She was one tough cookie. Jackson said she was their Ginger Rogers."

"Who's Ginger Rogers?" Madonna asked.

"I forget how young you are," Eileen said.

"Back in the day, the guy considered the world's best dancer was a guy named Fred Astaire. Ginger Rogers was his dancing partner. Jackson likes to say that Ginger Rogers did everything Fred Astaire did only backwards, and in heels. He said the pressure on Indigo to be as good as the guys was intense. He said, she knew she had to be better." Jimmy stopped talking to listen. The forest was quiet.

He started again. "The guys never talked about the jobs they were sent on. In fact they didn't talk about this at all. That old saying, if they told you, they'd have to kill you. Not quite that, but close."

"How did you get hooked up with them?" Evangeline said.

"I'm getting there. How many of you noticed that Jackson has only one foot?"

"I didn't," Eileen said.

"I saw him taking his prosthetic off at bedtime," Helena Jean said.

"I'll be damned," Robert said.

"They were on an operation, I'm not sure where, I think Afghanistan. Their instructions were to observe this Isis controlled village. Observe only, not to get involved. Then these Isis assholes buried IED's throughout the village and made the local men run through them. Just for sport."

"What's an IED," Madonna said.

"An Improvised Explosive Device," Robert said.

"Not many made it. Then to make matters worse this one jerk, clad head to foot in black, had a big shiny sword and he dragged the elders of the village into the village square and beheaded them. Then he went too far. He dragged a little girl, couldn't have been over twelve, out into the village square. Don't know why he picked her, but it was obvious she was next."

The women gasped. Robert groaned.

"According to Blackhawk, or I should say according to Blackhawk's woman, Elena, Blackhawk said that despite their orders, Jackson said, "Fuck this," and jumped into their open-air Jeep and started down the hill. Blackhawk jumped in behind him. Halfway down they switched places and Jackson opened fire to distract the guy with the sword. As they came roaring into the village, the jeep hit an IED, and it blew the Jeep up on two wheels. Jackson was flung out and sailing through the air, his foot dragged across the trigger of another IED and blew his foot off. Clean off above the ankle. But this is the remarkable part. At the same time, Blackhawk says that while he was in midair, Jackson shot the son of a bitch with the sword before he could hurt the girl. The team had followed them down, and shot up and routed the bad guys. They air evacuated Jackson to Germany, and he was done with the group. When he recovered, they gave him some state-of-the-art prosthetics, a bag of cash and a pat on the back, thanks for your service. He couldn't be discharged, let alone get a medal, because he didn't exist."

"What did he do?" Helena Jean asked.

"He decided he wanted to be a westerner. Not a cowboy, just someone who lived in the west. He went to Phoenix, bought a houseboat, and tried to have a quiet life. As you know he kept his code name."

"What happened to Blackhawk and the team?" Madonna said.

"The way Elena said Blackhawk explained it, the Colonel brought them a replacement and none of the team wanted him. The Colonel came to them and offered to try to find a replacement. Each member of the team had special skills. One was the computer guy, one was a master electrician. One was a professional hacker. Jackson was the strategy guy. Whenever things went wrong it was his job to figure out how to get them out of trouble and everyone out alive. Blackhawk said he was indispensable, and the team knew it. The team voted no to a new guy, and without a complete team, they were disbanded. Just by accident, Blackhawk ended up in Phoenix and bought a nightclub without knowing Jackson was also in Phoenix. I was bartending there, trying to go to college."

"I don't believe that story," Evangeline said.

"I do," Eileen said.

"I do too. What happened to that little girl?" Helena Jean said.

"The last Blackhawk heard, she was studying at Oxford. Remind me to tell you about Jackson saving a baby that fell off a three-story party boat in the middle of Pleasant Lake."

Then they all heard three shots way off in the distance. Then three more.

# 59

True to his word, it took Emil a few days to find the Blue Boy. But find him he did. He called Elena and Elena called Marianne. Emil wanted them to meet at the El Patron at 7 am the next morning. Marianne couldn't sleep all night, so she was waiting in the parking lot when Nacho opened the front door. Nacho had stayed overnight. Elena came down from upstairs just as Marianne came into the main salon. A couple minutes later Emil walked in with Emilio Garza, Manny and Willy. They all sat at the bar and Nacho served coffee.

"Have you heard from Jackson or Blackhawk?" Emil said to Elena.

Elena stirred honey into her coffee. She shook her head. "Not a word. Every time I call, I get a message that the person at that number is not available." She looked at Marianne. "How about you?"

"It's the same with Jackson," Marianne said. "I know they said it may be ten days, but I can't help but worry. It'll be ten days tomorrow."

"I looked it up on a cell tower website," Nacho said. "Where

Jimmy told me they were going, there are no cell towers up there. No people up there, so no cell towers."

"So, you found this little pissant?" Elena said to Emil.

"Found him last night."

"So you waited until this morning?"

Emil sipped his coffee. "These are night people. If I were going to pay a surprise visit to say, Miss Marianne, or even you, or any ordinary working person, I would do it at maybe three or four in the morning. These people just went to bed an hour ago. An hour from now we will surprise them."

"How did you find him?" Elena said.

Emil smiled. "In my work, I have many rivals. I also have many friends. Sometimes, such as this one, rivals with a common interest can become my friend. When our good friend Manny here was shot by our rivals, ordinarily that could have started a war between Mr. Garza and them. But over time, I have nurtured a mutual respect with the man in my position on the other side and found it was not them that ambushed Manny. And he expressed the opinion that a war would not be in anyone's best interest. So he found Mr. Ibanez for us."

"Where is he?"

"In his bed, surrounded by his whores, sleeping the sleep that only those without a conscience can have."

"And Tiffany is there?" Marianne said.

"I'm assured she is."

"So we go surprise him," Elena said.

"Not we," Emil said.

"Can I get some bourbon in my coffee," Willy said.

Emil, Garza and Manny turned to look at him. After a

moment of awkward silence, Manny said, "After the job is done, you can drink your bourbon."

Emil looked back at Elena. "As much as I have confidence in my plans, anything can happen. You two ladies can accompany us, but I'll want you to park at least two blocks away until the girl is safely in our hands, and Blue Boy has been dealt with."

"What will you do to the Blue Boy?"

"You can't confess to something you don't know about."

"How will you be armed?" Nacho said.

"We each have a personal firearm and the license to carry it. How about you?"

"I'm an ex-felon," Nacho said. "it's illegal for me to carry a firearm. I'm sure you three can handle whatever we come up against. If you get into trouble, I'll overwhelm them with my dynamic personality."

"I feel safer already," Emil said.

Elena shook her head. "Can we just go?"

# 60

The place Blue Boy had fled to was a twelve room, six bedroom, six bath, two story mansion. It was on Central Avenue, in the heart of Phoenix, just north of Bethany Home Road. In its day it had been a showcase built by a copper tycoon. But for the last thirty years his reclusive grandson had lived in it with his just as reclusive wife. They were all alone until they had grown very old and died within days of each other. They had never bothered to update any of it. Something had to be flat-out broken for them to even repair it. They had no family to leave it to. It was in such sad shape, no one would buy it. So the bank had put paint on the walls and made it a rental. Dos Hermanos had connections with the bank and rented it for a song. They used it for gambling and partying and a place for whores to ply their trade.

On the run, Blue Boy rented it for a month and moved everyone out. He brought in his stable of whores and porn queens and arranged for two Dos Hermanos soldiers to act as bodyguards. He also had Tiffany there. He had told the girls the protection was for them, but it really was for himself.

In Elena's car, Elena and Marianne followed Emil as he exited

State Route 51, west onto Bethany Home Road, turned right on Central, drove to a side street, pulled in and parked two blocks down. The girls pulled in behind him. Garza, Nacho, Manny and Willy pulled in behind them.

Emil got out of his car and came back to Elena. Elena rolled the window down. "You girls stay here. It may be a half hour, or even longer, but one of us, probably Nacho, will bring the girl to you."

"Which house is it?"

"The less you know the better." He went back to his car, got in, started it, and did a U-turn. Garza followed.

Both girls turned in their seats to watch as he turned right onto Bethany Home and disappeared.

"He's right you know," Marianne said. "I don't want to know anything about what is going to happen. I just want my Tiffany back."

Emil's frenemy had told him there were surveillance cameras around the building, so he parked around the corner on the next side street from the house. He opened the trunk and got out five wide brimmed hats and five pairs of dark glasses. They didn't hesitate. They donned the hats and glasses and walked to the house. They didn't hesitate and marched right up to the door and rang the bell. Garza stood in front of the door while the other four were on separate sides. It took a few minutes, then Garza could see the peep hole covered by someone on the other side. The door opened.

The guy had a Hawaiian shirt, unbuttoned to reveal a ribbed, wife beater tee shirt. His hair was tousled, and he looked sleepy. He started to say something, and Garza clubbed him with his pistol. The man fell back, and Garza followed him in and clubbed him again. The man went down. Garza reached down, grabbed the man's collar and dragged him out of the way.

It was a large room with stairs at the back that rose to a landing. No one else was there. They all looked around, just a little unsure of their next step.

"That door over there," Willy said, indicating a closed door to the right of the stairs, "is to a small room. They used it as a bedroom."

Manny looked at him. "How do you know that?"

"I've played poker here a couple of times."

"Do you know who rents this place?" Emil said.

"Hey man," Willy said. "I just played poker. They don't care who you are if you have the money."

Garza reached down and slapped the man he had slugged. The guy was conscious. When he groaned, Garza started to slap him again and he raised a hand to ward it off.

"Who's in the small bedroom there," Garza said.

The guy didn't answer right away, and Garza slapped him again.

"Matias," he sputtered. "He's sleeping. It's my shift."

"What's your name?"

"Alex."

"Okay, Alex, you can make it through this if you do what I say. I want you to go to that door and tell Matias he needs to come out here for a minute."

He didn't move right away, and Garza kicked him. "Now!"

Alex dragged himself to his feet and went to the door. "Hey, Matias! I need you to come out here."

There was a muffled reply. "Right now," Alex said, anxiety in his voice. He knew that if Matias hesitated, he was going to get smacked again.

Garza pointed with his gun to a corner. Alex moved to it. Garza waved his gun down and Alex sat. Garza stood close to the bedroom door. A moment later it began to open, and Garza hit it with his shoulder. A second later he was hauling Matias out by the back of his hair. Matias was wearing boxer shorts and a ribbed tee shirt similar to Alex's.

Emil walked over to Matias. "Do you know who Mateo Diaz is?"

"Everybody knows...."

Emil slapped him, almost hard enough to put him down. "If you want to live through the day, you will answer my questions as asked. Let's try again. Do you know who Mateo Diaz is?"

Matias nodded, "Dos Hermanos Jefe," he said.

"Have you ever met him?"

Matias nodded again. "Yes," he said.

"Would you recognize his voice, if you heard it?"

"Of course," he started, then changed course. "Yes," he said.

"If Mr. Diaz gave you an order, would you obey it?"

"Yes."

"No matter what it was?"

"Yessir. No matter what it was."

"Tell me who is in this house, right now."

He thought a second, "Rose, Marnie, Maria...."

"No, just tell me how many girls."

He thought. His lips moved as he counted. "Five, right now. The rest of them went home. These girls have nowhere to go. They are all asleep."

"Is one of them Tiffany?"

"Yes."

"What does Tiffany look like?"

"Blond, five seven, maybe 130 pounds."

"Is she pretty?"

"Very."

"Who else is here, are they all upstairs?"

"Only other one is Sally. Just him and the girls upstairs."

"Sally? Salvator Ibanez?"

"Yeah."

Emil turned to Garza. "Emilio, take Manny and go with Matias upstairs and bring Mr. Ibanez back down to me."

Garza pointed his pistol at Matias. "Lead the way. Anything funny, you die first."

It wasn't a long wait. Manny was manhandling Ibanez across the landing and down the stairs. He was protesting but Manny slapped him across the back of his head, and he shut up. As anyone might have guessed, the guy was wearing shiny silk blue pajamas. He made Hugh Hefner look like a bum.

As they got to the ground floor Emil said, "Was there anyone in his bed with him?"

Garza shook his head. "Surprisingly, no. Must have got his jollies earlier."

"What the hell is this…."

Manny slapped the back of his head again.

Nacho thought there was a whole lot of slapping going on.

Emil said, "Mr. Garza, I want you to wrap him up and tie him so he can't move. I want a gag on him so he can't make a sound."

Garza turned to Alex, squatting in the corner. "Is there duct tape in the house?"

Alex nodded, "In the kitchen. A whole roll of it."

Emil said to him, "Are there plastic garbage bags in the kitchen also?"

Alex said, "Under the sink. In a box under there."

Emil said, "Nacho, get the tape for Mr. Garza then grab a bunch of those bags. You and Willy go up and get all the girls. Get'm dressed. Tell them to put their belongings in the plastic bags. Tell them they are moving. Don't let them fuck around. Kick them in the ass if you have to, but get them dressed and packed and back down here in five minutes."

"Got it," Nacho said and followed Willy to the kitchen. In the kitchen Nacho handed Willy a wad of plastic bags, as he searched for the tape. Willy started to object, but then shut up. Nacho found the tape. They came back out, and Nacho tossed the tape to Garza. He and Willy started up the stairs.

Upstairs, they found two girls in one room, two girls in another and Tiffany with her own room. The girls had been partying all night, so it was difficult to wake them up. All but one slept in the nude. Tiffany slept in an oversized man's tee shirt. When Nacho finally got her to open her eyes, she was very grumpy. Nacho twisted her ear to wake her up. It brought her awake.

She didn't really look at him for the first several seconds. When she did, she stopped still. "Hey. I know you."

Nacho said, "Yeah, you know me. I'm here to take you to your Auntie Marianne." He handed her four plastic bags. "Get dressed, put everything you want to take with you in these bags and let's go. If it's important to you, put it in a bag. We aren't ever coming back here."

When they came back downstairs, the girls were dressed alike in very short cutoffs and flip flops. They all wore tee shirts with their sleeves cut out and their various colored bras fully exposed. Willy was subdued and sported a bruise on his cheek.

Manny looked at him, "What happened to you?" Willy was silent.

One of the girls said, "The creep was trying to feel me up. Grabbing my crotch and boobs and the big guy had to smack him."

Manny just looked at him.

Emil said, "Alex, do you have a car?"

"Yes."

"Can you fit four girls and yourself in it?"

"Yes."

"Go now," Emil said. "Take all the girls except her." He pointed at Tiffany. "Take them each to whatever destination they choose." The girls were staring at him in disbelief. "If," he continued, "you don't do that exactly, we will hunt you down and your death will be very painful."

Alex stood staring at him. "You didn't understand me?" Emil said.

"Yes sir," Alex said. "Come on girls." He herded them out the door.

Garza had Blue Boy trussed up to where he couldn't move. Now it was just them in the room. Emil, Nacho, Willy, Manny, Garza, Matias, Tiffany and the Blue Boy. Emil went to the window and watched Alex and the girls drive away.

Manny had his pistol in his hand. He was looking at Willy. "Willy," he said. "I know it was you that set me up for the ambush."

"Oh, no, Manny. It wasn't me."

Manny shot him in the chest. Then shot him again. Willy crumpled to the floor. Manny stepped over and shot him in the forehead. Tiffany yelped and covered her mouth with both hands. Nacho looked at Matias and had never seen someone look more frightened.

Emil looked at Matias. "There were two shooters when Manny was shot. Blue Boy here only has two shooters." Matias looked stricken. Emil continued, "I just let one of them drive away. Would you like an opportunity to save your life?"

Matias swallowed, "Yessir."

Emil pulled his phone out and hit a speed dial number. It rang twice and someone picked it up. "Senor Diaz, It's Emil. Yes, just fine." He listened for a minute, "Yes, that is why I'm calling. I have one of your soldiers here, his name is Matias. Oh, you know him. Good, that makes it much easier. I'm going to give him the phone, so you can give him his instructions." He listened. "Yes, that's right. It's good to talk to you, we'll have to have a drink someday. Here's Matias."

Emil handed the phone to Matias.

"Yessir," Matias said. Again, "Yessir. I understand sir. Yessir, you can count on me." He handed the phone back to Emil.

"Do you have a gun?" Emil said.

"Yessir, in the bedroom."

"Get it."

Matias was back in a second with an automatic.

"You have your instructions?"

"Yessir."

Emil said to Tiffany. "Young lady, our work here is finished. If you would be so kind as to follow Nacho, he will take you to your aunt."

They filed out the front door, led by Nacho and Tiffany. They got to the street and turned toward the side street they had parked on. They had almost reached it when they heard a shot. Then another one, and after a pause, a third one. When they rounded the corner, they heard a fiery explosion, which they later found out to be a very expensive blue sports car being blown to pieces. No one noticed Detective Boyce's city vehicle parked two blocks the other way on Central Ave.

# 61

Blackhawk and I carefully moved along the edge of the meadow in the dark. It would still be a while before the moon was up. It was cold but as long as we kept moving, it was bearable.

"Let's cross here," I said. I started across with Blackhawk following. My plan was to swing wide and see if we couldn't come up behind Deiter and his jerks. Once across the meadow I checked my compass. I headed us west. At first, we moved pretty swiftly, or as swiftly as we could. Once we sensed we should be getting close we slowed and stopped to listen more often. By now the moon was peeking through the tree limbs.

Then we heard them. Or at least two of them talking. Not making any effort to keep their voices down. As long as they kept talking, we kept moving. When they stopped talking, we stopped walking. I couldn't make out the words but by the tone I could tell they were pissed. We found them in a small ravine. They had a small fire burning. At least they were smart enough to keep it concealed, even though I'm sure they thought us to be no threat. They were the ones with the automatic weapons.

Blackhawk touched my arm. I could see him well enough to

see him make a circular motion with his finger. He was going to go around and come up behind them. He moved off into the dark. I moved closer and could finally make out their words. Evidently some of Blackhawk's and my wild random shots had hit one of their quads and put it out of commission.

"That son of a bitch better come back like he said he would."

"He'll come back," the other one said.

Like so many guys in the woods, once they had a fire, they were huddled close and staring into it. Now they were fire blind. I was careful not to look directly at the fire. I waited until I saw movement in the dark behind them.

I stepped into the fire light. "Howdy boys. What's for supper?"

They both jumped. One started to reach for a rifle. "I wouldn't do that," Blackhawk said behind him and stepped into the light.

"Where in the hell did you guys come from?" one said.

"You remember a little bit ago when you and your buddies were trying your best to shoot the shit out of some people over by that white truck? That would be us."

One guy stood up. He was tall and rangy looking. He had an ugly look on his face. "You're the son of a bitch that killed Diego," he said to Blackhawk.

"Diego's son killed Diego," Blackhawk said. "Diego's son was the guy that planted the spear traps that killed him. And I'll bet Diego's son guided Diego right to them."

"Think about it. If you can think, that is," I said. "What does Blackhawk get out of killing Diego? Diego was the only guy in the camp that treated him decently. If he did kill him, why didn't he steal a quad and vamoose. Then I want you to think about why Deiter might kill his own father. First, he has the hots for the woman that lived with his dad, Eileen, and her daughter Madonna too. With his dad gone he can get what he wants. Including being the head honcho in camp. Has he talked about taxes yet?"

"Taxes? Why would he talk about taxes," the tall guy said.

"Because that's what all dictator's do."

The other guy stood. He was considerably shorter than the first guy. "Why should we believe you?"

"Lord, you are stupid," Blackhawk said. "Think about it. You are still alive right now. If I did kill Diego, why wouldn't I just shoot you two before you even knew we were here?"

They looked at each other.

"He didn't kill you because he wants you to make it back to the Fremen and tell them the truth. But to keep from getting shot, you are going to tell us how to find Deiter and what's left of his boys."

"There's only two of you," the short guy said.

"Two of us is enough," Blackhawk said. "Where would he go? You think he's waiting for daylight?"

The taller guy said, "Two of the guys were hit. They probably pulled back to tend to them. Both of our quads were hit, and they left us behind. He said he would be right back."

"But you don't think he will be, do you?"

The tall guy said, "Diego would have been, but I don't trust Deiter."

"Smart man," I said. "How many are with Deiter?"

"We started out with ten," the tall guy said. "There are more

296

at camp, but a lot of them didn't want to go chasing this wild man," he nodded at Blackhawk, "in the dark."

"So, with you two here and two guys shot, he's left with six?"

"Yeah. He doesn't know who all is in your group. We got to the Redcoat camp, and they told us about the girls going with you. He had already figured that Robert Bruce was responsible for you guys having vehicles."

"Where would they go with the wounded guys?"

The tall guy said, "We crossed a creek about a mile back. He would go there. But he's not going to go too far out of his way for those guys. He was in no mood to help the wounded guys, and one of them already looked dead. We got left behind and Deiter just doesn't give a shit."

Blackhawk was looking at me. "Only six," he said. "I want Deiter's scalp."

Both of these guys looked at him, eyes wide.

"Listen to me," I said. "I'm going to back out of the light. Blackhawk will be covering you. Once I'm out of sight, Blackhawk will back out while I cover him. Don't be stupid and try to do anything. Don't be really stupid and try to follow us."

"Why would we do that?" The short guy said. "You don't have any vehicles either. We just want to get back to camp. And, as soon as I get back, I'm heading to Payson. I'm done with this militia bullshit."

"Smart guy," I said. I slowly backed out of the light until they couldn't see me. I went to my right several paces and leveled my rifle on them. I whistled and Blackhawk backed out of the light.

Once Blackhawk was in the dark, we waited to see what they would do. I heard the tall guy say "I don't want to be stumbling around out there in the dark. Let's just hunker here till we have light."

"We need firewood," the other one said.

"Flip you for it." A short time later the short one said, "Son of a bitch!" When we heard him stumbling around in the dark, gathering wood, we turned and headed toward the creek where they said Deiter would be.

# 62

At an easy pace, I can walk a mile in six minutes or so. It took us an hour in the dark and through the forest. Once we left the two guys by the fire, I pulled my Kahr and fired three shots into the air, then with a pause, three more.

We kept moving in the direction the guy had indicated. It took a while. Once we got close, they had made it easier for us. They had built a large fire. We slowed to a crawl and edged up on them. The first thing we noticed was there weren't six of them. Only two were at the fire. Another guy was seated, head hanging on his chest. He was leaned against the only quad in sight. He had a bloody bandage on his head. His eyes were closed, and his breathing was ragged. It was so quiet we could hear him.

I didn't like this. Where were Deiter and the other guys? We were squatted in the dark pondering this when one of the two guys by the fire stood up and came out toward us. Once out of the firelight he moved from tree to tree, touching their trunks. He was looking for just the right place to pee.

Finally, he picked it, and stopped. He unzipped himself and

began to do his business when Blackhawk came up silently behind him and pressed the barrel of his Sig Sauer against the man's cheek. The man yelped and peed on his own leg.

"Make another sound and you're dead," Blackhawk whispered. The guy was still peeing. A lot of men, once you get started you can't just cut it off. Blackhawk made sure to stand out of the way.

"Sorry," the guy said. "I can't help it."

"Shut up," Blackhawk whispered, pushing the barrel against his cheek.

The guy finished his business and Blackhawk prodded him toward the fire. "Don't say a word," he whispered.

The guy at the fire was bundled up, sitting close and nursing a bottle of bourbon. He saw me first, as I stepped into the firelight. If he had a rifle, it wasn't anywhere close to him. If he had a handgun, it was zipped in under his heavy coat.

"Keep your hands where I can see them," I said. He didn't move. One of his hands were already extended toward the fire, the other held the bottle. Blackhawk walked the other guy into the circle of light.

He waggled his gun at the guy, "Sit down next to your buddy." The guy did it.

I went over and took a closer look at the man in the bloody bandage. His eyes were half open but unfocused. He was moaning. The wound in his head was seeping blood onto the bandage. He was young, early twenties. "Forgot to duck," I said to him. He gave no sign that I was there.

I went back and squatted by the fire. It felt good. Really good. "Where are your buddies?" I said.

"Who?" the pee monkey said.

Blackhawk smacked him on the side of the head with his pistol. The guy had his parka hood up, but it still had to sting. "He's not going to ask again," Blackhawk said.

The other guy started to answer for him, but I stopped him. "What are your names?" I had experience asking questions and getting better answers if I knew the reluctant guy's first name.

The guy with the whiskey said, "I'm Keith, he's Long John."

Blackhawk laughed. "I saw it, it wasn't that long. Go ahead, tell us where Deiter and the rest are."

Long John looked at him. "Deiter wants you real bad. He left us here with one quad to stay with this boy until he dies. He is definitely going to die. When he does, we are supposed to bury him so no one would ever find him. Then he wanted us to take the quad back to main camp and get the rest of the guys and high tail it back out here."

"How many guys are with him now?"

"Ten or twelve."

Blackhawk hit him again.

"We talked with two guys back yonder who don't have transportation. They said there were originally ten of you. Subtract those two and that leaves eight. Subtract this guy," he indicated the guy by the quad," and that leaves seven. Subtract you two that leaves five. I think Deiter is losing his army. Now, Long John, you tell us where he went or there will be two more bodies to bury out here."

"They told you wrong," Long John said. "There was ten until you guys opened up on us. Two guys panicked and ran back toward camp. So Deiter only has three."

"You won't shoot us," Keith said.

"We won"t?"

"Hell no. You guys are cops. FBI maybe, or forest rangers or sheriff's deputies."

I shot him in the foot. He screamed and fell over holding his foot.

"You see, no cop would do that," I said. "But I did. In fact, if you don't tell me what I want to know, I will shoot you in the leg. Then in the gut, and you will be in so much pain you will beg me to shoot you in the head. You understand?"

He was crying.

"Do you understand? Tell me you understand."

He was nodding so hard his parka hood slipped down on the back of his neck. I looked at Long John. "Tell me."

Long John stood, holding a hand out, as if to ward me off. "Deiter is crazy. When he wants blood there is no stopping him. He's been out here for ten years. No one knows the forest better than he does. He is going to circle wide around that meadow where that truck was left. He knows you all are going to get on what quads you have and head down the mountain. He knows you are going to take the shortest route you know of. And he knows you will have to go slow in the dark. He's going to get ahead of you and set up an ambush. He was bragging that he was going to kill you," he looked at Blackhawk. "Then he was going to rape Madonna right in front of her mother. Then he was going to let the rest of the boys have a taste."

Blackhawk looked at me, his eyes troubled in the flickering firelight. I looked at Keith's foot. It was bleeding. He was moaning.

"With four legs and only three feet, it'll be a long walk out of here." We dragged the guy with the head wound away from the quad. He had died. We fastened our backpacks to the back rack. It was a nice quad with four lights and rifle clips under the handlebars. We climbed aboard with me driving and Blackhawk holding his rifle at ready. I started it up and we rolled out of there. I hated leaving the fire. It had felt mighty good.

# 63

Jimmy had Madonna holding on for dear life as he led the way through the pines, moving them downhill as fast as they could. Robert had Evangeline around the waist. Eileen had wrapped his leg tight, but it was obvious that it was paining him. Eileen and Helena Jean were bringing up the rear. The moon was finally up, and Jimmy was relieved by that. Once they had packed the quads and Jimmy got a length of rope and a small toolbox out of the truck, he spent a moment looking at his map. When we had been hunting, there had been a two-track dirt path that we had followed pulling the quads trailer up the mountain. The truck and trailer should be sitting, with the rear end pointing back at the path.

He found it and everyone fell in line behind him. Even with the path to follow, it seemed to be very slow going. He felt vulnerable. It was up to him to protect all these people and he wished Blackhawk and Jackson were there.

They rode single file, and they were creeping along. Jimmy calculated they were maybe making a mile and a half an hour. He tried to remember how long he had driven from Washington

Park to the meadow where he left the truck. He couldn't remember. He did remember, when he was planning the trip, he had calculated it would take six hours in the truck to get where he wanted to hunt on foot. And he also remembered that it had taken longer than he had planned.

They drove on into the night and the hours dragged by slowly. When the sky to the east began to lighten, he called a stop. Eileen took the opportunity to change Robert's bandage. They all took long pulls on the water bottles. Jimmy and Madonna walked back a hundred yards to listen for the sound of quads. They also wanted to be alone. When they reached a dip in the path, they dragged some small dead branches into the low spot and covered it with leaves and sticks. A surprising little drop for someone not expecting it. The snow was mostly melted, making the ground wet and soft. They cut off stout limbs and sharpened the ends to deadly points. They then forced the butt end of the sharpened sticks into the mud and made sure they were covered with sticks and leaves. If they were lucky one of the followers would drive into the camouflaged low spot and puncture a tire.

They stood, side by side, listening. The forest was silent. Madonna turned to Jimmy and put her arms around his neck. He leaned down and they kissed for a very long time.

They stood there silently, looking at each other. Finally, Jimmy said, "We have to get back." Reluctantly they separated and started back.

Eileen and Helena Jean were standing in the path waiting for them. Evangeline was hovering over Robert. Eileen and Helena Jean were looking expectantly at them. Jimmy said, "Nothing."

"Let's keep moving," Eileen said.

"Everyone is exhausted," Helena Jean said. "Maybe we need to take a break."

Eileen shook her head. "Honey, you don't know Deiter like I do. He would have already raped Madonna and me if it weren't for his dad. Now his dad is gone. We'd like to think Deiter got tired and went back to camp. He didn't. He's still out there and the more we hesitate, the faster he will find us."

"What about Robert?" Madonna asked. "How is he holding up?"

"He can make it. I gave him more Ibuprofen. He's a tough cookie."

"Eileen's right. Let's mount up," Jimmy said.

They were moving again. In the east and so slowly it didn't seem it was happening, the sky began to brighten. When they reached the largest creek Jimmy had pulled through on the way up, the melting snow had made it a raging river. The bank on their side, which had been manageable, was now cut into a steep cliff. No way to cross there.

Madonna leaned up and spoke in Jimmy's ear. "What do we do now?"

Jimmy shook his head. He felt trapped. "We go left, or we go right. We have to find a better place to cross." He scooted around to look at the others. They were all watching him.

"Let's go left," Madonna said.

Jimmy mentally shrugged. One way was as good as another. He revved the engine and started left. It was very rugged going. Several times he had to detour away from the creek to find a way around heavy foliage.

306

An hour later he found a wide spot in the creek where the bank had a gradual decline. Once in the water, they would have to travel downstream for fifty yards before they could come up on the other side. The good news was the creek was wide enough here that it spread the water out and it appeared to be only about a foot to a foot and a half deep. The water was fast, but at worst would only come up to the top of the wheel rim.

Jimmy held his hand up to halt everyone. He slid off his seat and walked back to where they all could hear him.

"This appears to be our only choice to get across," he said.

"What if we kept going," Evangeline said. "These creeks don't go on forever. Sometimes they just disappear into the ground."

"You're right," Jimmy said. "But I know this creek. We keep going this way, we eventually end up in a canyon and there's no way out of that except to turn around and come back. I'll need all of you to follow me. Stay close up to each other. Stay right in my track. If there is trouble, you'll see me have it first."

"What about Madonna?" Eileen said.

"I'm going with Jimmy," Madonna said.

Jimmy looked at her. There was no arguing. "Like I said, I'll lead off. Robert, you and Evangeline follow me, Eileen and Helena Jean follow them. If Robert goes into the water with his leg, he's in trouble. With Madonna and me in front and Eileen and Helena Jean behind, we should be able to help him."

Jimmy looked at Robert and Robert met his gaze and didn't say anything. Jimmy knew it was hard for Robert to take the invalid role and admired him for it. He looked up to the sky. It was beginning to spit snow.

"We all on the same page?" They all nodded.

Jimmy mounted up and started into the water. The current was powerful enough that Jimmy had to keep the tires moving forward or the quad would slide. He kept it moving forward. He glanced behind and Madonna said, "They're coming."

He aimed at the spot up ahead that looked to be the best place to exit. He doggedly kept the quad digging into the bottom fighting the current. He was over halfway there when he knew he was going to make it. Then, ten yards from the exit a large boulder loomed barely under water. He was lucky to see it in time. If he had hit it, it would have been disastrous. He swung wide left and at the same time pointed his arm to the left to indicate to the others to do the same. He cut around the boulder and got to the bank. He came roaring up out of the water. He heard a yell behind him, and he swung around. Evidently Eileen had not seen his arm gesture and she had gone to the right, around the boulder. The left side of her quad rode up on the rock and the current got her, tipping her into the freezing water. Helena Jean and Eileen both screamed as they went in.

# 64

Jimmy got Madonna off the quad. He grabbed the coil of rope from where he had wrapped it around the duffel-bag secured to the back carrier. He unraveled one end of it and tossed it to Madonna.

"Tie this to that tree," he yelled, pointing. Without waiting he climbed aboard and charged back into the water. Robert and Evangeline had made it to shore and had to dodge him. Both women in the water were holding on to the quad. Jimmy fought the current and headed to them. Now he was driving with the current instead of against it and that was much more difficult. Bucking and pitching he fought the machine until he was next to the women. He handed his end of the rope to Eileen.

"Tie this to the front axle, by the front right wheel," he shouted to her. He shouted to Helena Jean, "Can you climb on with me?"

She didn't answer, she just started climbing. She damned near pulled him in.

Jimmy shouted at Eileen, "Make sure it is as tight as you can get it!"

Eileen wedged herself against the quad and tied the rope around the wheel that was sticking up out of the water. The water was freezing, and the cold was binding up her hands. "Now get on!" Jimmy yelled. Eileen scrambled onto the back of Jimmy's quad with Helena Jean pulling her. Jimmy gunned the motor and somehow got turned around and headed back to the shore. As he reached the shore he yelled at Madonna, "Give me the rope. Untie it from the tree and give it to me." Madonna raced to the tree. Jimmy yelled at Robert and Evangeline, "Get a fire going. A big fire. Quick! Against those rocks," he pointed at a group of huge boulders jumbled up just away from the shore. They made a fifteen-foot-high wall. He hopped off his quad and tied Madonna's end of the rope to the back rack of his quad. Eileen and Helena Jean bailed off the quad. He jumped on and gunned the motor as he kicked it into gear. At first the quad in the creek didn't budge. His tires were spewing dirt and rocks. Then it broke free and shifted and tumbled back onto its tires. He began to drag it until he finally pulled it onto shore. He got off his and shifted Eileen's into neutral. He, Madonna and Evangeline horsed it up onto dry land.

Robert had a flame started and he expertly fed it bigger and bigger pieces of deadfall. "Get the wet clothes off," he said to the two drenched women. "Hyperthermia will only take a few minutes."

Madonna grabbed the women's soaked bags. She emptied them onto the ground. Everything was sopping wet. Jimmy noticed that Eileen didn't hesitate to start stripping. Helena Jean on the other hand was hesitant.

"Get our sleeping bags," Jimmy said to Madonna. She

grabbed the two back packs from the back of Jimmy's quad and hurriedly pulled the sleeping bags out. She grabbed two pairs of Jimmy's spare socks. They were the heavy winter ones.

She unzipped a sleeping bag and handed it to her mother who wrapped herself in it. Eileen then sat on the ground and pulled the socks on. Madonna unzipped the other sleeping bag and held it as a shield so Helena Jean could undress. When she was naked, Madonna wrapped her and helped her with the socks.

With the women taken care of, Jimmy went back into the brush and using his Green River knife, he chopped some bushes off at their base. They were thick and bushy and winter dead. He dragged them over to the fire and piled them on top of each other. Madonna didn't have to be told what to do. She draped the wet clothes over the bushes and got them as close to the fire as she could without catching them on fire. They almost immediately began to steam. Jimmy gathered more wood to pile on the fire. Jimmy chopped stakes to drive into the ground by the fire and hung the women's wet boots on them. With more stakes he draped their socks to dry.

Eileen was watching Robert. She stood up and went to him and felt his forehead. "You look flushed. You feel like you have a temperature."

"I'm fine," he said.

"Jimmy," Eileen said. "Where's your medic bag?"

"It's in my backpack."

"Here it is," Madonna said. She pulled it from the pack and handed it to her mom.

Evangeline took Robert by the arm. "Come sit by the fire," she said. He let himself be pulled by the small girl. She picked a small boulder so she could sit him on it. The heat from the fire would bounce off the big boulder behind him. She helped him sit down and sat beside him. She put her arms around him. He was beginning to shiver.

Eileen gave 1000 milligrams of ibuprofen to Robert and handed him a canteen. She looked at Jimmy. "Hey Jimmy, do you have any whiskey?"

"I did," he said. "But that big gorilla of Francis's took it."

"Jerry's a prick," Evangeline said.

"Eileen and I need to look at that wound," Jimmy said.

"You have medic training?" Eileen said.

"Got a badge in Boy Scouts," Jimmy said.

"Hell, he's practically a surgeon," Helena Jean said. She was sitting on the ground, as close to the fire as she could get. She was holding the sleeping bag open soaking in the heat. It looked like she was flashing the boulders. Jimmy sat next to the fire, to the side of Helena Jean. Madonna came and sat next to him.

"She has a really good body for an older lady," Madonna said in a low voice.

"I heard that," Helena Jean said.

"First of all," Jimmy said. "I wouldn't know, I'm not peeking. I don't want to get in trouble with my girlfriend." Madonna grinned and squeezed his arm. "And she's not old." He paused, smiling at Madonna. "At your age, everyone is old, including me."

"Jackson was the lucky one," Madonna said. "I'll bet he gotta peek. I'll bet you would've peeked. Wouldn't you?" Jimmy felt his face flush.

"Oh my God, you would." Madonna laughed.

Helena Jean said, "I tried to catch Jackson peeking, but I never could."

"What are you guys talking about?" Evangeline said.

"Absolutely nothing," Jimmy said. He stood and joined Eileen with Robert. Earlier Eileen had sliced Roberts pants to expose the wound so it could be dressed. Jimmy sliced more so it wouldn't lie on the wound. He then sliced that cloth into strips. Eileen had done a good job of wrapping the bullet hole, but blood was still staining it. They took Robert's boot off to ease the strain on his leg.

"Should we try more sulfur?" Eileen said.

"Definitely," Jimmy said. Jimmy dug through the medicine kit and found more packets of sulfur. Eileen opened one and spread the sulfur on the wound.

"Evangeline," Helena Jean said. "I packed a small pan. It's there with the stuff Madonna is drying. Fill it with water and put it on the fire to boil. Once it boils put in those strips Jimmy just cut. Then get fresh water and we need to wash the wound on both sides of his leg thoroughly. Then we can re-sulfur and rewrap. "

"There should be a small bottle of hydrogen peroxide in the kit. We can wash the wounds with that. In the meantime, I'm going downstream to listen. See if I can hear quads."

"They know where we are," said Robert.

"How? How do they know?" Evangeline said.

Robert was looking at Jimmy to supply the answer. "The firewood is wet," Jimmy said. "Look at the smoke it's putting up." Sure enough, as soon as the wood caught, a billowing plume of smoke was rising into the sky.

"You knew it would do that, didn't you," Madonna said.

"We have no choice. Take the chance or let your mama and Miss Helena freeze. I'll be right back."

"I'll come with you," Madonna said.

"We'll be just a minute," Jimmy said. "If we hear something, we'll be more prepared. If we don't hear anything, we'll be more prepared." Once again, Jimmy was wishing Blackhawk and Jackson were there. He unstrapped his rifle from the quad and checked the load. He pulled his pistol from its holster and checked the clip. Madonna slung her quiver across her shoulder and picked up her bow.

"Locked and loaded," she said.

"Be right back," he said. They began working their way down the shoreline. They walked for a hundred yards or so then stopped to listen. He could hear birds, which was a good sign. They walked for another hundred, then stopped again. It was still quiet. Madonna took his arm and pulled him to her. They embraced and kissed. Then they kissed again for a long time.

"We have to get back," he said.

They turned and started back when Jimmy suddenly stopped.

"What is it?" Madonna said.

"Listen," he said. They stood listening. "I thought I heard something."

"Heard what?"

"Don't know. Something different, but I don't hear it now." He took her arm, "Let's go."

As they neared the others, something was different. They were all standing. Even Robert. They were all watching them approach. Thinking they must just be nervous, Jimmy shook his

314

head to indicate they hadn't heard anything. By the time he and Madonna reached the edge of the quads Jimmy knew something was wrong.

Before he could ask, Deiter and two others stepped out from the trees. They all had automatic rifles and were pointing the rifles at them. Deiter was grinning broadly. One of the guys had a red stocking cap. The second had tattoos on his face and neck.

Deiter pointed his weapon at Eileen. "It doesn't look like the gang's all here. Where's the Indian asshole and his buddy?"

Jimmy took a step to the side, and Madonna stepped behind their quad. Jimmy said, "They are out scouting around. Looking for you. The women dunked in the creek, so we had to stop to get them dry."

Deiter looked at the two women wrapped in sleeping bags and then their wet clothes drying on the bushes next to the fire. He laughed. "Well, well, this is an interesting predicament."

# 65

The four lights made it better. The fuel gauge indicated three quarters of a tank. It was still slow going with the cone of light only illuminating maybe an eight-foot splash of light in front of us. The moon was up to the top of the trees but the trees we were winding our way through were so close it didn't help much. Then it started spitting snow. The good news was, maybe that would allow us to track Deiter easier. The guy said Deiter knew the forest, and he was circling to get in front of Jimmy. It was just a wild guess on my part, but I tried to think like Deiter. He had his blood and his lust up and would want to catch them quickly. I turned more southward.

I drove slowly through the trees for over two hours then stopped and cut the engine. We sat listening. Nothing. We started forward again. It was starting to get just a little lighter.

"Do these quads have an alternator?" I said above the sound of the engine. I began wondering how long the battery would last.

"I'm just a poor Injun that owns a saloon," Blackhawk said. "I'm no mechanic. If you would catch up to Robert the Bruce we could ask him."

"Good idea."

I would rather catch up to Deiter first. Get that battle out of the way. I wasn't even sure that was possible now. We moved along. Faster than if we were walking. Saved our energy too. After a while we came to a creek that was obviously rising with the recent rain and the snow melt. Hard to see if we could cross with just the headlights. I knew we had to cross.

"I remember this," I said. "Jimmy called it Big Creek. I remember because it wasn't much then. We crossed it easily then. This doesn't look so easy. We'll have to move along it and find a place to cross."

"Cut your motor. Let's listen again," Blackhawk said.

I cut the motor and we sat there. Still heard nothing. We started on. We traveled along the creek for an hour, periodically stopping to listen. Finally, there was enough light and with the lights of the quad we found a place, we both agreed, we could cross.

It looked like the shore on our side was a gentle enough slope, we could enter the water easily. Blackhawk slid off and cut a pole about seven feet long. We started into the water and even though we had to keep our feet up we did pretty good. When the water got a little deeper, I stopped and Blackhawk handed me the pole. I leaned out front and tested the depth. It was a little over two feet.

"Mark Twain," I said, referencing the safe depth on the Mississippi where Samuel Clemens had taken his pen name. Blackhawk took the pole and I moved on. It looked as if the best place to exit was about forty feet in front of us. I could barely make it out, but the reach of our lights was helping to illuminate it.

When we got about ten to fifteen feet closer the right front wheel went into a hidden hole. It threw us down and sideways.

317

The water came up to our seat. Blackhawk immediately thrust the pole straight into the water and pushed against the bottom with all his might. I gunned it and with Blackhawk keeping us from going over we climbed out of it. By then we were at what we hoped could be our exit spot and I goosed the quad into the slight bank and up onto dry ground.

We found ourselves surrounded by thick brush, and it was tough going. I cut the engine and we listened again. Again, we heard nothing. The cold water had soaked our pants legs and it felt like my leg was freezing. I started the engine, and we kept moving.

It had seemed forever, but the sky began to brighten. I was tired. I couldn't remember the last time I had a decent sleep. We kept moving, then stopping and listening, then moving again. I was beginning to get discouraged. Were we even going the right direction? I was thinking about stopping and having a powwow with Blackhawk about our course of action, when he tapped me on my shoulder. "Stop," he said.

I stopped. I cut the engine. "You hear something?"

"No," he said. "But, is that morning haze up ahead?" He pointed to the sky. "Or is that smoke?"

"I believe I smell smoke," I said. "Very faint, what do you think? Can you smell anything?"

"I believe I can," he said. "Let's get closer."

Just for stealth, I thought about getting off the quad and walking. But if it turned out to be nothing, we'd have to walk all the way back and waste time. At least now, I had a target to shoot for. The closer we got, the more we knew it was smoke. Now it was a question of why there was smoke? How close could I get to it before I alerted someone I didn't want to alert? Finally, when it was heavier in the sky, I stopped again.

"We're close enough, we should scout around, see what we can see," Blackhawk said.

"Why start a fire?" I said.

"Let's think about it. First to get warm. Second, maybe to signal someone."

"I think it's beside the creek," I said. "Maybe someone got wet. In this cold, you aren't going to last long if you are wet."

"Let's go find out," he said.

"You're the Injun, you lead off."

"You never have believed I'm a real Indian."

"Now's the time to prove it," I said, shoving his shoulder to get him going. I have to admit, he moved through the forest like an Indian.

As we got closer the smoke smell got stronger. Blackhawk stopped us.

"If this is Deiter," he said. "We don't want to come straight at them. I suggest we swing out wide, so we come at the source of the smoke from the woods instead of from the creek."

"You got it, Kemo Sabe. Lead the way."

We moved quietly and slowly. An hour later when the sky was much lighter, we came on three quads. There had been an effort to hide them in a stand of short pines. Not a very good effort. We figured that Deiter thought we were still all together. He didn't know Blackhawk and I were stalking him. We took our sweet revenge and slashed the tires and cut the wires. Payback's a bitch. Now we headed straight to where the smoke was coming from.

# 66

Deiter was standing hip-cocked with his hunting vest open over his heavy coat. He said, "Eileen darlin', I've always wanted to see you naked. Why don't you drop that sleeping bag and give us a look."

Jimmy said, "You need to look at what I've got pointed at your belly."

Deiter turned his head. "It's a 30 ought 6," Jimmy continued. "And it will make a hole the size of a dime in your belly, but coming out the other side it will be the size of a silver dollar. It will mess you up."

"You don't even have the safety off," Deiter said.

"I clicked it off the moment I saw them all standing and looking worried."

Deiter turned slowly and raised the barrel of his rifle to point at Jimmy. "Looks like a Mexican standoff to me. But there's only one of you." Without looking at him, he said to the guy with tattoos, "Pogo, put your AK on Eileen. If he shoots, or even twitches, you shoot as many as you can, starting with her."

Pogo turned and trained his rifle on Eileen. Then he made a

mistake. He could have held it waist high and killed her and some of the others, but he thought he was badass and wanted to scare her. He jerked his rifle to his shoulder and sighted down the barrel.

Madonna's arrow hit him in the neck with a solid *thwok*. He gave a hoarse scream and dropped his rifle and went to his knees digging at the arrow. Deiter was fast. Real fast. Jimmy shot but Deiter had already moved. Blackhawk stepped out of the pines and shot at him. I was beside Blackhawk. I shot the red cap. Deiter was gone into the foliage. I could hear him crashing through the woods. Except for Blackhawk and me, everyone stood in stunned silence. They were staring at the bodies. Jimmy looked at Madonna as she stood staring at the body of the man she had just killed. She began to shake. Jimmy took her into his arms. He looked at Blackhawk. "He's getting away," he said.

"I'll get him," Blackhawk said and handed me his rifle. He turned and disappeared into the forest.

Jimmy looked at me. "Should you help him?"

"He works well alone," I said. "Help me drag these assholes into the brush out of sight and cover them up. But not too much."

"What are we going to do," Helena Jean said.

"About what?" Robert said.

"These men are dead."

"There are more dead men back there," I said, nodding the way we came. "And, if they had their way, you, me and the rest of us would be dead now instead of them. Listen to me and think about this. First of all, we are a long way from any sheriff's station. Madonna thinks Deiter bragged about murdering an

FBI guy that had infiltrated the Fremen. I have a picture on my camera of a man's skull I found in the forest, with a bullet hole in it. This was before any of you found us. Proof the guy was shot in the head, probably murdered."

"If we did feel like we had to notify the authorities, they would have to come up here and find the bodies, which will be bones and dirt by spring. And I'd be willing to bet if they did find them, they couldn't identify any of them. Then to make it worse, they would feel obligated to find and roust not only the Fremen but the Redcoats as well. All your friends would be homeless again. And they would run them out of the forest and destroy their camps so they would have to find a way to live in civilization again. Go ask them how they'd like that?"

Helena Jean had tears in her eyes. She came over and hugged me. "You're right. I know you're right."

Finally, when she broke away, I said to Jimmy, "Gimme a hand here." He let go of Madonna. She went over to hold her mama. He came to help me drag the bodies into the forest. We dragged them far enough back that we were well clear of the camp. We unceremoniously rolled them into an old creek bed. We covered them with leaves, needles, and brush. The wolves and bears would smell them out soon enough.

The falling snow was getting thicker. It made me happy. I knew snow on the ground would help Blackhawk track Deiter. When we finished, Madonna was dragging more logs onto the fire. I walked over and felt the clothes that were drying. They had been sopping wet, so they were still damp. The boots would take longer. I finally looked at Robert, who had sat down again. He was pale and sweating.

"I'd like to take a look at that leg," I said.

"Be my guest," he said.

I gently unwrapped a very professional job of bandaging. The hole wasn't bleeding anymore and that was good. The edges of both the entry wound and the exit were inflamed. The sulfur had helped retard more inflammation. I poured more hydrogen peroxide on both wounds and added sulfur. I then wrapped the leg with gauze and taped it tight. We were running short on gauze.

Eileen came over beside me. "That's a good job. Did you have training?"

"You did a good job yourself," I said. "When I was in the service I was trained. I was the designated medic in mine and Blackhawk's team. When we were in together."

"I'd like to hear about that sometime."

"You'd just be bored."

"I doubt it." She stopped and was listening. "I don't hear Blackhawk."

"Neither does Deiter," I said.

# 67

Blackhawk didn't bother to listen for Deiter. He knew the panicked man was heading for his quad. Blackhawk raced through the broken ground, careful not to twist his ankle. By now it was light enough to see. The snowfall was heavier and Blackhawk knew that would help him. But not for a while. He had his Sig Sauer in his right hand and the long, super-sharp skinning knife in the other. He had pulled his camo bandanna up around his mouth and nose to protect his face from the small slashing limbs.

Deiter's quads had not been far from the creek, maybe two hundred yards. Twenty yards away were Deiter's prints in the light snow, heading directly towards the machines. Within a few yards Blackhawk could see Deiter's new prints leading away from the quads. Blackhawk veered to his right, moving at a ninety-degree angle. Deiter might have swung back around to ambush him.

When Blackhawk was far enough away from the machines, he swung around to intersect Deiter's track. Sixty yards from the machines he saw the tracks again. By the length of the stride he could tell Deiter was running. Blackhawk didn't care. The man had nowhere to run to. Maybe back to the two guys where Jackson and he had taken the quad. If he made it that far he was in for a surprise. There would be no quad. It didn't matter. Blackhawk would follow the son of a bitch to the ends of the earth.

Now Deiter was following the quad tracks they had made earlier. Raised a city boy, Blackhawk had found he was surprisingly good in the woods. He found he loved it. The quiet, the one with nature. The sense of accomplishment when you harvest your own food. When he bought the El Patron he had married it, 24-7. He had not been in the woods for a long time. He found himself really enjoying this. And he had a score to settle.

He began to notice that Deiter wasn't traveling in a straight line. He was beginning to utilize the terrain to make Blackhawk's pursuit more difficult. Ducking in and out of ravines. Climbing bluffs, only to drop back down. This guy was dumb. None of that would change the fact that Blackhawk knew where he was going. All he had to do was follow the quad tracks. He had no worry Deiter would take a sudden turn north or south. He knew that Deiter's ultimate goal was to get back to the safety of his people. Blackhawk pushed forward harder.

He, Jackson and Jimmy had studied Jimmy's map pretty thoroughly before they even left the El Patron, and Blackhawk remembered it. If Deiter, for some reason, did head due north, after several miles, he would end up way to the west of Blue Ridge Reservoir. Nothing out there. The same for east and west.

The snowfall was heavier now. When he did see Deiter's

tracks they had no fresh snow in them. He knew he was getting closer.

The one thing Blackhawk did keep an eye out for was a way to get back on the north side of that big creek. He knew Deiter would have to cross it too. Deiter had not roamed too far from it and every once in a while, Blackhawk could hear it roaring along. When Blackhawk did spot a place to ford the creek, he stopped himself at the edge. He studied the other side. The quad tracks had led down into the water. It was a great place for a trap. He would be a perfect target halfway across. He skirted along the bank, keenly aware of the other side. He could see no sign of Deiter. Just before he decided to go ahead, he noticed the twelve-inch diameter log leaning against the tree. Right where he would be coming out. He cautiously waded out into the water, his pistol ready. Because he was looking for it, he saw the para-line two inches off the ground. Deiter had picked a great spot for it. It was where he had to step up. A trip line. Set to trigger the leaning log to fall on whoever tripped it. A heavy and deadly dead-fall trap.

Blackhawk carefully stepped over the line. He kept low in the brush, cautiously moving slowly, circling. Expecting Deiter to be there. He wasn't. Deiter had made a lot of overlapping tracks as he had set the trap. There was one set that led away into the forest. Blackhawk chose a spot that gave him good cover. He kicked the trip-line and the log fell with a loud crunch. Blackhawk yelled like he had been hurt. He backed into his hiding spot and waited.

# 68

With the imminent threat neutralized, Eileen and Helena Jean began to rummage through the packs looking for food. They hadn't brought much, not expecting to be stopped like this. Helena Jean emptied some mason jar canned vegetables into the skillet to heat. Eileen put dry beans and water on the fire to boil. Madonna cut elk jerky into small pieces and dropped them into the beans.

Robert had a fever and was sleeping. He was groaning in his sleep. Evangeline wouldn't leave his side. Jimmy always kept a spool of fishing line and some spinner lures in his pack, and he dug them out. He went down by the water trying to get lucky.

"You think Blackhawk's okay?" Madonna said.

"If anyone would be, it would be him. I've been in many a skirmish with him and he is the most competent man I've ever met."

"Competent in what way?"

"He's not a carpenter or an electrician. He can't fix a car. He's no mechanic. Has no interest in it. I guess If he did, he would probably be the best mechanic in the world. But up against the

Deiters of the world, no one can match him."

"Jimmy said he kicked the shit out of Deiter while he was tied to a post."

I smiled. "Yeah, that's what I mean. He's quick, smart and deadly. You be glad he's on our side."

"He owns a nightclub?"

"The El Patron. Below the I-17 in Phoenix."

"And he has a girlfriend?"

"Elena. She's a salsa singer at his club. The best entertainer I've ever seen."

"Is she good looking?"

"Very."

"So is he," Madonna said, looking down at the creek, towards Jimmy.

"He doesn't even know it," I said. "Or at least he doesn't think about it. The most self-contained man I ever knew."

We were quiet a minute when she said, "Do you have a girlfriend?"

I didn't answer right away. I had to think about that. Finally, I said, "I don't know. A short time ago, I would have said yes, but lately, I don't know." I was whittling a piece of wood, trying to fashion a spoon out of it. "We've been seeing each other for a couple of years now. Her name is Marianne. She's a singer at the club. She's very good also. And beautiful." I smiled at Madonna. "My God, she's beautiful. But I don't think we have as much in common as we would like."

"*We* would like," Madonna repeated. "Most people would have said, '*I* would like. Are you engaged?"

"Oh, no. Maybe that's the problem. I don't think I'm the

marrying type and maybe she is."

"Why aren't you?"

"I've been alone my whole life."

"Jimmy said you don't have family."

"I'm an orphan. I'm unemployed and live on a boat at Lake Pleasant. Have you heard of Lake Pleasant?"

"I think so."

"I don't think I could change my lifestyle. I sure don't want to. She hasn't said a thing, but I think she would prefer I lived in town and had a job. Have children, that kinda thing."

Madonna looked at me slyly. "Women are like that."

"Are you like that?"

"Probably." She sat there for a minute. "Mom and I talk about it. What kind of life we want. My father left her when I was little. She couldn't make enough money to have a normal life. She was evicted because she couldn't pay rent. We were homeless for a while." She was quiet. Then she said, "Why is Jimmy only a bartender? He's very smart."

"Yes he is. But like me, he makes his own choices. I've known him for a while now and I never thought about it. He is what he wants to be. I don't know anyone happier than Jimmy. Besides that, Blackhawk loves him and pays him twice as much as any bartender in town. Jimmy is like a son to him, even though Blackhawk's not old enough for that. At least to have a son Jimmy's age." I thought about it. "You know hon, I've not really analyzed it before. But Elena and Blackhawk treat Jimmy like he's part owner of the bar anyway."

She hesitated, "Does he have a girlfriend?"

I laughed. "I think he does now."

She blushed. She said something under her breath.

"Sorry, I didn't hear that."

"That's what he said," she said not looking at me.

Jimmy came walking up from the creek empty handed.

"No luck?" I said.

"Water's too cold. They're not moving. Have you heard anything?"

"No. I don't know that we will. Depends how long it takes Blackhawk to catch Deiter."

"Deiter's mean," Madonna said.

"Deiter's a coward. All cowards are mean. And he'll be mean up until he is faced with the danger he is in. Then he will revert to being a coward."

"How long do we wait?" Jimmy said.

"Not much longer. Get some food. Get a night's rest. Start early in the morning. Even if Blackhawk's not here yet, we need to go. He can move faster than the rest of us. He'll catch up."

# 69

After a while, Blackhawk had waited long enough, and he knew Deiter wasn't coming back. He didn't know why he was surprised. The guy would run for home as fast as he could. At least he would run back to the two guys that had a quad. Surely the asshole would figure out that he and Jackson had taken that quad, but maybe the guy was too stupid to figure it out.

He began to follow the tracks and once he was assured Deiter wasn't doubling back, he began to move as fast as he could. He remembered the way they had come. But, of course, it all looked different coming from a different direction. It took a while, but he finally began to smell the wood smoke from the two guys' fire. Now it was daylight, they had built a large one and the wood was damp so the smoke would be large. As soon as he got closer, he slowed to listen. Then, two shots rang out spaced a couple of seconds apart. Blackhawk froze in his tracks. The shots had been in the distance, but close enough to be alarming. He finally veered away from the direct line he had been on and began to circle through the woods. Everything was melting and his outer garments were sopping wet.

With the pistol in his right hand and a knife in the left, he

331

moved quickly and silently through the brush. He stopped to listen, then moved again. He kept moving until the smoke was coming from his left. He listened. He began again. He gave it another couple of minutes then turned slightly south and kept moving. He became aware of a grunting, groaning sound. It was the sound of desperation. It was just ahead of him. Then he could see through the brush. Up ahead, Deiter was on his knees digging through the packs of the two guys, throwing what he didn't want away from him. Blackhawk had no idea what he was searching for. Deiter pulled out a box of ammunition and stuffed it into his pocket. He put something else in his pocket, but Blackhawk couldn't tell what it was.

The two men were lying sprawled by the fire. One of them had a leg in the fire and it was smoldering. Both had been shot in the head. The hoods on their parka's was saturated and dark with blood. The wounds were in the back of the head. He had circled to come up behind them, then shot them point blank.

Blackhawk took two quick steps forward and kicked him in the head. At least that was the intention. Deiter must have sensed him and lunged sideways as Blackhawk kicked. Blackhawk's foot glanced off the back of Deiter's head as Deiter moved. Deiter rolled and scrambled to his feet. He had stuffed his pistol into his belt. He was trying to yank it clear. Blackhawk charged him, wondering why he hadn't just shot him to begin with. Deiter danced backwards. His heel caught on a root, and he tumbled backwards. He was quick. He rolled and bounced to his feet. He had the gun in his hand now. Blackhawk clubbed at it with his. He connected and the gun flew into the brush. Deiter swiped at him with his wicked long knife. The blade caught his coat sleeve, sliced it and cut into his forearm. The cut was deep and his hand went numb. His blood made the pistol slick and with the numbness, it slid from his hand.

Deiter started to charge him, but with his knife in his hand Blackhawk thrust the blade at Deiter's belly and Deiter dodged back. Now they warily circled each other.

"I'm going to gut you like a fish," Deiter growled.

Blackhawk laughed. "I'm going to take your scalp." He took a step backward and Deiter followed. Halfway through the step Blackhawk lunged forward, holding the knife straight out like a rapier and narrowly missed the jugular. He kept charging, driving Deiter back into the trees. Deiter dodged behind a bushy pine. Blackhawk kept after him. It was slick and wet and both men had trouble with their footing. Both of them knew it was useless for Deiter to try to run. Both of them knew that one of them wasn't going to make it.

They had moved away from the bodies of the two men. Their pistols were lost in the underbrush. Deiter snagged up a deadfall branch, and charged Blackhawk with it swinging wildly. Blackhawk dodged away. Lesson #1 in a knife fight is to cut the closest part of the opponent. This is usually hands and arms. Every time Deiter swung the branch at him Blackhawk would swipe his blade at his hand. He finally connected and Deiter howled in pain and the branch flew from his hand. The cut was on the top of the hand where the skin is thin, and blood splattered.

Blackhawk didn't give him time to suck his wound. He went after him. Relentlessly thrusting the blade, closer and closer. Putting the man in full retreat. Blackhawk could feel that cold exhilaration he always felt in combat. Other men might feel fear or dread or sometimes on the other side, excitement or even an ebullience. With Blackhawk it was more an endorphin high. Almost an ecstasy. With Black Mamba he had found it to be addictive. His new life at the El Patron didn't give him the opportunity to experience this much anymore. But, right now, right this moment he was loving it. It showed with an almost maniacal grin on his face, and it scared the hell out of Deiter.

Back and back Deiter went until he found himself backed into a thicket of brambles with no place to escape. Without options, Deiter charged Blackhawk and they grasped each other. Like sumo wrestlers they struggled back and forth. Just like sumo's, and almost all forms of hand to hand combat, the trick is to use the other guy's weight against him. Blackhawk was trained. Deiter was not. As soon as Deiter pushed his bigger body against him, Blackhawk pulled him and swung them both around, slamming Deiter to the ground. He wrapped his legs around Deiter's and held his hand with the knife trapped against the man's body. No matter how strong Deiter was, Blackhawk had the leverage.

Blackhawk's knife tip was pushing against Deiter's chest. Deiter could barely hold it off. Blackhawk used his arm strength and his own weight to push the blade harder though the man's clothing and against the man's chest. The tip cutting into the man's skin. Deiter was groaning and sweating and millimeter by millimeter Blackhawk pushed the tip of the knife deeper.

"Okay, okay," Deiter cried. "I give up, I give up."

Millimeter by millimeter the tip of the knife pushed deeper.

"Please, I give up! Don't do it."

Millimeter by millimeter the knife tip went deeper.

"For your father," Blackhawk whispered. Another millimeter.

# 70

Marianne found a one-way flight to Columbus on Southwest Airlines. It was a red eye. She booked it two days out so Tiffany could get plenty of rest. She didn't leave the girl's side for that entire time. Packing for Tiffany was easy. She didn't have anything to begin with. For herself, Marianne found it to be harder. She had lived in this house for a while and like everyone, had gathered things. Now she had to make choices. What did she have to have? She wasn't coming back.

She knew she could ask Elena to hire someone to pack it up and ship it to her, but she wanted a clean break. She would be cancelling her phone service before she boarded the plane. Once she decided she didn't really need anything more than her legal papers, birth certificate, passport, college diploma etcetera, the packing became easier.

She paid for early boarding but that didn't help much when the plane was late. They had been sitting next to the gate for over an hour and a half. They hadn't had an argument since the first day Tiffany was home. That may have been because she still had residual cocaine in her. They had another forty minutes before the plane was due at the gate.

"I'm going to the ladies room," Marianne said. Tiffany just grunted. Marianne set the J.D. Robb mystery she was reading in her chair to keep it and walked to the restroom. When she came back, Tiffany was gone. Marianne's book still sat where she had left it. A thrill of fear ran up Marianne's back. Tiffany's carry-on was gone. She looked up and down the concourse. The shops were to her right, so she started that way. Halfway down was a pub. She looked in and Tiffany was sitting at the bar. Marianne came and sat on the stool beside her.

"You scared me," Marianne said.

"Sorry. Didn't mean to. I would've come back to the gate." She had what must have been a triple bourbon on the rocks in front of her. She stirred it with a twizzle stick. "I figure when I get back, between you, my insane mother and the teetotaling grandparents, I may not get another drink for a while."

The bartender came to Marianne. "Glass of Chardonnay please," she said.

When he brought it, Tiffany said, "I've been wondering about something."

"What's that?"

"What about your boyfriend? You just walking away?"

Marianne ducked her head and took a drink of the wine. "I don't know what else to do. We really care for each other, but we are too different. It just wouldn't work in the long haul. He lives in a different world. I just couldn't adapt."

Behind the bar, up on the wall the television was showing a picture of a bombed-out car, then a picture of Blue Boy.

"Hey, bartender, turn that up, please."

He picked up the remote and brought the sound up.

"......*identified as Salvatore Ibanez. He was a known playboy in Scottsdale and was reported to have ties to local drug cartels. In what was called a gangland execution, his body was found in a rental home on Central Avenue. Neighbors reported an explosion at that location two mornings ago. This was where the destroyed automobile was found. The automobile, identified as a Bugatti Chiron, was valued at one hundred and thirty thousand dollars. The Scottsdale police say that they have no suspects identified at this time. In other news...*"

Tiffany took a drink. A tear ran down her cheek.

"You are crying for that son of a bitch?"

She looked at her aunt. "I'm crying about what he did to me."

Marianne was silent for a long time. Finally, she said, "Because of Elena, we got you back. But that was the kind of world that Jackson was involved with. Not the drugs and girls, but he could rub elbows with those people without blinking an eye. You have heard the old saying, *honor among thieves*? Jackson had done things, good things, not bad things, but dangerous things, things you and I couldn't possibly understand. Jackson had the respect of all those people. Even their top tier bosses." She finished her Chardonnay. "Do you remember Eddie? The old guy that lives out at the same marina Jackson lives at?"

Tiffany shook her head.

"Well anyway, one time, when we were all together, Eddie told me Jackson stories that brought the hair up on the back of my neck. Come on, finish your drink, it's time for us to board."

# 71

The eastern horizon wasn't light yet, but the impenetrable darkness of the forest was just coming to the point where objects could be identified. Instead of a black wall, it was a black wall of trees. When I opened my eyes, I could feel the warmth caused by Helena Jean's body, in her sleeping bag, rolled up against me. There was something wrong. In an instant, I recognized it. The fire had been stoked and was blazing. I turned my head to see Blackhawk sitting beside the fire, sipping coffee, and looking at me. He had the coffee pot hanging from a tripod over the fire.

I slipped out of my sleeping bag, careful not to disturb Helena Jean. I picked up my boots one at a time and shook them to dislodge any critter that had crawled in for warmth. I grabbed my heavy coat and joined Blackhawk. I sat on a thick log and pulled my boots on. I laced them up and slipped my heavy coat on. Blackhawk handed me a coffee cup and I poured a generous amount. No one else was stirring.

In a low voice, I said, "Any trouble?"

He shook his head. He sat his coffee cup on the ground. He fumbled in his coat pocket and finally came out with something.

He held it up, so I could see it. At first, I couldn't recognize what it was. I reached over and took it.

"Oh my God," I said. "Deiter's?" He nodded with a grin.

It was bloody strands of hair attached to a patch of pale skin. "A scalp?"

"I told him," Blackhawk said softly.

"Best to not show that to the ladies."

"I have no intention to. I don't think even Elena would enjoy it."

"Might even be a little much for Jimmy."

"I don't know. That boy was a stand-up guy. He handled his own."

I sipped my coffee and looked over at Jimmy's slumbering form. "You know we are going to be asked a lot of questions about all this. There are too many people here to keep the whole thing quiet. I think it's best that anything you and I did, that wasn't witnessed, needs to be kept between us."

Blackhawk held his cup out and I touched it with mine. A few minutes later it began to get light, and Jimmy and Eileen arose at the same time with the same thought. They went to Robert and woke him so they could check him over. He had no fever. They set about changing his dressing. Soon everyone was up. They all wanted to hear from Blackhawk. They all were talking at once.

"Did you catch him?" Eileen said.

"Did you kill him?" Madonna said.

Blackhawk held his hand up. "We will have no more trouble from Deiter, or any Fremen."

"Tell us what happened," Jimmy said. Everyone gathered around; even Robert sat up to listen.

Blackhawk took a breath. "Yesterday, when Jackson and I went hunting, we discovered two of Deiter's men plus one that was still alive but didn't last. They had one working quad and one that didn't. When Deiter ran out of here, and after he found that Jackson and I had disabled his quads, I knew he would head for those guys. What he didn't know was that we had the quad he wanted."

Helena Jean got up and started to fix some food. Eileen joined her. "Go ahead," she said. "We can do this and listen too."

Blackhawk continued, "I chased Deiter for a long time. It was made easier since I knew where he was going. There was nowhere else out here for him to go. When I got close to those guys, I could smell their fire smoke. So, I snuck up as quietly as I could and suddenly there was gunfire. Two distinct shots. Then it was dead quiet. I came into their camp just as carefully as I could. They were all dead. Deiter had come in to take their quad and shot them, but one didn't die fast enough and shot back. Killed Deiter dead."

"They are all dead?" Jimmy said.

"All of them."

"So, we're free?" Eileen said.

"Free as anyone can be."

"Let's get packed up and get out of here," I said.

"Let's eat first," Eileen said.

Five hours later we pulled up to the Rim. We sat looking down at the two-wheel track we had used coming up. It was almost straight down.

Jimmy looked at me and I said, "Lead the way."

He and Madonna started down and the rest of us followed.

340

It was rough but Jimmy took his time and made sure we all were good. At long last we pulled into the campground at Washington Park. We just sat, grinning, looking at each other. Evangeline got our attention. She was looking at her phone. "Hey, guys, I've got service."

I said to Blackhawk, "Call Nacho. Have him get Ben and rent two vans with hitches and two quad haulers. Tell him to get his ass up here and get us." I looked at Robert and he was very pale. "We need to get Robert to the Payson hospital."

Blackhawk said, "I better call Elena first." Smart move. He dialed the number. Just when he thought the thing was going to go to voicemail, she answered.

"Hello darlin', we're back.," Blackhawk said.

He listened. "No, we're still up above Payson. In a place called Washington Park." He listened again. "Well, that's the problem. We ran into a group of off the grid assholes and they shot the hell out of Jimmy's truck, so we are stuck with four quads and five extra people." He listened. "No, we didn't do anything to them. They attacked us. Why would you think that?"

I had moved over by him and I could hear Elena chattering at him. "Wait, wait. Wait hon, I'll tell you all about it but first we'll need Nacho and Ben to rent two mini-vans and two quad haulers and come get us." He listened. "I told you, they shot it to pieces. All we have is four quads. I'll give you directions, you write them down, Nacho won't remember them." He slowly and patiently told her how Nacho could find Washington Park. "Okay," he said, when he was finished. "Okay, hold on."

He offered the phone to me. "She wants to talk to you."

"What'd I do?"

"Take it," he said, thrusting the phone at me.

I took it. "Hi," I said.

"I could wait and tell you later," Elena said. "But I know you'll want to know. We found Tiffany and Marianne took her back to her mom. I don't think she's coming back. She told me to hire another singer. She left a letter for you on your kitchen counter."

I didn't say anything. "You okay?" she said.

"Yeah, I'm fine," I said. "Thanks for telling me."

"Nacho can't stand it. He wants to talk to Blackhawk."

I handed the phone to Blackhawk. I could hear Nacho's voice.

"Hey Boss," Nacho said. "We've been wondering about you. Did you get any elk?"

"No," Blackhawk said.

"Too bad. Boy, you should have been here. You won't believe the amount of excitement we've had around here."

# 72

It was well after midnight by the time I got back to my boat. Tiger Lily had never looked so good. It took four and a half hours before Nacho and Ben showed up. Our first stop was Payson and the Emergency Room, where we reported Robert had been accidentally shot by a lone hunter. The doctor decided to keep him overnight. He was impressed by the care we had given him. Helena Jean and Evangeline decided to stay with him. Well, not with him but in a motel close by, at least for the night. Elena arranged for them to stay at the motel for a week. She had sent Nacho with a wad of cash for whoever needed it. So one of the vans wasn't needed except for transporting the quads. The rest of us made it back to the El Patron, sleeping most of the way back. Jimmy borrowed Elena's car and took Madonna and Eileen to stay with him. I got my car and made the long drive home.

I was bone tired and there was no shuttle. I was so used to sleeping on the ground I could have just laid down and gone to sleep. I toughed it out to the boat. I disabled the alarms and went in. It was stuffy so I opened the windows and the front and back doors for the cross breeze. Elena had told me there would be a letter from Marianne on my galley counter, and there was. I looked at it. I fixed a very large scotch on ice then went to the master stateroom and stripped down. I took a very long shower. It felt so good, it was almost like sex. I toweled off, slipped on a faded pair of swim trunks, and fixed another drink.

I picked up the letter and carrying my drink, I hopped up to the captain's cockpit. The envelope was sealed. Across the front, in Marianne's immaculate script, was just the word *Jackson*. I sat looking at it for a very long time. I drank half my drink. I looked around at the middle of the night lights of the marina. I was thinking it had been nice having a girl. I walked over to the stern overhang. I looked across the lake. I took the envelope between my fingers and tore it in half, then again. Then again. I let the pieces drift from my fingers into the water below. I finished my drink and went to bed.

# EPILOGUE

Summer had come and gone. It was the time of year that the evening and nighttime hours were hinting at the cool months to come. I went back to my old habits of fishing, reading and hanging out with Pete Dunn and Old Eddie. Pete's movie had crept closer to becoming a reality. I would go down to the bar once in a while. Sherrie had taken the summer off and had gone somewhere. No one was sure where. That was okay.

One day, on Jimmy's day off, he had brought Eileen and Madonna down to the boat and we had spent the day on the lake, floating and swimming and inventing new and wonderous cocktails. I took them to the northern reaches of the lake and showed them the wild burros that roamed the shoreline. We grilled steaks on my little hibachi grill, and they spent the night. I gave Eileen the spare stateroom. Jimmy and Madonna took my master stateroom, and I slept up top on one of the chaise lounges. I ignored the sounds that drifted up the steps.

The two women had moved in with Jimmy, and Jimmy had gotten Madonna enrolled in ASU. She was studying for a Wildlife Management degree. Elena had given Eileen a job as a waitress at Rick's American. Jimmy was teaching her the art of bartending and occasionally, on heavy days, she would help. Nacho liked her a lot. It seems that Nacho and Esperanza had taken a break. Elena hadn't replaced Marianne, and Marianne's band had formed a jazz quartet and had become quite popular.

Helena Jean, Evangeline and Robert had stayed in Payson. Helena Jean got a job in an insurance office. Evangeline enrolled as a senior in the high school and Robert worked as a mechanic in an all-purpose garage. He barely limped anymore. At first, they had separate apartments, but Evangeline and Robert spent so much time together they had decided to combine their resources and rented a house on the outskirts of town.

Unbeknownst to me, Captain Rand and Maureen, the marina manager, had visited Elena at the El Patron and proposed having a party on Captain Rand's party boat. They wanted to kick off the new season on the lake with a party for all the regular employees. They also wanted to do something for me for saving the little girl. They were both fans of Elena's and wanted her and her band to perform. Since Elena knew it would make me very uncomfortable, she readily agreed to it.

The first inkling I had was when Pete came over and invited me to have a drink with him in the bar. Maybe insisted is a better word. He said he had a couple friends from the movie industry meeting him there and wanted me to go along. I should have been suspicious when he thought I should change into some nicer clothes. Since when did he give a damn what I wore?

When we got to the bar, he pretended to take a text and told me his friends were running a half hour behind. He said that was okay because he wanted to talk to Captain Rand about another

Hollywood party. Again, he insisted I go along. Dumb me, I didn't notice a thing. Even as we passed people on the way to the boat, I didn't notice they turned to look at me as I went by.

The steward on the main deck told us Captain Rand was on the next level. We went up the stairs and as my head cleared the deck, and I could see all the people waiting, Elena and her band broke into, *For He's a Jolly Good Fellow.*

I turned to flee. Nacho and Blackhawk had come up behind me and blocked the stairs. Blackhawk hugged me, which was a rare thing for him. He said, "Just go along. All our deep woods friends are here."

And they were. Eileen and Madonna. Helena Jean and Evangeline and Robert the Bruce. Helena Jean looked like a million dollars. She came and hugged me. I hardly recognized Evangeline without her Army camos. She had a summer dress on, and had her hair professionally done. She kissed my cheek. Robert shook my hand. Our trek through the mountains seemed like ages ago.

Elena burst into one of her most requested numbers and the area spaced off for a dance floor was instantly filled. Jimmy and Madonna took to the dance floor, and I was shocked at how well they danced together. Nacho was dancing with Eileen. Pete Dunn pulled a reluctant Helena Jean onto the dance floor. Toward the stern, I noticed a large group of people standing together, staring at me with large grins on their faces. Maureen and Captain Rand stood beside them, wearing identical grins.

A man and a woman came up to me. He was carrying a toddler.

"Mr. Jackson," the man said. The woman began to cry. The

baby just stared at me. "This is our baby. Her name is LaDonna Marie. This is her birthday." Now he began to cry and couldn't speak. I looked around for help. Blackhawk was watching with a smile. He was there when I needed him in a gunfight. He was of no use now. The mother hugged me around the neck. She held on so hard I thought she was going to hurt me. "You saved our baby, and now she has a birthday," she blubbered.

"This is LaDonna's family," the father said, indicating the people standing around us. The group began to applaud. Then everyone else joined them. I was at a loss. I stood there like a bumpkin.

Finally, Blackhawk saved me and took me by the arm. "I think you need a drink," he said. He pulled me and I followed him to where the bar was set up. Sherrie was behind the bar. She was grinning. She already had a rock glass with one cube, filled with Ballantine's.

"My hero," she said, handing me the glass.

The sun was down by the time the party was over. All good things come to an end. It was dark, the band had packed up. Helena Jean and Evangeline and Robert had to drive back to Payson. The El Patron would open tomorrow for business as usual. Madonna had classes. In fact, both of the young girls had classes in the morning. One in Payson, one in Tempe. Pete had disappeared. Blackhawk, Nacho and Elena had headed back to El Patron. Old Eddie, Maureen and Captain Rand had left early.

I emptied my glass and carried it over to Sherrie. She and the steward were putting everything away.

"Would you like another?" she asked. The steward picked up a tray of dirty glasses and headed down the stairs.

God, she was pretty. She had dressed in a cute little sailor top with an anchor embroidered above her left breast. Her shorts were crisp and white and her legs long and tan.

"No thanks."

"What are you going to do now?" she said.

"Guess I'll go back to the boat and have a night cap up top and watch the moon."

She looked at me through hooded eyes. "Would you like some company?"

Did I say she was pretty? I mean really pretty. "I'd be a fool not to."

Do you remember how good it feels to do something nice for someone. Did you enjoy Deep Woods Warrior? If you did, or if you like any of the Jackson Blackhawk books, please do something nice and go to Amazon.com and search for the book. Click on reviews and leave me one.

Amazon chooses how they pay me based not only on sales but also largely on reviews. The more reviews I get, the better they place me in their advertising schemes. I will be extremely grateful. I want to spend the rest of my life writing these novels. There isn't a writer in the world that appreciates his readers more than I do.

Sam

Made in the USA
Las Vegas, NV
09 December 2023

82373303R00208